Out of Hibernation
The Creatures

Out of Hibernation

The Creatures

Robyn J Hunter

ISBNs:
978-1-3999-4958-3 (paperback)

In remembrance of Abraham

CHAPTER 1

July 9ᵗʰ, 2015

A rural country house located in the isolated dirt tracks of the Peak District was a perfect location for a premeditated murder, or so Detective Goodrick thought. Could it have been the pothole-riddled lane he climbed or the shattered stained glass windows that brought him to that assumption? One thing he knew for certain was that whomever he found in there was not invited.

Slamming the door shut on his SUV, he stood for a moment with his hands in his pockets, observing the house that loomed over this beautiful landscape. If you closed your eyes and took a deep breath, you would feel instant tranquillity. A soothing breeze stroked your face, protecting you from the harsh July sun. *Bliss.* He dropped his shoulders, exhaling, lifting his eyes towards the front porch. Even with the crime scene tape wrapped around the perimeter with the glare of dancing blue lights, it was a magnificent sight.

Reaching his hands out of his pockets, he retrieved a pair of latex gloves and strolled towards the front door whilst stretching them over his hands. The constant shift in his balance, caused by the rumpled overgrown weeds, tangled their way around his feet, making this simple task near impossible. With a final hurdle, his feet found level ground at the bottom of a series of cracked concrete steps. Above him were officers he recognised, each with their heads down and leaning against the rotting timber beams. Even to an untrained eye, you could see the anxiety imprinted in their expression's.

"Alright, boys, taking a little break are we?" Goodrick cheered as he bounced up the steps. Not one of them turned or acknowledged his presence.

1

An odd feeling he'd never encountered. Being the district's leading homicide detective, he usually turned heads when his expertise was called upon. Plastered on his face was a trademark cheeky grin, that could instantly make anybody smile, but it soon disappeared when nothing was reciprocated. With a frown growing between his brows, he clapped his hand on the shoulder of the closest policeman and made his way through the decrepit door.

Before him laid a grand staircase to the far-right. It would've been much more elegant in its day had it not been missing most of its balusters. With the ones left, it's a wonder it could uphold the decaying handrail that was snapped in three places. The dirt on the once-polished mosaic floor blew in the air and sparkled around the room like a squalid snow globe. To his left, an antique mirror stretched across the wall, giving the eye access to the three adjacent rooms, one before the staircase and two behind. Goodrick positioned himself, staring intently into the mirror. Was it peculiar to see an ornate, well-looked-after piece, polished and gleaming in such a run-down place? Perhaps, or maybe he much preferred the view it rewarded him.

In the far room, if he could battle his way through the waves of white suits, stood a poised, assertive woman, Louise Allman. Her file did her no justice; a book nerd who skipped through the ranks primarily based on her hard work. Goodrick scoffed. *It'd have nothing to do with her protruding chest.* Her pursed lips rested on a humbled expression whilst long strands of mousy brunette hair guided a wandering eye. Sure enough, that smirk was imprinted on his face, ogling at how her loose trousers would transform when she took a closer look. Mesmerised by the curvature of her behind, she formed a superb hourglass to gaze upon.

A distant chatter became increasingly louder from outside the house, bringing Goodrick crashing back into reality. Two policemen passed behind him and into the room as a flash blinded their entrance. Sulking now she was out of sight.

"Best get to work then," he murmured to himself. Rocking the knot of his tightly fastened tie around his neck, giving himself a once-over in his egotistic reflection. With a nod of acceptance, he was on his way.

"Here he is, the man of the hour," a colleague bellowed. Rolling her eyes in frustration, she attempted to tunnel her concentration on the task at hand; a literal hand. The fingers were limped naturally towards the palm as it rested on a large centrepiece rug. The tapestry of the woollen furnishings created a contrasting canvas for the gruesome discovery. Royal colours of gold and purple entwined, depicting songbirds flying around a tree but from the right perspective, now sat on a cold, detached hand.

Cracked portraits mounted every inch of the walls with no escape from their unsatisfied glare. If only walls could talk, these 18th-century witnesses could disclose the grisly tales that transpired. The grand piano, sitting by the spacious bay window, would have usually been the focal point of the room, had it not been for the distressed sheet outlining a corpse.

Promptly levitating herself, she placed her knuckles on either side of her hips whilst chewing on her bottom lip. It wasn't the first time she'd examined dismemberment, but something was unnerving her. Her thoughts were interrupted by a baffling, cheering eruption coming from the doorway. Two policemen entered the room, shortly followed by a series of camera flashes. A tall, well-groomed man stepped behind them. A few colleagues noticed, what they thought, was a celebrity stepping out on stage and huddled around him like a gaggle of adoring fans.

The moment she'd been dreading was here, meeting the know-it-all detective, Gregory Goodrick. He wrote the manual for crime scenes for dummies and knew everything there had to be known about the: who; what; where; when and why. Only three hours late, but judging by the Breitling watch around his wrist, he could clearly pay for time. Maybe if he responded to her letter six years back, when she was an aspiring detective, offering advice more than: 'good looks will get you there' she'd have more admiration for the man.

Wrapping her arms around her torso brashly, she headed towards the doorway to invite Detective Goodrick onto the scene. It was as though she interrupted a few good pals catching up at a bar, the smiles and the back and forth chuckles, an uninvited casual demeanour descended when he waltzed in. Clearing her throat loudly, silence waved over the group.

"Ah, Detective Allman, how rude of me. Please, let me introduce-"

Abruptly, she broke the noose her arms had knotted and, with a dissatisfied expression, extended a hand towards Goodrick. It may've been bad taste to interrupt a superintendent, but so was the decision to backstab her by allowing Goodrick here in the first place.

"Detective Goodrick. I'm well aware of who you are. I'm sure you'll be a great credit given your experience with this type of..." She sighed, looking down and back up at him before finishing.

"Homicide. I've personally never seen anything quite like it."

To her amazement, his soft hand caressed hers and shook intently, looking directly at her. Maybe it was his piercing blue eyes that forced hers elsewhere. Maintaining eye-contact with the physical stroke of his palm made talking difficult. She was grateful her superintendent and a colleague were whisked away before stumbling over her words. The last thing she needed would be any reason to doubt her competence.

"The pleasure's all mine, Detective Allman," Goodrick smiled before releasing his grip.

"Please, Louise will do. I'm sure you've read the files I emailed you this morning?" Extending her arm outwards, inviting him to walk alongside her as she turned towards the centre of the room.

"Ah, about that, I'm not much of a reader, you see Louise, more of a, turn up, tell these pillocks what happened, and be on my merry way, leaving the paperwork for some bozo to do." He said smugly.

Giggling in disbelief, with a shake of her head.

"Well, this bozo might need more from you. Tell me, Detective Goodrick, have you seen anything quite like this?"

A gentle waft hit his body with disturbed dust punching the back of his throat when a sheet was dragged. Catching his breath, he turned away briefly with a tight fist covering his mouth, coughing repulsively. Returning his vision back to the corpse, his eyes were stitched to the horror laid before him. His white-knuckled fist was attached to his mouth to disguise his complete shock. Salvaging his other hand from his pocket, he rubbed it tediously against his thigh, concealing any evidence he was sweating.

Allman floated around the body with excessive hand gestures, presumably explaining in great detail what they knew thus far. If he'd read her email, as he should've, maybe he wouldn't be so inquisitive right now. Battling with his thoughts, he shook his head and tried focusing on what Allman was explaining.

"White female, aged between twenty-one and twenty-five. Estimated to have been here no longer than two days,"

Of course, he could identify the petty details himself; she was following protocol, after all.

"Severed left hand, large abdominal laceration, face carved out, ribcage and all internal organs removed."

Her eyes tensed on him, waiting for his highly anticipated reaction. With a clear gulp, he dropped both hands back into the safety net of his pockets and tiptoed around the body.

"Blood?" He stuttered.

"None. The body has been drained."

"Cause of death?"

"Asphyxiation, perhaps."

Goodrick came to an abrupt stop in alignment with the body's feet. The bruising around the legs and bloodshot eyes, that floated on top of exposed muscle and tissue, were tell-tale signs asphyxiation was the most probable cause of death. He gawked intently at the torso; grey, shrivelled skin stapled to both sides of the hips, displaying the lack of contents within. Only thing left behind were small strands of ripped organ tissue and the skin of the back. To the side of the body was a sawed-off hand, roughly ten feet away.

Lost in speculation, Allman's voice became a distant nuisance, tearing him away from his thoughts. *For what reason could they have to scoop out the internal organs, leaving the skin to collapse? The significance of the left hand, was it placed strategically? No blood, why drain a body, for what purpose?* He dwelled further into his puzzle before Allman's voice roared, shaking his eardrums back into her presence.

"Did you hear what I said?" Allman barked.

With a subtle shake of his head, she continued.

"Like I was saying, we found faeces trapped in her windpipe." Goodrick waved his hand in a concerning motion.

"Sorry? Faeces?" He challenged.

"Yes. Truly unique. There's one more thing you should see."

Goodrick curled his top lip. *What more could there possibly be?* Allman squatted directly in front of him. It would've been a compromising position for them, if it weren't for the mangled corpse at their side. With his eyes locked, growing in curiosity, she carefully hooked her hand under the knee of the body, pivoting a leg outwards, displaying the genitals.

Goodrick smacked his lips apart, taking a hand to his forehead.

"What the fuck is that?"

―――――ᶲᶲᶲ―――――

His reaction concerned her. Fair enough, it wasn't a pleasant sight, but surely, he must've come across worse. With doubt twinkling in her eyes, she leisurely gazed up at him. From this angle, she couldn't help but engulf herself in his presence. Starting with his polished, pin-holed shoes which led to the pinstripes on his smart trousers. They created traffic lines, allowing her eyes to weave in and out.

A salmon, tightly tucked shirt was a nice feminine touch, roughed up by the crumpled sleeves stretching over his forearms. His hand that caressed his forehead was shadowed by luscious chocolate locks of hair, laid perfectly back. Chiselled jawline was pricked with fine stubble, stretching from ear to ear, adjoining around puckered lips. *That's a pleasant sight.*

Stunned at her own ineptitude to keep her mind focused, she unhooked her hand away and stood upright by Goodrick. Silence fell around them as the room began to empty, filling with tension instead. She almost missed the upbeat atmosphere he brought to the scene, which she'd loathed moments earlier.

Gulping, she found the confidence to begin talking again. "It's a magazine." Rocking back and forth on her heels, stretching her mouth into a closed smile, making jest of the statement. It almost threw her off balance when she looked over at Goodrick, who had his eyes affixed on her. The slight squint and the curve of his raised eyebrow proved he was less than dissatisfied with her reaction. Guilt and anger grew in the pit of her stomach. How can the laid-back la-de-da detective make her feel inadequate in all of this? She couldn't understand how, but he did. Suddenly stopping her rocking motion, she gained her assertive posture back and attempted a complete summary.

"What you're looking at is a very tightly rolled, hard card magazine measuring seven and a half inches in circumference. Guessing from the two inches visible to us, there's another ten inside. We won't know fully until we get the coroner's report. We're ready to send the body, so we can expect it by lunchtime tomorrow."

She delicately patted her fingertips together; the clattering of her nails created a ticking clock, waiting for a response. Not only did he leave her hanging, but two white suits stood around sheepishly awaiting instructions. After a few awkward seconds, she moved her head lower to break the connection between his eyes and the body. Refocusing his gaze, he sighed heavily before looking behind him. A wiggle of his index finger is all they needed to jump into action. The thrashing of a metal trolley hammering its way towards them almost made it difficult to hear what he said next.

"Well then, Louise, dinner's on me tomorrow."

With a wink of his eye, he spun away, taking a hand through his impeccable hair, and the cocky demeanour descended again. She chuckled to herself, holding the side of her face. She didn't hate to see him go, but she loved watching the jiggle in his perky round arse leave, nonetheless.

CHAPTER 2

July 10ᵗʰ, 2015

Brushing her eyes open, she felt the rough-dried patches of mascara flaking down her cheeks. Her throat was parched, and her lips were cracking from lack of moisture. The soft breeze from a fan, positioned at the foot of her bed, caressed the bare bottom half of her body. The clattering of its blades, with a persistent knocking noise, were the regular morning sounds. Beige walls transformed into a warm, orange glow as the sun rose, but sure enough, a cloud shadowed the apartment. Once more; she lay in a bleak greyness.

Glancing across to check the time on the clock, 08:15. She hardly ever overslept; a natural built-in alarm would've woken her up hours before. Frustrated, she whipped her legs over the side of the bed, sitting up abruptly. With her eyes seized shut, she focused on abnormal shapes floating side to side. It began a ritual morning game, flicking her closed eyes from left to right, watching the floaters crash either side, an impossible Tetris level she'd never win.

Curling her toes, expecting to feel the fluffy texture of the carpet, instead was a slippery surface that slid under her foot. Unclasping her eyes, she peered downwards at the floor. Pictures and papers spread at every angle, ricocheting around her. She heard the flapping of an opened file at the foot of her bed, papers thrashing in the generated wind, held together by a paperclip. Stretching across, she retrieved the tattered brown folder and flicked through its contents.

Actions from the previous night flooded her memory, researching for connections from her crime scene to all those that had happened previously. Any young female that was mutilated in the past fifteen years within a hundred-mile radius now laid bare on the floor. The empty vodka bottle stood soberly on the window sill, proving there could only be so many pictures she could face before seeking help. No matter how many she researched that night, there were no leads. Her crime scene was first of its kind.

A sudden buzzing noise echoed from inside her bedside table, aggressively becoming louder as she pulled the handle. Scrolling across her screen was an unsaved number ending in 7675. Instead of answering, she fogged her head with those numbers trying to put a name to it, another one of her impossible games. The number soon disappeared, and the picture of her late mother flashed on her screen. Her infectious grin was all she needed some days. Allman smiled down at her mother before it faded to nothingness and the all-familiar alone feeling washed over.

Grabbing her mobile and shuffling to her feet, she anxiously tiptoed around the disturbed piles of paper and hopscotched out of the room. The morning sun greeted her into the open plan living area, where floor-to-ceiling windows overlooked a busy park. Clicking the button on the kettle, that perched on the edge of the breakfast bar, she sat herself down by one of the panelled windows and began her only hobby; people-watching. Her apartment gave her the ultimate vantage spot, too high to be overlooked but not too far away to see.

She enjoyed being a director, creating storylines for passer-by's. Unknowing members of the public had a role within her morning breakfast show. A suited and booted middle-aged man who spent more time narking at his phone, most probably late for a meeting, was in such a rush, he didn't care to notice the swing of his suitcase hit an arm of a passing woman. Instead of stopping or slowing down, he bulldozed on, leaving the fragile woman looking behind in disbelief. He'd go on and miss the train to the meeting he'd waited six months for. Arrogance could only travel so far, after all. For the woman, she'd accidentally walk into an attractive man, and years on, they'll laugh over how they 'bumped' into each other.

The kettle's screaming distracted Allman from her plot; she detached herself from the window screen and poured herself a much-needed cup of coffee. Sipping softly, she retrieved her phone and checked through her messages. Two missed calls from the mysterious number, one text message from her friend Jay and an email. Opening the text message: '*I saw the news report last night about that girl, fucking hell, heavy!*' Rolling her eyes, he's always one with words. Due to her job, she couldn't work a typical 9-5, allowing her time to socialise. Jay was her only remaining friend who understood, given he worked away for months on end. They were thick as thieves and their weekly Skype chat was the only thing she could look forward to. The email, from the coroner's office, read that the magazine had been removed, successfully. With anticipation growing in her stomach, she took a large gulp of her coffee, slammed the cup back down, and strutted into her dressing room. Scrolling through the neatly lined clothes that hung tidily, all too common, the same white blouse and black trousers repeated across the rail. She was a creature of habit and didn't stray far away from her norm. Crossing her arms, she grabbed the bottom corners of her oversized pyjama top and began to pull the fabric over her head. It did her no favours and didn't compliment her hourglass figure, but she only had herself to impress; much preferring comfiness over sexiness. Gazing at her reflection in the mirror that centred the room, she bit down on her bottom lip as a wicked thought crossed her mind. *Would I have time?*

With a smirk, she excitedly opened the first wardrobe door. Inside was her erotic playground of fast and wet attractions. At the bottom was a mechanical contraption, you wouldn't know what the bolts or the steel rod were for, but the fleshy dildo attached gave the intentions away. Inside the door exhibited stringy lingerie that didn't leave much for the imagination. Lace in all kinds of bright colours, from hot pink to tiffany blue, was accompanied with a shelf full of toys in all shapes and sizes.

Her heart raced when she'd gazed at her inventory to see what would take her fancy. Passion grew, but at a steady pace, so did anguish, for the fact all these toys were for singular use. She'd been occupied after leaving school with building a career whilst caring for her mother, there was no time for men. Pottering around at a yearly works gathering was the only excitement she indulged in. Midnight promises, stained whiskey kisses, dreaded walk of shame; it felt that's all she'd have. She realised mixing work with pleasure was not a recipe for success, so began her collection instead.

Squeezing her legs together, each toy she studied would reminisce a steamy rendezvous. She reached her hand outwards and grasped the shaft of a dildo with a suction cup: perfect companion for in the shower. With a smug smile, she collected a fresh combination of her uniform and carried them through into the en-suite. The lights flickered on automatically as she used the dial on the wall to set the shower temperature. With a few presses, the jets began erupting on either side of the cubicle, casting a vortex of water.

As she opened the shower door, her phone that laid on the side, flashed and began to shake uncontrollably. The reflection in the mirror above showed it was the same number, ending in 7675. She should've returned the call by now, but given it was her personal phone, she didn't sense any urge of importance. Sighing, retrieving her damp foot from the shower, she sluggishly made her way to the sink and answered.

"Hello?"

Pushing and shoving your way through a busy high street teaches you to always lean with a hard shoulder to get where you need to be. The concrete pathway was full of busybodies that morning, all heading for an early grave, judging by the anxiety on their faces. Just when you are beginning to make headway on your journey, a wall of people bring you to an abrupt stop. Common courtesy would be to part their chain to allow you through, but instead, their dissatisfied snarls would make their bond stronger. All in a pact with their first mission of the day; purchase an overpriced coffee from the kerbside parked van.

Shaking his head, Goodrick crab-walked around the back of the queue and continued on his way. Finally, he could see the red wall sign gently rocking in the wind, Clod's Café. It was an Irish family-owned café that was established in the late 70s, introduced to him by his old man. His morning cup of tea with a full English breakfast served at eight had never strayed for the past decade. The brass bell chimed that hung above the door as he swung it open, greeted by the same cheeky grin from Eileen. Always his first chuckle of the day, observing her trying to hide a half-eaten cupcake with the daily explanation.

"Just checking for poison, dear."

With a grin, he made his way to his regular seat. A sturdy, walnut circular table tucked away in the back corner; an ideal spot. The daily papers hung on the wall behind him and it was the closest table to the kitchen, saving on Eileen's legs. Within the first flick of the paper, his cup of tea was placed in front of him with a saucer full of biscuits. She always made it her goal to try to encourage him to eat more than the day before, which he appreciated. Even Goodrick wouldn't lie to himself; he was a greedy bugger. Scoffing his first ginger biscuit and washing it down with a large gulp of tea, his prepared breakfast made its way to him. Staggering side to side, Eileen struggled to pick her feet up from under herself, let alone try to balance the enormous oval plate of food. Goodrick jumped to his feet and retrieved the weight from her, placing it down; he pulled out the closest chair and waited until Eileen was seated. With a big sigh, she threw herself down and gently wafted her face using an embroidered handkerchief; always keeping one handy in her floral apron.

"Oh, tell me, Gregory, is it four o'clock yet?" Eileen huffed.

Goodrick chuckled whilst digging into his first runny egg, "I've told you once, and I'll tell you again, you shouldn't be working at your age. It's about time your Charlie took over. You deserve a rest." He said assertively, shaking his knife in her direction.

"If only. Cars, cars, cars. That's all he's interested in. I'll be sorry to see the back of this place, but I think it's time to sell up, give it a new lease of life, you know?"

Goodrick paused eating, peering over at the sadness ageing on Eileen's face. She was lost in thought, looking around the ceiling border at all the bric-a-brac treasures she'd collected through the years. As a young boy, he'd love nothing more than a trip to the café, sitting on the bar stools that lined the counter, choosing his favourite chocolate frosted cupcake, and listening to the stories each item derived from. Placing his cutlery down, he extended a hand outwards and gently stroked Eileen's forearm with a reassuring smile. She clasped her hand over his, reciprocating the kind gesture.

With the chime of the bell, their moment was shaken away. Eileen jumped up out of her seat and shuffled behind the counter to greet the customer. Goodrick began shovelling mouthfuls of his breakfast quickly, for every time he heard the bell, a waiting customer needed a seat. The café was a popular establishment on the busy high street. However, Eileen was humbled by every punter that the thought of extending never occurred to her.

Swallowing the last of his breakfast down, he folded the paper under his arm and neatly shelved his plate on a tray stack. He appreciated the fifteen minutes of quiet the place provided him, a little piece of sanctuary from his regular hustle and bustle. The quirky café was now as busy as the street, full of hungry and impatient members of the public. Wrestling his way through the crowd, he'd no chance of transferring parting words to his dear friend, but she knew the score, at eight on the dot, he'd be there tomorrow.

Greeting him were the loud sirens of the town, constant horn beeping, distant chatter with the odd occasion; an ear-splitting child screaming. He retrieved his mobile as he bounded down the steps. A highly anticipated email was waiting; the magazine was ready. Attached to the email was Allman, no doubt she may already be on her way to gathering the evidence.

By the time he finished reading the email, he was standing by the side of his vehicle. Climbing in the driver's position, his phone automatically connected through the radio conveniently. Using the dials; her name would display first Allman, Louise. Voicemail. Disheartened, he tried again, voicemail. He scoffed, turning out of the side street and making his way to the coroner's office. *Maybe she's already there?*

"Louise, it's Goodrick. Where are you? " he barked down the phone. Astonished at his arrogance, she replied.

"At home, I'm about to grab a shower. Why?"

"No time for that. I'm collecting the evidence now. I'll head straight over."

The line went dead, she held the phone outstretched in front of her and stared, gobsmacked. *Does he even know where I live? How did he get my personal number?* Slouching her shoulders, she turned the shower off and regrettably took her belongings back into the dressing room. Her dildo took its pride of place back inside the wardrobe, safely locked away until next time. Allman quickly threw on her clothes and tied her hair back in a low ponytail.

She clicked the kettle again, anticipating Goodrick may want a hot drink when he arrived. Presuming he was already at the coroner's office, his ETA would be less than ten minutes to reach her apartment block. She turned on the TV and slouched into her spacious corner couch.

"An anonymous tip-off to the police resulted in the finding of a young female's body in a remote house in the Fiddlers View area, Peak District. Police have yet to disclose any information relating to the discovery but are asking-"

Taking a deep breath, she clicked the television off and sat quietly engrossed in her thoughts. She could feel a migraine brewing, common side effect alcohol has on patients, but she blamed it on her overthinking instead. She couldn't bare another minute of rethinking her case. She's used the overthinking excuse for the past several months but her overactive mind along with an obsessive imagination are what made her good at her job.

BANG!

A heavy thud rippled through the walls that enclosed her, her heart thumped briefly as her eyes ripped open. Jumping to her feet, she paced towards the front door, anticipating another loud thud; she steadied her body before peering out of the peephole. There he stood, in a long overcoat, one hand nestled inside his trouser pocket with the other gripping an evidence bag. He was looking over his shoulder at her neighbour who began watering the potted plants on a nearby windowsill.

Bloody nosey parker. The old lady, Edith, had lived in the same apartment pretty much all her life. Always inquisitive when Allman would bring people home. She can't remember a time where Edith wasn't present during a goodbye kiss at the end of her many first dates.

Flinging the door wide open, almost knocking it off its hinges. She wanted to prove to Edith there was nothing to hide with this one. She exhaled and, maybe, over-exerted her efforts.

"Detective Goodrick, good morning. I see you've brought the important evidence for our case."

She flicked a fake smile over Goodrick's shoulder, directed at Edith while standing poised with both hands on either side of her door frame; she waited for either one of them to break their silence. With a steady turn of his head, Goodrick broke away his fixation with Edith. A detective's eye would humour the sight of a woman watering fake indoor plants.

"You look like shit." He gleamed at her, pushing his way through her barrier.

Her arm fell to her side with her smile deteriorating. It was due to Edith's poor attempt at hiding a hissing laugh that brought Allman back from her sinkhole. The hissing soon transpired into a disgusted huff when Allman flicked her middle finger up towards Edith. Slamming the door shut, she leaned back grinning, happy with herself. *Totally worth it.*

Pushing her body forward, she felt ready for the next battle. A clinking from a metal spoon circulated around the open room. *Of course, he's already helped himself to a drink. Why wouldn't he?* Slumping her body on the couch, she peered across at his overcoat, now draped over an arm, like it'd been there all along. *Make yourself at home Goodrick.* The evidence bag soon caught her attention. It laid bare on the glass coffee table, in-front of her. She sat nervously, staring intently, waiting for instructions. Her glare was obstructed from Goodrick's forearm, placing a cup of brewing tea on her edge of the table.

From the smell, she picked up a hint of ginger that was whooshed away as he stepped over her, taking a seat by her side. He sat at an inviting angle with his legs spread with entwined fingers hanging in the middle. He contrasted against the sheepish body language she was portraying; legs tightly squeezed together, forearms tucked into her sides and wearing a vacant expression.

She was arguing with herself within her thoughts, agitated for thinking rude of him, helping himself but only to come back with a drink for her. She never asked for a drink and the first words out of his mouth was an insult! *He's made himself right at home. Since when did he become the host?* Transpiring into a downward spiral, she contradicted herself with every argument, seeing the good and the bad within a minimal interaction.

"It's ginger tea. It'll help," Goodrick smiled at her.

She mirrored the gesture back, grateful for the clarity although, bewildered by the thoughtfulness. Leaning to his side to retrieve gloves, the movement made his knee naturally brush against hers. Frustrated by having her play interrupted, Allman took great pleasure from the touch. It'd been pushing a year almost, but whose counting?

"Well, do you want to do it?"

Almost choking on her tea, she coughed intrusively at his question, completely rendering its initial meaning. With a small laugh, he smacked her back with a series of direct hits, helping her clear her throat, along-with her mindset.

"Sorry?" She asked, turning her body towards him, ignoring the scorching heat on her back where his hand rested.

"You're in charge. Open it." With a gentle nod of the head towards the magazine, he replaced the cup she was gripping with a pair of gloves. She couldn't decide if the hand on her back was there for reassurance or persuasion now.

Anxiety and excitement churned in the pit of her stomach. *Could this be a breakthrough in the case?* Glancing behind her, Goodrick slouched with both arms draping over the couch, carefree, awaiting her next moves. With a single huff, she opened the bag and dragged the contents out, placing it delicately on the table.

"Well?"

CHAPTER 3

The smell of the ginger brew singed the hair from his nostrils, thumping him hard in the back of the throat. He'd taken a sip prematurely, without allowing it time to cool down. Tucking his now scolded lips inside his mouth, he attempted to squeeze the heat out. Always Goodrick's problem: prematurely doing something without thinking of any consequences beforehand. He only worried about issues when the time came to worry, but for him, nothing was worth worrying about.

"Ah," the country's acceptance for a good cuppa.

He exhaled a cloud of hot breath before placing the cup on the corner of the table. Smirking slightly, he appreciated the artwork on the coaster. Four in total, perfectly aligned to their assigned corners, displaying Kama Sutra positions. One on the far-left; the bridge position. *Maybe if I was ten years younger.* Far-right, the bow-down position. By Allman, the snail position and under his mug so happened to be his favourite; speed bump.

As he watched on, staring at the back of Allman's head, he morphed the imagery from the coasters to anticipating affairs. Being a well-paid, well-dressed, good-looking man in this town wouldn't surprise anyone; Goodrick could charm his way through any g-string easily. What did surprise everybody, including himself, was when he proposed to one of those g-strings. The announcement of the pregnancy, during the reception party, answered the rumours as to why the bachelor suddenly settled.

He hadn't worn his wedding band for some time now, but reminisces of his attempts of becoming a better man, embedded his flesh. The novelty soon wore off for Goodrick; just another one of his many poorly, premature decisions. He didn't have the characteristics to becoming a husband, especially to a one-night stand. He could only tell friends she liked to drink expensive wine and was good at giving head. *That was some wedding speech.*

He'd waited patiently for Allman's response, but she seemed completely engrossed in whatever she'd found. Leaning away from his comfort, he peered down at the (much to his surprise) unblemished magazine. He struggled to see anything due to the paper creasing from her tight grip. Gently, with a caressing stroke of her hand, she obliged, tilting the magazine towards Goodrick so he could catch up.

'One of our planet's most feared venomous lizards. They don't often need to hunt their prey; they can detect a carcass as far as six miles away. Keep in mind, they've been known to take down enormous prey. They're the ultimate ambush predators, lulling you into a false sense of security, and then they attack.'

Allman shuffled the papers of the magazine frantically across with imagery of Komodo Dragons flicking quickly from side to side. Some photography included a collective group of dragons, ripping apart a preys entrails. Another image depicted two dragons standing on their hind legs, fighting presumably. Goodrick took a liking to it for in his mind, the creatures were doing a reptile recreation of the distinctive dance; the tango.

Allman held the magazine outstretched, allowing them both to examine the cover. The outer card was heavily creased from the tight rolls. The inside was printed on thin, flexible paper could bend effortlessly. Blood smears were noticeable on the cover from the dried, flaking patches between the cracks. There was no front cover imagery, only the magazine's name, *Out of Hibernation*, with the subheading, *The Creatures*.

Becoming tiresome from the eerie silence, he clapped his hands together.

"So, it's just an animal magazine then?"

———

Huffing, she glared at the evidence; there had to be more to it. There must be, otherwise shes faced with another dead-end. Oddly to her, a wildlife magazine without an animal on the front cover? *Why a blank, black cover, why so unauthentic?* Goodrick's clap pierced her ears, making her flinch. She didn't want to admit he might be right; it's *just* a magazine.

"It must mean something to the victim, but what? She rhetorically asked the room, before directing it towards Goodrick. His intense stare suddenly made her felt self-conscious regarding her appearance. Barely given any time to dress, never mind an attempt to redo her makeup. The crust from her favourite lipstick had dried in the corners of her mouth, scratching her upper lip when she talked. Chunks of mascara clung onto the end of her long eyelashes, obscuring her vision. A pink complexion wasn't due to unwashed blusher; the intensity of Goodrick's eyes caused that. She'd never gazed upon that colour before; deep and dreamlike.

"Your eyes are *so* blue," she blurted.

A crease formed between her brows, becoming cognizant at what she'd said. If there was ever a time for the ground to swallow her whole; now would be a pretty good time. Goodrick's chuckle broke the awkwardness. She was appreciative for the break between their eye-contact when he glanced away briefly. It allowed her a few valuable seconds to fully recoup herself.

"I really don't know what that has to do with anything, Louise." Goodrick hooked her attention again.

There was something in the way he'd look at her. With eyes slightly squinted and his bottom lip would occasionally drop, invitingly. She liked hearing his northern Manchester accent, especially when he'd say her name. It was soothing how his monotone pitch could keep her enticed with every word.

"Sorry, just an observation. Sometimes it's difficult for me to keep my mouth shut. Always saying what I see before I've thought about it." She shrugged her shoulders, attempting to convince them both, there was nothing in it.

"Well, what do you see?" Goodrick inquisitively asked.

Allman gulped, not quite sure she understood his intentions clearly. Was he that big-headed he'd gloat over her slight ineptitude to hold her tongue from time to time? Well, she wasn't going to give him the satisfaction if so.

"A narcissist who enjoys hearing how great he is," Allman said smugly. She wasn't only referring to this instance, she'd observed him from afar for months. Always carried himself highly above everyone else with a self-importance arrogance. He loved the attention, and she was more than happy to knock him down a peg or two.

"I was talking about the magazine, you idiot."

She observed him in disbelief, as he chuckled, he had the better of her again. How can you attempt to insult someone, and yet you become the brunt of the joke?

His laughing intensified whilst he leaned over to retrieve his phone that had begun vibrating and jingling in his pocket. Allman glanced across, wanting to thank the caller for their impeccable timing. *Caller ID: The Witch.*

With a confused expression, she peered up at Goodrick, who'd quickly lost his sense of humour. He was transfixed, staring emotionless at the flashing white LED in the corner of his phone. Awkwardly, they both sat in silence, waiting for the ringing to stop. It felt time stood still as they waited: it was up to Allman to break the tension.

"I think we should make a few copies-"

"I need to go."

Goodrick abruptly jumped to his feet, and with one swift movement, phone; back in his pocket, overcoat; draped over his forearm and his ginger tea; chugged in a mouthful. Allman remained silent, bewildered by the sudden emergency. *Who was ringing him, whose The Witch?* Of all the times for him to be brash; he'd pick the time they're beginning to delve into their one and only clue.

"Seriously? You're leaving?" Allman asked with a hint of disgust, making it clear she wasn't pleased.

"Yes, call me if something *else* catches your eye." He said mockingly. She couldn't think of a snide, clever comeback in time before he slammed the mug down.

"Oh, and another thing..."

Allman looked up, rolling her eyes. *What smart-arse comment has he thought of now?* A repetitive noise drifted her attention to his index finger, tapping the coaster.

"That one's my favourite."

With a cheeky grin, he made his way towards the door hastily.

A look of horror came over Allman's face when she'd realised, hearing the door slam behind him. Living alone, she decorated her apartment with furnishes she thought tasteful and that included Kama Sutra coasters. It'd never occurred to her to tidy them away giving the far and few occasions she'd welcome visitors, especially to this area of the apartment.

The illustration depicted an outline of a woman lying flat on her stomach with her legs closed together, being mounted by a man. It's a position Allman found herself in regularly. It meant she'd never be faced with her mistakes, directly. She could bury any moans of pleasure into a pillow, receiving deep thrusts from, well, as far as she was concerned, anyone she could think of at that time. That's why she found it her favourite position too.

CHAPTER 4

July 20th, 2015

Her palms were clammy. The relentless stroking down her thighs may have helped remove excess sweat, but it left burn marks down her skin. The quick, short breaths only made her heavy heart thump harder within her chest. The uncontrollable shaking of her legs thrashed the file resting on her lap into a frenzy. This type of behaviour only happens on two occasions; either she was experiencing extreme pleasure, or she was fretting.

Gulping, she glanced ahead at the clock facing her, 09:35. The meeting should have started at 09:30, and being her punctual self, she'd already been sat there for an hour, gathering dust. She welcomed small chit-chat with passing officers beginning their dreaded Monday morning. Allman couldn't think of anything worse than to live by a strict schedule, starting your day at nine, finishing at five, repeating for the next four days, and then for the next forty-odd years.

Allman did envy their capability to switch off at five o'clock on the dot. Even in the early days, when her work wouldn't come home with her, she'd work extra hours, tying loose clues together into the night. She was deluded; thinking that she'd have less to do in the morning if she worked the night before. She learnt the hard way: crime doesn't have a stopwatch. It was a rough seven years sitting behind a desk, but it'd be all worthwhile, she convinced herself.

To waste the time, she counted the vinyl tiles across the office ceiling; she could count as far as forty-three. It frustrated her it wasn't an even number so, to be sure, she recounted them; four times. The pinboard opposite displayed useless mediocre leaflets on crime prevention. Top ten tips to keep your house secure, local adverts for self-defence classes, and her favourite one: 'How to Find Your Stalker.' *The irony.*

She squirmed uncomfortably, sweating under the pressure. Her white blouse peeled from the chair and slapped her on her back. Dripping wet, the transparent piece of cloth now displayed an ill-placed dolphin tattoo. The sweat droplets, dripping from the nape of her neck, made it appear the dolphin was back in it's natural habitat.

"Allman! Get in here!"

A roaring voice snapped behind her. She peeled herself from the chair, leaving a wet stained silhouette of her dignity behind. Staring through the glass panel, she could see a great oak desk carved with elephants. It would've been a beautiful piece of furniture if it wasn't ruined by the dickhead sitting behind it. He was happily huffing his pungent breath on the silver name plaque with the engraving: Chief Superintendent Chadwick.

Chief Superintendent Flatdick, more like.

"Well, come on, I don't have all day in 'ere you get."

Allman shuddered at his lack of professionalism. Always late, always wrong, and always ruder than last time. She regrettably found him charming when he moved to her office years prior, but that was a ploy to get her onside. *Yes, Chadwick, of course, Chadwick, I'll lick your arse Chadwick.* Driven to please her new boss, she bent over backwards, adapting to an incessant work load with the promise she'd make superintendent by 2013.

"Are you going to stand out there all day, or will I have to drag you in by your hair?"

Creaking the door open, she tiptoed inside. She didn't want to turn around, no doubt he'd mention the saturated blouse. Instead, she reached an arm behind herself and gently pushed the door shut. Flatdick extended a finger, instructing her to sit in the spacious leather chair opposite him. Regrettably, she did what she was told.

"Well, what have you got for me?" he asked, knowing the answer already.

"Nothing yet, but I-"

Allman was interrupted by the abrupt smash of his hand on the desk, she jumped unexpectedly with shock.

"Nothing, that's right! You have produced no leads, no motive, and no suspects! Have you even identified the body yet?"

The hatred in his eyes burned through to the back of her skull. She couldn't tell if the subtle shaking in his closed fist was due to pure rage or that he didn't anticipate the hard-wooden surface to bite back. Trying to defuse the situation, she shook her head, looking down at the flimsy case file sitting on her knee. No matter what he said, she was giving herself a grilling; feeling like a failure.

The autopsy report confirmed what they already knew; death by asphyxiation. The girl suffocated on faeces, some her own and some with others, whose DNA aren't recorded on any forensic database. The numerous tragic mutilations had never been seen before: this was no copycat. How did they expect Allman to find a new, off-the-grid killer? The house she discovered hadn't been occupied in over a century. The last registered owners died in 1907, with no heirs, hence the decaying condition it's in. Not one missing person report matched their body; she wasn't missed.

They pleaded on every national news asking for witnesses, begged whoever called in the initial tip-off to come forward but chances are; they never will. They used a burner phone, untraceable, perhaps intentional. They could be in danger themselves, or they were dealing with a boastful psychopath. Which one did she want to admit to? Either she's suddenly incapable of her job, or she'd finally been outsmarted.

"And Goodrick, where's he? He must've something by now."

"I don't know. He abruptly left my apartment ten days ago when we received the evidence, I haven't heard from him."

"Well, you have tried calling him, haven't you?" Chadwick sneered.

"Of course I have. Every day, at least five times. Sometimes rings out, and sometimes it's off. I asked for his personal file and for some absurd reason, was refused."

"Maybe he found something and is following a lead?"

"I doubt it. He only glanced at it, whereas I dissected it inch by inch. I know it's linked to the crime scene."

"Well, no shit Sherlock. It was removed from the corpse's cunt. How can it not be linked?" Chadwick belly laughed.

Allman shook her head in disbelief at his vulgar choice of words, given the delicate situation it was subjected to. Flicking through the file on her lap, she pulled photocopies of two pages from the magazine and placed them next to each other on the desk facing Chadwick, pointing to the barcode on the back page of the magazine.

"What are you trying to show me here?"

"Look at the barcode."

"Looks like a standard barcode to me, 9, 7, 8, 0, 0..."

Chadwick said mockingly.

"I mean the actual lines of the barcode. Does it not seem strange to you they're elongated?"

"It's clearly a bad print, been caught on the printer, and that's why it's all stretched."

With his stubby index finger, he tapped to the front cover, trying to prove his point. The title of the magazine was indeed stretched also.

"Look at it from a different perspective, hold the paper at eye level. It's an optical illusion."

He raised a concerning eyebrow in her direction but continued lifting the piece of paper above the protruding hook of his nose. From this angle, she couldn't help but find it comical. Even if she was having him on, which she wasn't, it'd have been worthwhile seeing his dull eyes drift in and out of focus. She hid her smile beneath her hand, attempting not to laugh, unable to imagine him looking any stupider. His eyes would cross over with a gormless frown, he was on the peak of seeing what she wanted him too, but then would lose it.

A few hard-concentrated minutes passed until he finally gave up, shaking his head in frustration. With tremendous force, he threw the piece of paper at her, to her amusement, it backfired. Gleefully watching it gently rock back and forth, falling effortlessly between them whilst he sat stiffly with a resentful expression.

"53, 10, 28, 4, N, 1, 49, 39, 8, W, 53, 1, 7, 4, 5, 6, 8, 1, 8, 2, 7, 7, 1, 1," Allman recited cheerfully in a musical way; it helped her memorise the barcode. His movements didn't knock her off her rhythm while he stood up, closed the blinds to the window and one over the door. She'd about finished her chant when he returned to his desk, standing upright. As much as she was a great detective, she didn't notice his movement. Much more distracted with the prospect she had a breakthrough with the case.

"Some lines are closer together, purposely. I wasn't sure what they meant at first until I began writing them down. I noticed what they were then. They're coordinates to the house."

She excitedly smiled, waiting for her well-done appraisal speech. Instead, she was awarded unenthusiastic clapping as Chadwick sarcastically slapped his hands together slowly. Allman readjusted herself in her seat, trying to hide any disappointment growing in her expression. She tearfully watched as he took great pleasure in the discomfort he was forcing her into.

"Well done, Miss Louise Allman, you found the exact same coordinates you used in your sat-nav to find the house."

Trying to regain what was left of her dignity, she stood upright so he didn't have the upper platform anymore.

"You don't get it. This girl followed those coordinates to that house. Someone lured her there intentionally!" Allman desperately shrieked.

"Sit the fuck down." Chadwick spat through gritted teeth.

Allman had never seen him so angry before. He always tended to lose his temper and was known to other districts as a hothead. Rumours that Internal Affairs were investigating him, which was no wonder with the way he held his own. In the beginning, Allman knew of the rumours but tried to give him the benefit of the doubt. She was never one to judge someone from hearsay but knowing she'd overstepped the line, she quickly sat back down; remembering her place. It was never like Allman to speak over superiors, but she was exhausted after years of trying to prove people wrong. Sick and tired of being mocked and made to look like a fool.

"You know what, Louise, I like you, I do. When I first came here, I knew it would be difficult to fit in, but you helped me. I'd like to return the favour. How about I take you off this case? You're clearly clutching at straws and exhausted your efforts."

Allman fought back the tears and blinked up towards the ceiling. *This can't be happening.*

"I just think your efforts would be appreciated elsewhere."

The sound of a zipper sent a lightning bolt through Allman's body, paralysing her. *No, not again.* She blinked away tears of frustration and turned her gaze towards him. He smirked from the corner of his mouth, lifting his belt strap up. The clash of the brass buckle felt like a punch to Allman's stomach. She continued watching the horror unfold with his trousers falling to the floor. Kicking them under the desk, he beckoned her over to him with the curl of his index finger. Internally, she was screaming no, positive the door wasn't locked. *Walk out, you don't need to do this anymore,* but before she could convince herself to be brave, she was already standing before him. She tearfully gulped as his measly erection probed her in the stomach.

"You know what to do," Chadwick stated.

Slumping to her knees, she crawled on all fours backwards until the sides of the desk fully enclosed her. Sitting back on her heels, she saw his briefs fall to the floor. He kicked them inside the cave she found herself trapped in. The enclosed space in such a hot office made breathing difficult. The only airflow she had was through the shallow tunnel between his legs, contaminated by the grotesque smell from his profoundly hung balls.

A claw forced its way under the desk, pinching at the back of her neck, dragging her trembling face towards him. His tip rubbed aggressively across her cheek, wet with precum. Strands of her hair began to knot around her neck, clinging to drenched skin, suffocating her further. Jabbing the end against her lips, she could taste the saltiness, from the tears beginning to run down her face, along with a potent onion-like aroma. Prising her jaw apart, she regrettably took his dick, sliding it inside her mouth. He wasn't a fortunate man; it could stretch all the way inside, and she'd still have the room to tell him so.

Closing her eyes, she tried to picture herself anywhere but here, doing this. A sunny beach in a hammock with her body rocking back and forth. The burning sensation on her shins; from the sun, not from the grazing on the carpet beneath her. She couldn't think why her throat had a dry and bitter taste. The sensation felt like swallowing shards of glass, different from her usual ice-cream beach treat.

Sensing his discomfort from the lack of tongue motion, mixed with a roughness of chapped lips, he pulled her head away. She gasped in joy; maybe he'd had enough of her intentional lousy job?

A muffled snort was followed by the sound of a singular splash. She flinched, knowing what's to come. She daydreamed the sound was a wave, caressing the shoreline. Snapping out of her abyss, she painfully watched him rigorously yanking, stretching it uncomfortably whilst his balls jiggled back and forth. The phlegm gathered on his palm as he pleasured himself with the thick lube. The squelching was enough to make Allman gag, let alone when a droplet landed on her forehead.

He was quickening his pace inches away from her. *He's almost finished.* Sweat was pouring down his legs whilst a twitch in his knees intensified.

Allman braced herself for the finale, anticipating a jet stream to spray across her face.

"Excuse me, Chief, do you have a minute?"

Allman's eyes shot open to the soothing voice of a woman she didn't recognise, the creaking of the door hinges meant whoever it was, was now inside the room. Before the woman finished her question, Chadwick jerked Allman's head into his crotch, taking his length back into her mouth. The slimy texture of his mastered lube stabbed her taste buds. She began to slightly choke, unintentionally tightening her throat, which seemed to please him.

"I'm a little busy at the minute. Can this wait until tonight?"

"Oh, but Danny, you promised you'd make more time for me. I'm not wearing any panties..."

The more Allman wriggled for air, the tighter he yanked her in. Her face began to sting from unruly pubic hair, pricking her across her mouth as he continued to muffle her.

"Oh, come on, baby. You can't tell me things like that at work. You'll get me in trouble."

"I told you, I am trouble." the woman giggled flirtatiously.

"Yes, you are, but I'm sorry, love, you *really* need to go. I'll make it up to you," he promised.

The woman huffed, not satisfied but understood perfectly, like any controlled woman would: she obeyed.

"Alright then, you best had."

Allman heard the door shut and knew there'd be trouble. He wouldn't take it lightly; a disturbance during his pleasure time. With her face pinned onto him, he pushed backwards, dragging her along. A waft of fresh air brushed across Allman's face, intensifying the penetrating taste and smell. She glared up at him, with tears wobbling on her lashes, to his disgruntled snarl.

"Well, that could've been awkward, couldn't it?"

He placed the phlegm coated hand through her hair, clamping his fingers behind her neck.

"How would I've explained to my girlfriend why you're sucking my dick, eh?"

He began thrusting against her face aggressively.

"Eh? What would I've told her? How this slut, you, slut, can't keep your hands off me?"

Allman began feeling herself go limp, the relentless head jerks and the ache in her jaw, she was struggling to breathe, and although there was more air to cool her down, the room was scorching.

"You like sucking my hard cock, don't you?"

Allman resisted giving him any more satisfaction. She was already trying to hinder any movements to avoid touching him further. She shook her head in defiance. The side of her face throbbed from the provoked slap he delivered.

"You fucking like it, don't you?" Chadwick hissed.

She again; shook her head, refusing to give him what he wanted.

"You're going to fucking have it!"

Flinching as his final grunt pulsated through him, a tangy hot sensation gathered at the back of her throat. *Swallow; get it out!* His grip loosened on her head and the restraints slipped away. She wasted no time hurrying to her feet, marching towards the door, wiping sweat and spit from her face.

"Before you leave, Louise." He chirped up. She stood motionless with her back towards him, waiting until he finished gathering himself.

"If Goodrick doesn't get back to us by end of tomorrow with at a positive lead rather than your *delusional illusions*. I'm handing the case over."

With a final tear dropping from her tired eyes, she quickly jolted to the nearest bathroom. Flinging the door wide open, she looked nervously around. *Coast is clear.* She erupted into a frantic episode of uncontrollable sobbing. Her heart wrenched with each breathtaking cry as she leaned into the sink. Running the tap, she splashed cold water repeatedly on her face. She clasped her mouth around the stream, allowing the unfiltered liquid to run down her stinging throat. Collecting enough to gargle, she attempted to spit the evil out of her.

Panting, she looked up at her reflection. She didn't feel herself shaking but could see the wobble in her elbows, struggling to hold herself upright. Closing her eyes and taking deep breaths, managing to calm herself down. In no way was she to blame for this. She spent too long blaming herself. *This stops right now.* Opening her eyes, beginning to recognise the woman in the mirror again.

Digging her phone out of her pocket, she looked up the call history; only tried Goodrick twice today. *Third time lucky?* Crossing her fingers, she dialled and waited. *Please answer Gregory, I need you.*

CHAPTER 5

July 19th, 2015

"Is this enough?"

"More to the left."

Huffing, Goodrick dragged the thick fabric of the living room curtains until he heard a rip.

"Oh! See what you've gone and done now, you silly boy. They were an anniversary present from my great nana!"

"Yeah, you can tell." Goodrick joked.

The rip in the old, frayed fabric made the green and yellow eyesore pattern a little less distasteful in the artex room. The only thing that brightened the room was the sun's light beam that began seeping through. Dark wooden furniture cluttered the room, glass cabinets overflowing with ancient artefacts, everything mummified by an inch-thick coating of dust. Everything except Ida Stone, a name to match her heart. Stern, assertive, and an arrogantly, opinionated old hag.

"You watch your tongue around me, young man, I may be old, but I'll give you a good hiding! Now hurry and fetch my handbag will you? I'd receive better treatment in a morgue!"

He could hear her babbling away to herself as he walked into the adjoining bedroom, collecting a tattered handbag as instructed. With only one strap remaining, he scooped the aged leather bag with both hands to keep all the useless tat contained. He never understood why people needed to use money bags in this day and age. Every coin was collectively confined to its own sort, divided into multiple bags. Somewhere in there, she held onto her blue ration card used in World War II. Everything found a permanent place, he couldn't even remember any details of the wallpaper. Picture frames stretched the entire surface, strangers making the home décor, nameless people who were either dead or simply didn't bother with her. He gave up trying to find one single picture of himself or his late father: there isn't one. Her relentless mumbling became louder as he made his way back into the musky living area.

"Bloody lazy good-for-nothing. I told your father he smothered you, babied, that's it! No wonder you turned out how you are."

Dropping the handbag by her feet, Goodrick walked to the other side of the room with both hands in his pockets, looking down at the ghastly red carpet with a kick in his step. He had to admit, the five years living with her were hell. He couldn't wait to move out. It was exceptionally hard when his father died four years after that. The only reason that kept him visiting her every month was his wayward thinking; if his dad loved her, he could too.

Fast forward sixteen years, he's fetched her home from the hospital after a nasty fall. Of course, none of her, as she calls them, true children came to her aid, with their love as dormant as it was all those years ago. Goodrick came to the conclusion that some people were just born evil. After meeting many criminals in his career, he was a good judge of character. *Why did my father marry such a heinous bitch?*

"Coming here in your flashy motor vehicle, showing off!"

"Are you about finished, Ida?"

Goodrick interrupted her ranting. Disgruntled, she turned her face in a downward snarl.

"Right, I must be off. Your tablets are by the sink. District nurse, Anne, is coming today, so be nice. She almost quit last week."

"That lard arse, she's stealing from me she is! Soon as I catch her, god help her. I'll ram this stick so far up her-"

"Alright, Ida! That's enough! I'm going to be busy for the next few days. Only call if it's an emergency, okay?"

With a stiff nod of the head, she understood. Goodrick started making his brisk escape towards the exit. He pulled the chain from the door before hearing her screeching parting words.

"Tell that café slut, Ida Stone's still alive and kicking. Tell the home-wrecker I win!"

Goodrick shook his head before slamming the door behind him. Growing tired of the tedious spat between Ida and the rest of the world. As awful as it sounds, he was looking forward to the day he'd receive a phone call, announcing her death. Her two offsprings, who she had before she married his father, would cash in on their fortune, and his promise to his dad will be fulfilled. Until then, the past nine days he spent with her would easily justify an absence for the next six months, thankfully.

He pressed the fob to his car, startling a huddle of school children gathering around it. Gawking inside, trying to see through the blacked-out windows. Goodrick presumed they were looking for anything worth stealing. Maybe he was wrong, but nonetheless, he didn't appreciate the handlebars from their BMXs so close to his BMW.

"Shouldn't you lot be in school?" He shouted across the communal car park; housing an overflowing skip and remains of a decayed mattress.

"This your car mate?" one of the kids asked.

"Yup." Goodrick gleefully smiled, patting the roof.

"How much did that cost you then?"

"Oh, I don't know, at least five years studying and then a decade of hard grafting."

"You some sort of cop?" Another kid nodded towards Goodrick's badge that dangled around his neck.

"You could say that."

"Fucking pig."

The biggest in the group held his head high, took a deep nasal snort, and spat down at the concrete floor towards his feet. Goodrick watched the droplet of phlegm land inches away from his polished shoes. Lucky for the kid, he had poor aim. Arching an eyebrow, Goodrick looked towards him with a slight smirk.

"What's the matter? Your parents not teach you to respect the authorities?"

"We respect our own. You're in the wrong fucking neighbourhood, pig!"

Goodrick chuckled, rubbing his hand across his jaw. A coping mechanism he regularly used to deflect his anger.

"I see. Well, stay out of trouble, and I won't be back here."

With a fake smile across his face, he jumped in the drivers seat, switching the engine on. Hearing the muffled insults the teenagers bounced back and forth, erupting in laughter; he couldn't blame them. He was the same at their age, probably worse.

This neighbourhood was his stomping ground, which he gladly grew out of. His father paid for him to attend boxing lessons, thinking it'd be a good way to punch out his frustrations. Not realising it only made him stronger, more tactical. Someone only had to look at him the wrong way; didn't take much for a right hook.

The turning point for Goodrick; his father suddenly dying from a brain aneurysm, so he traded the gloves for books. Instead of throwing parties, he attended late classes at the college. His neighbourhood gave him the perfect step ladder to kick-start his career, picking off corner drug dealers he once bought from. Bit by bit, he tore apart his old life and dragged the scum down with it. Every criminal he caught was a new, more rewarding high for him. He always had a competitive streak, and by his first year, he set a record for arrests made. Goodrick may be good at what he does on paper, however, luck and knowing where to find a criminal played a part.

Turning his phone on, it was flooded with disregarded notifications. He knew he should've been in touch with Allman sooner, alerting her to his situation. He felt guilty after his abrupt departure but selfishly thought she had it all in hand. Dealing with Ida consumed all of his attention and efforts. He couldn't leave her bedside without being bombarded with ludicrous questions and accusations. Being mentally abused was draining: comprehending work with the ongoing case made him shudder.

A familiar name flashed on the screen: Nicole. Goodrick smirked, gleaming down at the picture. Taken from a confident angle, it displayed her protruding chest. Her grin proved she wasn't shy about displaying her assets. They bulged to their limits under a tightly fitted tank top she teasingly pulled further down. Excited butterflies fluttered in the pit of Goodrick's stomach, just the distraction he craved.

'Hey sxc, think u could tear urself away from the wicked witch for an hour? I have a surprise for u.'

'I'm coming now, be ready!'

He found himself in a busy side street, littered with takeaway joints. A lonely red door with an intercom stood before him. He nervously glanced around, it wasn't uncommon to see familiar faces this side of town. He tossed between a couple of excuses in case he was seen but always settled on the most convenient one; witness statement. The door unhatched with a sudden buzz, giving him permission to enter.

Jolting up the stairs, he paused briefly outside her door, pushing any unruly hairs backwards with his palm. He raised his fist to knock, but with gentlest of touches, the door squeaked open.

Greeting him was a heavily used sofa with sagging cushions. The coffee table stacked with old pizza boxes consisting of her weekly diet. The kitchen, if you could call it that, consisted of: a battered under-counter fridge; a broken microwave; a kettle (for the pot noodles of course) and a toaster used as a makeshift lighter. Goodrick didn't come here for the pleasantries: the constant hopping to avoid the clutter land mines didn't bother him. Giggling became increasingly louder as he reached a closed door; he intently knocked three times.

"I believe you have something to show me."

"Why don't you come in and see for yourself."

He stood still as he watched the door swing back to reveal the room. Before him laid a double bed, metal silver bars as a headboard. What lay on top of the colourful duvet interested him the most. She was restrained with bright pink fluffy handcuffs.

"And how did you get yourself into those?" He jested whilst ogling at her.

Nicole laughed flirtatiously before responding.

"I don't know, it's a mystery detective."

Loosening his tie, Goodrick confidently prowled up to his prey with hunger thumping his stomach. Waves of adrenaline pulsated through his body as he began to crawl over her. Her legs squirmed until he straddled her, pinning her tightly between his thighs. Looking down at her with a menacing look, she smiled up at him with desire. Tracing the cute dimple on her cheek with his thumb, he held her head forward and, with the other hand, wrapped his tie around the back of her head. Pulling both ends of the tie, matching their lengths, he crossed them over and under the other.

"What are you going to do with that, detective?"

With a snap of his wrists, he ripped his palms apart, creating a knot in the tie that forced downwards across her mouth. He quickly took the ends of the tie and repeated the motion. A second knot accelerated towards her, rendering her speechless. With the remains of the tie, he pushed it into the gaps of her mouth, gagging her.

"No talking."

She gently quivered as he ran his lips across her cheek, under her jawline, and pressed his lips together over the delicate skin of her neck. Using his knees, he pried her legs open and knelt between her trembling thighs, beginning to pinch her skin with tender bites. Reaching his hand down and unzipping his trouser pants, his growing penis could hardly breathe, suffocated by his trousers.

She jerked forward and pressed her chest into him as he kissed her neck intensely. He pulsated from the sensitive touches of the wet lace material that seeped between her legs. With his index finger, he hooked under the bodysuit and delicately slid his finger along the shape of the material.

Biting down aggressively when he felt the slippery substance on his finger, forcing the material to the side. Thrusting inside her silk-like vagina, gasping at the immediate pleasure.

"Fuck!"

CHAPTER 6

July 20th, 2015

"Louise, how are you?"

She sighed with relief from hearing his voice.

"Gregory! Where've you been? Are you alright?"

"I asked first, are *you* alright?"

She fought back any bubbling tears, not wanting to let slip she'd been crying. As good as she was at acting everything was fine, when someone bothers to ask her how she really was, she'd crumble. She could sense his characteristic sarcasm in the question, surprisingly, she's grateful to hear it again.

"Of course, only losing my mind wondering where the fuck you've been!"

"Sounds like you've missed me?"

She could hear the smile in his voice. Loosening up, she tilted back and forth on her heels, childishly. A much-needed grin stretching across her face.

"That's a little pedantic of you, isn't it?"

They both simultaneously chuckled.

"I'm glad you think so, but to answer your question, yes, I'm fine, a little family trouble, that's all."

"Oh no, is everyone okay?"

"You're a very concerned woman Louise. Didn't I just say everything was fine?"

"Well, to be exact, you only said *you* were fine."

"Now, who's being pedantic?"

She let out a slight giggle and began pacing the seven-foot room. It might have been an awkward silence, but thankful for an excuse to smile again, she didn't care.

"You don't have a comeback, do you?"

"No, I was never good at them, so I'll just take it."

"I bet you do."

Pausing from her stride, she thought she knew what he was insinuating by his sarcastic tone but, surely not. Maybe it was her dirty mind that felt every conversation could be interpreted in that manner, but Goodrick was a professional.

"Have you had a chance to catch up on my emails?" Allman asked, diverting the topic.

"Well, I've made a start on them this morning."

"You've only started this morning?!"

"I'm glad my English is fluent. Yes, this morning, that's what I said."

"Goodrick, I've sent you over twenty emails and five reports. You can't have read everything properly?" Allman shouted back.

"Oh good, we're onto surnames again. I've read them, maybe skimmed through, but I thought you'd like to catch me up."

"We don't have time for you to play catch up. We've less than thirty hours to come up with a lead."

"Who says?"

"My superintendent! He's not happy we have nothing yet, I'm against a ticking clock, and I really needed you to have something for me!"

"What about the optical illusion with the coordinates, I remember reading that?"

"He called them my *delusional illusions.*"

"Delusional illusions: I wish I'd thought of that," Goodrick said, laughing. He must've taken the silence as a warning and quickly tried to continue the conversation.

"Well, it's a difficult case, that's all. Every great detective hits a brick wall. You need fresh eyes and a clear head. I'm sure something will come to you."

"I'm sure it will but like everything that comes, too little, too late."

"Does that include men?"

"Now I know you are trying to be rude, Goodrick."

They both laughed, equally contempt with the break in the seriousness of their conversation.

"But truthfully, Gregory, I really need your help. They didn't call you in if you'd be good for nothing."

"Wow, that almost hurt. If you ask nicely, I might have something for you."

"Don't play with me, Gregory. Tell me if you have something!"

"It's no fun if I tell just you."

"I don't have time for this. Where are you anyway?"

"What do you want to know first; where I am or what I might have?"

"Is it always going to be a game with you?"

"Rule one: one question at a time."

"Gregory! Fucking tell me something already!"

'Rule two: ask nicely."

Allman angrily huffed, burying the phone into her chest to muffle her frustration. Closing her eyes, she took three deep breaths and began to play along.

"Gregory, what do you have for me? Please tell me. I'd be ever so grateful to you."

"Rule three: don't take the piss."

"Goodrick!" she screamed in annoyance.

"Alright, alright." He began laughing.

"In the house, did you thoroughly check the upstairs?"

"Well, no, they said due to the handrails condition, it'd be a safety hazard, so I was never there when they searched it."

"You only needed to lean heavily against the wall on a couple of steps. It's fine."

"Are you telling me you're at the crime scene? They told me they found nothing upstairs."

"Yeah, well, I think you have some lousy people working for you."

"What do you mean? Is that where you are? What's there?"

"I'll remind you of rule one again: one question at a time. You have either lazy or inept people working for you."

"What are you trying to tell me?"

"I'm only saying, I think we might have something. Something your people clearly missed. If I had my team, this wouldn't have happened."

"Well, now's not the time to talk about recruitment. What is it?"

"I'm not sure."

"What do you mean?"

"Well, there's six bedrooms, right?"

"Right, and?"

"Each one has been decorated differently."

"Most bedrooms are, I really don't-"

"What I'm trying to say, if you let me finish, each bedroom has been decorated *recently*. The rest of the house is in a decaying state, despite that large mirror, but all the bedrooms must've been lived in."

"How recent? The house hasn't been registered to anyone for years. Maybe squatters?" Allman offered reasoning.

"I don't think squatters would go so far as to wallpaper each room and assemble four-poster beds."

"No, I agree. I know they swabbed the bedrooms but there was no mention of their condition."

"They're immaculate, except one of them having scratch marks by the door, the duck room."

"Sorry, the duck room?" Allman questioned.

"Yeah, there's a duck carved into the door."

"What's on the others?"

"So far, I've only seen three of them. One looks like a bug or a beetle, and I've seen one that looks like a lizard."

"I need to be there. Don't touch anything, okay?"

Allman began swinging the door open, she heard a loud thud coming from the other end of the phone, followed by Goodrick's signature chuckle.

"What did I just say?!"

"I promise, I won't touch anything... from now on."

With an exaggerated sigh to express her concern, she hung up and began marching her way down the corridor.

The intense noise of phones ringing, constant chatter, and the occasional desk bang – which seemed to most officers their only release of frustration – hit Allman hard in the face. Scrunching her nose in anguish, she soldiered on walking along the outskirts of the room, trying to keep her head down, until she reached her office.

Her small office consisted of a sturdy desk with the only window behind it. Shadowed by the building's hedges, never overlooked. The room displayed a lonely, cold feel to it that Allman knew all too well. She placed the flimsy file inside the top drawer, slamming it shut. She felt embarrassed that she had convinced herself it would've impressed Flatdick. A sudden knock on the door spooked her, making her jump slightly.

"Come in!" She panted, quickly gathering her belongings and throwing her coat over her shoulders, eager to get to the crime scene.

"Louise, it's only me!"

Allman grinned when she saw the gap-toothed smile from a young woman, Jade. Standing at only 5'1, Allman towered over her with her skyscraper-like height. She shuffled into the office with both arms outstretched trying to balance her tiny frame on top of what only could be described as ankle breakers. Allman laughed at the sight, thankful she didn't need to indulge herself with such ridiculous fashion statements.

"You're going to break your bleeding neck in them!" Allman shrieked.

"Well, If I do, I'll at least go down looking fabulous." Jade laughed, hovering herself a few inches in front of Allman's desk. She placed a hand down flat to balance herself and, with the other hand, placed it casually on her hip. The control and effort it must take to stop herself going arse over tit with every step took its toll on her. Allman could hear the rasped breaths and see the soreness in her expression.

"You should take those shoes off, Jade."

"Are you crazy? These bad boys cost me five-hundred quid in the sale. I'm bloody getting my money's worth."

"Remind me, how much are intern photocopiers on nowadays?" Allman asked sarcastically.

"Oh ha-ha, a big fancy detective now, I do more than photocopy, you know. I sometimes have to send a fax to the other office, easily a five-minute job. We all can't break out of the administration role like *some*."

"Well, I guess *some* of us are made for bigger things, clearly not you, without the help of those."

Allman laughed, walking past her friend while pointing at the sleek black shoes with the signature red underneath. Ironically, Allman thought that represented blood seeping from Jade's feet.

"Alright, alright, I only came in for a quick hello anyway. You're never around these days."

"Yeah, I've been busy and I'm going out now, sorry. Just got off the phone with Detective Goodrick, who thinks he's found a breakthrough in the case."

"Oh! Gregory Goodrick? That fit guy that used to sit by our Paul?"

Allman had reached her office door when Jade finished her question. Turning around, she'd climbed up on Allman's desk, sitting patiently for a response. Clearly not understanding the urgency Allman was in.

"Yeah, the very same. Flatdick asked for his help." She said, rolling her eyes.

"Since when did you need any help from a man?"

Allman chuckled at Jades sarcastic question, beginning to engross herself in the conversation.

"Well, never, but he seems different."

"He's not an arrogant fuck anymore?"

"Oh no, he's still that, but I'm growing to like that. He's, how can I phrase it, witty and sarcastic more than anything."

"Hmm, I think it's those eyes and arm muscles that are doing it. Remember, he took what was yours, you deserved that promotion, not him!"

"Yeah, but he wasn't to know. The faster I work with him and solve this case, the quicker he's out of my hair anyway."

Allman opened her office door to entice the departure of her friend, eager to get going. Jade lowered herself from the desk slowly, creasing her face when her feet hit the ground. The pain from the pressure inflicted on the soles must've been crippling.

"He may be a dick, but he's a definite smash from me," Jade laughed as she staggered through the open door.

Allman smiled, reminiscing their game: smash or pass. Choosing, unknowingly to other colleagues, people into their game, where they'd giggle and debate reasoning for passing or smashing on a colleague jokingly.

It helped pass the time during brain numbing tasks by describing steamy, sexual scenarios. Working within a male dominated workplace, they had plenty of contestants to choose from. Goodrick, being one of Jade's favourites, however, Allman used his arrogance for passing, denying the obvious. Allman would be quickly shut down when she began providing her go-to smash: Paul, Jade's cousin.

"You know what Jade, Goodrick's a smash for me after-all."

CHAPTER 7

"**F**uck!"

Goodrick cried out, wafting his hand to reduce a throbbing sensation pricking his fingertip. Maybe that'd teach him not to be rifling with a mysterious box. He found it placed front and centre on a chest of empty drawers in the duck room.

Small, rectangular shape made from dark mahogany, with the carving 'Ducky' on top. Piquing his interest enough to investigate what's inside. A small ballerina wearing a silver sparkling tutu sprung up. The lid unexpectedly snapped shut onto his thumb, causing him to drop it instantly.

The thud as it hit the floorboards echoed into a sweet lullaby as it creaked open. Goodrick recognised himself in the mirrors reflection, obstructed by the twirling figurine. The music sounded familiar; a slow, soft harmony of chimes. He couldn't place his bloody finger on where he'd heard it before but knew enough to hum along.

Captivating him for a short duration, until the ballerina came to a stop. Only now he noticed the wet sensation seeping from a small cut on his finger. He opened his hand to the sight of fresh blood pooling in the creases of his palm. A droplet formed, running through the indent of his deeply curved heart-line. Goodrick shuddered at the less-than-desirable sensation from the warm substance. Surprisingly for a homicide detective, he couldn't stomach blood. The look of it, the feel of it, the smell of it: repulsive. He'd recount a handful of crime scenes that'd pushed his limits, luckily, a sick bag was never too far away.

He'd crease reminiscing a time he stumbled across an axe victim. A young girl who'd a nasty run-in with her psychotic boyfriend. Accused of cheating; he took matters into his own hands. The punishment: dismemberment.

Goodrick stood over her detached head that had an eerily bleak expression. It was determined she'd died during the first couple of fatal swings. What sort of monster could look down at such a pretty face and deliver another ninety-two blows, completely tearing and ripping her apart?

That was the first time a crime scene caused him to violently heave. Attempting to overcome his weakness for blood, he found himself volunteering for the real gritty crimes. The logic was simple, the more he saw of it: the quicker he'd become used to it. When that coping mechanism failed, he sought help from a shrink, practising hypnosis to tackle it. That technique only resulted in bringing his past traumas to light. One being a severe attachment issue caused by the abandonment from his mother.

He vividly remembered the horror on his dad's face whenever his mothers eyes glazed over: drunk again. His dad tried his best to explain the mysterious daily disappearances. It didn't take long for baby Goodrick to not miss her at all. The weeks soon turned into months, seven years had passed until Goodrick questioned her whereabouts. To avoid the difficult conversation, his dad would take him window shopping. Goodrick used the distraction to his benefit but when the retail therapy subsided, he demanded answers.

"Your mum's gone, and she isn't coming back, Gregory. We don't need her anyway, do we mate? We're alright just you and me."

His dad encouragingly smiled, teasingly punching Goodrick on the shoulder. The sleeves from his dad's bomber jacket accidentally brushed against his fresh brew, smashing the china cup into pieces. A chubby woman, wearing a colourful floral apron, stumbled towards their table. Placing a delicate touch on his dads back, she stopped any attempt for him to pick up his mistake.

"I'm so sorry. I didn't mean to knock it off."

"It's fine, dear. This sort of thing happens all the time. You stay where you are, and I'll be back with a dustpan and brush."

"Great, thank you...erm-"

The woman smiled warmly at him.

"Eileen, dear, my names Eileen."

Tearing up, he refocused his mind, determined to find something Allman could use to make up for his absence. It might have been the memories from his childhood that began to bubble any guilt he felt. From his distasteful antics with Nicole from last night, to the ignorance he showed for the case. Selfishly only looking out for number one: himself.

A creak from downstairs alerted him with the realisation, he was alone, unarmed, where a girl was brutally murdered. Feeling vulnerable, he carefully tip-toed out of the room, avoiding any of the squeaky floorboards. A shadow forming as somebody, something, attempted to climb the decaying staircase. He tuned into the echoes of scratching, a struggle becoming apparent. Cautiously, he lifted himself towards the gallery landing to peer over the staircase, hopeful to catch a glimpse of an intruder.

Exhaling thankfully, the brunette hair gave her identity away. Dropping his shoulders, he casually leant his arms over the handrail, observing her frustrations at the obstacle.

"I thought you'd be longer!" he bellowed from above. Amused he spooked her, he began to chuckle. Allman unexpectedly jumped, frantically looking around to source his voice before looking straight up.

"How the bloody hell do you get up there?"

Goodrick leisurely walked around the perimeter of the handrails before stopping at the top of the stairs.

"Would you like some help, Louise?"

"From you?" She scoffed.

"Well, who else?"

Goodrick graciously took a step downwards, extending a helping hand; presenting himself as her saviour.

"What on earth have you done?" Allman asked worriedly.

Goodrick clenched, forgetting about his dry, bloodstained hand. Whipping it quickly behind his back, he offered his alternative hand for assistance.

"It's nothing. Now come on."

He wiggled his fingers in a beckoning motion, enticing Allman to grab him. With one big heave, he yanked her upwards. The force of the pull, catapulted her so fast she'd barely the time to find her feet. Luckily, Goodrick was quick with his reactions and held her steady. Flicking her hair over her shoulder in a swift movement, she welcomed Goodrick to a pleasing up-close view.

A smile grew, noticing her sparkling hazel eyes looking back at him. She was different from his usual type, difficult to believe, as Goodrick had a list as long as Allman's hair of past lovers. All of which came in different shapes and sizes but consisted of the same persona; needy. Goodrick loved seducing women to the point they'd end up heartbroken, hooked on his charisma and charm. Their relentless begging for his attention enforced his wayward need for acceptance. He didn't see the much-wanted look of desperation in Allman's eyes. Instead an independent, assertive woman glared back at him, intriguing him enough to sway his victim profiling.

"If you've got any blood on my coat, I'll slap you," Allman threatened.

"Let's hope I have," Goodrick smirked, releasing his grip. Mesmerised by her taking her final step unassisted. She stretched the sides of her jacket tightly, hugging her figure.

"Well? Is it alright?"

Goodrick bit down on his bottom lip, raising an eyebrow, exaggerating his studying pose. Unfortunately for him, no transferable blood stains.

"Perfect," he smirked.

Allman rolled her eyes, stepping onto a creaky floorboard, flinching unexpectedly at the sudden noise. Goodrick brushed his hand over her shoulder, desperate for the touch, but also to lead her away from further nuisances.

"Come on, this way," he directed.

He led her to one of the bedrooms, consisting of a grand four-poster bed and a chest of drawers with the music box. With no natural light, the room was eerily dark, easy to miss any distinctive details. Goodrick allowed Allman to inspect the room in silence. He waited patiently by the door, where the carving of the duck rested above him.

"What are you thinking, Louise?" He asked, believing ample time had passed for her to gather her thoughts.

"The lack of dust unlike downstairs, hardly used mattress, someone was staying here alright."

She thrashed out of the room, narrowly avoiding a collision with Goodrick, surprising given the small proximity of the doorway.

Following her stride into the next room, carved with a reptile. Exact same layout as the last, the bed stripped from all linen, chest of empty drawers but no box. Allman paced around the room, examining every millimetre, before quickly rushing to the others. She darted back and forth across the landing, returning to the duck room for analysis. Goodrick had a skip in his stride, attempting to keep up with her pace. Each animal depicted door was smashed open during Allman's raid. She abruptly stopped her stampede, tapping her finger on a carving of a Komodo Dragon.

"What is it?" He asked.

"I think it's the room we're after."

Allman turned the handle, allowing it to swing open. Both detectives stood waiting patiently, panting from the relentless searching.

"Thank fuck for that," Goodrick said, stumbling into the final room, grateful to not be chasing Allman's tail anymore. Nothing. No bed. No drawers. No window. The only light source came from Allman's phone flash as she shined it around the empty room. They both sighed collectively, standing in complete darkness as Allman nestled her phone away. Perhaps to hide her disappointment. Goodrick began to hear muffled, distorted breathing. *Was she crying?* He peered towards where he believed she was standing, impossible to know indefinitely. He extended a hand outwards into the abyss, hopeful to delicately touch her.

Surprisingly, he felt a warm embrace of her body pushing against him. A sweet smell of coconut radiated up his nostrils as he felt her nestle into the crevice of his chest. Her body began to tremor, confirming what Goodrick thought. He wrapped his arms supportingly around her, squeezing them close together.

He knew the difficulty of being a detective in her office, unhealthy competitiveness and a hierarchy made up of ride-or-die friendships. He knew of the urban office myths, detectives demoted within their first case, due to impossible expectations and unrealistic timescales. Some had been caught tampering with evidence just to make things fit, desperate to impress. Sometimes, they needed to admit, they've been outsmarted, easier said than done.

That's why Goodrick was delighted to hear the news he was transferring to Tannoch. A specialised, much more rewarding office, working as a relief detective for other districts. Each one was hand-picked for their individual strengths; for example, Lil' Laura was small but mighty. She could manipulate the holiest of men to admit forbidden sins with her words, the best interrogator in the country. A blood analyst, Stuart, gladly helped Goodrick on a few of his cases, which he couldn't stomach. He'd bring a crime scene to life with a use of singular thread, creating complex webs.

Tannoch's superintendent, Adriana Cross, assured him he was chosen for his unique perspectives. Perhaps because he wasn't schooled like other detectives, common sense and logic rather than textbooks, helped him to know what happened instead of using an over-analytical mind. That's where the popular opinion of his arrogance perceived from: turn up; state the obvious; be right and then mic-drop on his departure. He could sympathise with Allman, despising the system capable of breaking down such a dynamic detective like her.

"It's alright. We've more to work on now, don't we? You couldn't expect the killer to be sitting in here waiting for us, could you?"

He tensed, knowing he should've chosen a more delicate way of phrasing what he meant. Although, that was Goodrick's hand-picked strength: saying it exactly how it is.

"Of course, I didn't. I wanted more, that's all." Allman sounded defeated.

"I'm sorry, Louise, I really am."

Goodrick stumbled feeling her head tilting upwards, delicately, she stroked her nose against his. *Where's she going with this?* Bewildered, he froze, anticipating her next moves in the pitch-black room. Her puckered lips brushed past his as she spoke softly.

"It's okay, Gregory. It wasn't your case to solve anyway."

His chest deflated as she tore away from his grip, leaving him alone in the dark. Sighing, he was in disbelief over the intensity of their 'friendly' hug. He felt a heavy sinking sensation at the loss of opportunity. Unaware to Allman, Goodrick was up for a cat-and-mouse chase, and she became his new mouse.

CHAPTER 8

July 21ˢᵗ, 2015

"Lou!"

An excited familiar voice roared from her laptop speakers as Allman sunk down into the corner of her sofa, blowing on a freshly brewed black coffee. Sat on the table was the happy smile from her old friend, Jay.

"Hey, you! Have you finished work for the day?"

"I bloody wish! It's only half-four here. I keep reminding you I'm nine hours ahead. It's not that hard to work out."

"You know maths was never my strong subject Jay."

"No, I heard, eh? Was it DT? Design Technology or rather a deep throat with Mr Lark?" Jay winked into the camera and animated the actions of a blowjob. Allman erupted in a fit of laughter, tucking her legs close into her body.

"Those were only rumours! They were all jealous I was the only student that got an A-star." She said smugly.

"Hmmm, well, you were the only goody two-shoe student I know of that spent detention for, what was it, wearing the wrong blouse?"

"I wore a black knitted jumper under my blazer that was not part of my school uniform. That's why I was given detention."

"And I bet Mr Lark loved peeling that off you."

They both chuckled, knowing the indecency of their chat would be to some people, bad taste.

"It's too early in the morning for that. I need to keep my head on. I have an important meeting later today with Flatdick."

"Oh yeah, I've been trying to follow it on the news, but you know what it's like around here. If a man's found shagging his exhaust pipe, that takes priority."

Allman giggled, knowing all too well even though she agreed that would make for more interesting reading than her dead-end case.

"Did you find your run-away detective, George Goodrick? The one we don't like."

"Gregory, yes, I found him. Family issues apparently, he didn't go into much detail, but I really can't see how a whole week's justified."

"Someone die?"

"No, but is it horrible for me to say that would justify it?"

"Course not. Sounds like he's taking the piss. Is he that big somebody detective you told me about a few years ago?"

"Yeah, he's even bigger now, his reputation, I mean." Allman rolled her eyes, knowing how her friend's mind worked.

"Hey, no judgement here, you know that girl. Have you got this Saturday written down in your diary anyway?"

"I don't recall having anything to do that day. Why?"

"That's when I'm down! Me and Mike are surprising Julie for her 60th birthday. I thought you were picking me up from the airport? Mike said he gave you the invitation to the party last time he was over."

Allman could see the confusion on her friend's face. She did receive the invitation from Mike, Jay's older brother and her childhood crush. She can remember sneaking upstairs after dinner, excused for a bathroom break, and peeping through the crack of Mike's bedroom door. The loud rap music that bellowed through the hallway masked any noise she could potentially make. He wouldn't have heard her tiny footsteps or heavy breathing as she peered through the gap, indulging herself in the unflattering scene of a teenagers bedroom. Band posters covered the entire wall and ceiling, and dirty laundry and muddy football boots littered the floor.

A reflection in the mirror showed Mike lying down on his bed, pillows piled high, duvet slung off with his trousers ruffled, scrunched at his ankles.

Allman remembers gasping at the sight of her first one, ecstatic it was his. She must've been too close as Mike eyes darted onto hers through the reflection. Allman remained still, paralysed with fear that she'd been caught spying. Maintaining her stance, terrified that any movement would prove her existence, clinging onto the hope he hadn't seen her.

"You like watching, don't you?"

They never discussed their perverted game that became a weekly occurrence. It only stopped when they were older and her visits to the Andersons' household fizzled down. So, imagine Allman's surprise when he brought it up over a quick morning coffee.

"Surprise party in the garden, not a big do, some close friends, our family, her work colleagues. We managed to track down some of her old university friends as well, who said they could make it."

"Well, it certainly sounds like a lot Mike."

"Well, you know, Julie is loved by so many it's difficult to have a shortlist. And I know she's upset she hasn't seen much of you, but with Jay working away and you busy with your career, it'll be nice to get everyone together again, talk about the old times, and maybe, relive some past experiences."

Allman remembers staring blankly at Mike across the small, round table. With a rise of his eyebrows and a smile to the waitress as she placed their drinks down. He took a sip of his coffee and peered over the rim at Allman.

"I mean, you still like to watch, don't you?"

"Lou, you look spaced out. Did Mike give you the invitation?"

"Yeah, sorry, I remember now. With everything going on at work, I completely forgot. Remind me, your flight arrives at noon?"

"Yeah, that's right, but need to collect my luggage first. I was worried he forgot then for a second. I'm going to dart off anyway; it was only a quick one to ensure everyone was good. I cannot wait to party!"

"You bet, I wouldn't miss it for the world."

"I know you wouldn't. Speak to you soon, yeah?"

"Absolutely, if I don't speak to you beforehand. See you Saturday."

His friendly face disappeared with a wave and blown kiss to the screen. Now distracted with memories from her childhood 'romance,' she lost her train of thought. Coming up to 7:40, she calculated the time she had left to coordinate her next moves.

Okay, shower, twenty minutes max, give myself half-hour to get ready, take the expressway, that will save at least ten minutes travelling, that should get me to the office with five minutes to spare at 8:55. Perfect.

Like a flash, she jumped into action, gulping the final mouthfuls of her coffee, ripping her dressing gown off, and leaving it dumped in the middle of the room as she jolted towards the bathroom. A familiar sound stopped her in her stride. The slow chimes of her ringtone echoed behind her. She scrunched her face in annoyance. Whoever it was clearly didn't consider her tight timescale. Disgruntled, she marched back into her living area and snatched the phone off the marble countertop. The drawn open curtains didn't phase her. Even in the nude, she regularly walked around her apartment carefree. *Anybody would need binoculars to see anything worth seeing*, she arrogantly thought.

"Goodrick! Really?" She shouted in disgust. After their brief encounter the day before, he had sent her five leads based on his findings. She would've been grateful if he had done that at the very beginning, not the late evening the day before their meeting to produce such leads. Two of them she'd already visited herself, one being a family down in Dagenham, London, who claimed the body could be their runaway niece who ran away three years prior.

Allman saw it as a dead end with no explanation for why they were so convinced it was her. All the facts they provided didn't match their body: age; height; eye colour; ethnicity. It was a poor family desperate to find closure to their heartache. Allman couldn't imagine what toll a loss like that would've had on a family, where the findings of a mutilated body could bring better news rather than the ongoing, relentless, unknowing search they battled.

After thirty or so emails back and forth to the family, she gave up replying. There's no helping some people. The other was an unused train ticket, purchased at the closest train station, Buxton, for Friday, 3rd July, returning to Birmingham new street. Discarded train tickets didn't normally flag up on the police radar. This one, however, related to the station's CCTV footage of a drunken brawl that happened moments earlier.

What intrigued the policeman who forwarded the footage to Allman was the figure at the ticket machine. Somebody clearly trying to avoid the cameras and acting shifty. The person matched the height of their body, but with the layers of dark clothing that swallowed their frame, it was impossible to go off anything else other than the walk was feminine, thus presuming it was a woman hiding.

Within three minutes, she'd purchased the ticket, thrown it on the floor deliberately, and then walked away with both hands buried in an oversized jacket, hood up, with her face tightly tucked into a scarf. Hardly the outfit of the day with a recorded high temperature reaching 36.7 °C. They issued her as a person of interest regarding the assault and urged her to come forward with information. However, Allman couldn't go on a wild goose chase helping other detectives and policeman do their work if they couldn't be bothered. Since her case opened, she'd been bombarded with people of interest. All were sent to her team with elaborate explanations of why they thought it was linked to her case and why it'd be of importance to her teams resources. She entertained the first few dozen, but without the help of Goodrick, or the support of her superintendent, she decided to follow her gut instinct instead. The magazine was everything. Whoever did this left the magazine on purpose. That was the only thing that would break this case.

After her ordeal with Flatdick, she couldn't even bear looking at the magazine for further hints or clues. The big breakthrough, the coordinates; she really thought he would've started looking at her as a true detective, not some disposable plaything. After months of trying to prove herself worthy, meeting him at the odd hotel here and there, taking shot-gun lifts home, everyone knew of their little 'romance' but never said a word.

Allman tried using her new superior as a step ladder to further her career but instead, all the under-desk blowjobs or wanking him off at red lights didn't help her one bit. Instead, he played on her emotions and desire to please. After a while, she enjoyed sucking his cock under his tightly restricted desk while he had conference calls with the other office. She was always in the loop of what was happening, and all she'd have to do was keep her mouth open and breathe through her nose. The highly anticipated conversation came up one late evening that she'd been waiting for.

"So, Daniel, had any thoughts about who'll join my team? An internal transfer would be ideal, like the board proposed, but I need someone who can take charge, be assertive, and, most importantly, work well under me. Not many detectives favour having a woman telling them what to do. You know where I'm going with this, don't you?"

That was the voice of Adriana Cross. Allman didn't really know much about her. She was rolled in years prior, only briefly meeting her at inductions. Allman picked up that she wasn't a woman who stood for any bullshit, not one for chit-chat either; she'd a face like a slapped arse, red and bruised. When she made superintendent at Tannoch, Allman was gutted. Maybe she'd be best staying where she was, plodding through paperwork on minor crimes, rather than working under a sadist old hag.

That impression changed one morning when Allman opened an email from Adriana, expressing her gratification after she helped assist on one of her team's cases. The emails had been sent to Allman's prior superintendent, who didn't seem to appreciate the gesture, he replied with, it was Louise: 'doing her job,' and the appraisal wasn't necessary. Allman remembered sniggering at her desk when Adriana responded to his ignorance and continued to school him. Detailing how important it is to praise up-and-coming detectives on hard work.

Allman couldn't remove the grin from her face all day. Not only did she have an unbelievable appraisal, but she also had it in black and white. She appreciated Adriana's comments but most importantly, the way she belittled Allman's superintendent, calling him out for his lack of gratitude, was sheer brilliance. It was the only piece of encouragement she ever received from her job, inspiring her to become better, get on the Tannoch team, and get that pay rise. Now knowing, she'll work under a passionate, courageous superintendent, she wanted it more than ever.

To get there, here she was, doing what she knew best, sucking on an egotistic, pompous twats bellend. Through her excitement, hearing the conversation turn towards her new job opportunity, her pace quickened as Daniel Chadwick spoke.

"Yes, I do, and I feel I've appointed the best person for the job. They are very, very hard-working. It'll be an awful shame to have them leave my team as I depend on them greatly."

As Chadwick spoke, he reached his hand under his desk and delicately brushed Allman's cheek, which was burning hot from the suction tugging on his penis.

"So, who is it you have in mind? Are we thinking of the same person?

"Well, you do already know of them. Whether it's the same person, I don't know. They are, how can I say this without sounding like a record, they go the extra mile every time, and they're really, *really* good at what they do."

Allman smirks as she drags her tongue through his ballsack and up his shaft as he's talking. The cracking in his voice egged her on to become more ruthless with the act.

"Well, come on, you might as well spit it out then." Adriana pushed.

"I've decided to promote Gregory Goodrick."

CHAPTER 9

"Ah, Greg, come in, come in!" An excited Daniel rose out of his leather chair and pushed his hand through the air to greet Goodrick. Slapping his hand against Daniel's palm, they shook simultaneously, each with a slightly intensifying grip to establish dominance. Goodrick crushed the sides of his former superintendent's hand, tilting it slightly to gawk at the gold sovereign ring that strangled his middle finger.

"That's a nice-looking don ring. I'm not interrupting your daughter's wedding, am I?"

Daniel snatched his hand away and clapped enthusiastically. Goodrick's ears were ringing, even after Daniel's deep belly laugh elapsed. Daniel slumped himself back into the comfort of his bucket seat, shaking his finger at Goodrick, who stood admiring his audience.

"Oh Greg, how I've missed you. You really are a funny guy." Daniel struggled to say, pulling an used tissue from his sleeve, wiping away the happy tears. Goodrick stretched a smile, picking either side of his blue tailored jacket apart at the button and exposing an exquisite flawless ironed white shirt.

He delicately pulled the top of his trouser legs up and sat down across from Daniel, who stared intently at his every move, absorbed in his grace. Pushing backwards, he effortlessly moulded the chair's curves and crossed his leg, balancing his ankle on his knee. Now comfortable, he nodded at Daniel, instructing him to continue.

"So, how's it going over at Tannoch then? Anything I should know about? Any girls?" Daniel asked with a gaping mouth whilst pushing his protruding gut onto the table. He appeared like an eager dog, wagging his tail behind him as he studied Goodrick, who was shaking a big, juicy bone. Goodrick missed his little chats with Daniel. He was the perfect gormless idiot to feed his ego. Being the same age, he used him as a mirror to prove how much more accomplished he was. Sure, the man had a better-paid job, but so would Goodrick if he decided to become a detective sooner.

Daniel's receding hairline was a great starting point compared to Goodrick's thick locks. Daniel's gobble chops were scattered with ungroomed hair, whereas Goodrick's showcased the perfect barbered beard, caressing a chiselled jawline. He was everything Daniel craved to be, trying to keep up with his charm around the office, pretending they were the best of mates. He was amused by the idea Daniel believed they both sat on the same social pedestal.

"There's always *women* Daniel. You just need to know where to find them."

"Munters, they are here. Every single fucking one of them."

"Doesn't your girlfriend work in this office?"

"Like I said, Greg, munters: all of them."

Goodrick smirked, looking down and swallowing hard; finding amusement in Daniel's audacity.

"Anyway, I see you're not showcasing the eternal ring of love."

Goodrick looked up to Daniel pointing at his left hand. Goodrick stretched his fingers, extending them outwards and up towards the light to exaggerate Daniel's finding.

"Ah yes, you noticed. What are we doing having such a great detective wasted behind this *measly* desk?" Goodrick mocked, tapping the gigantic wooden surface. He watched the oblivious buffoon profoundly gloat in his imaginative greatness, stretching his hands behind his head and leaning back, mimicking Goodrick's laid-back demeanour.

"Well, I hate to say it, Greg, but I didn't win the regional recognition award at the police federation ceremony twice in a row by not being the best."

"Is that why you framed the awards, so you don't have to say it?"

Goodrick pointed sarcastically towards a sparse wall with only two hung frames. Formal declaration, stamped and signed, awarding the one and only, Daniel Francis Chadwick, as the best. The achievement was awarded to whichever superintendent spent most of their time signing off paperwork. Stealing the spotlight from the hard-working detectives under them.

"Oh, those! I almost forgot they were there." Chadwick sprung up, grabbing a glass cleaner with a cloth that ironically sat on a dusty glass cabinet. Goodrick had detected the only polished surfaces in the office were the awards and Daniel's name plaque.

Daniel was busy huffing his dog breath onto his awards and wiping the smut away as the clock was ticking. *8:53, she'll be here soon.* He spent the night tossing and turning, and it wasn't due to sleeping on a sofa causing his insomnia. He couldn't work out if he'd imagined their close encounter or read the situation wrong. Frustrated, she wasn't playing into his hands, no returning his calls, or even responding emails that regarded this very meeting. He was being ghosted by a woman he was convinced wanted him, so why wasn't she offering it on a plate like all the rest?

A gentle knock behind him ended his turmoil. Daniel abandoned his daily chore and, at a pace, squeezed through the extremely tight gap between the cabinet and his desk, catching the inside of his thigh on the corner sharply. Goodrick clenched on Daniel's behalf, feeling the bruise already beginning to sting.

"Mr Chadwick, Louise Allman's here to see you."

Daniel nodded and wiggled his fingers, granting access. Goodrick wasn't sure if the lack of speech was due to arrogance or Daniel was withholding a crying yelp, following his on duty injury. Goodrick stood for attention to formally greet Allman, taking a quick second to give himself a brush down, wanting to impress. *There she is.*

She floated into the room graciously, effortlessly beautiful, Goodrick admired. Looking to equally impress, she wore a fitted pencil skirt that hugged her extremely small waist tightly. A teasing, cold-shoulder blouse, tucked in to reinforce her curvaceous hourglass figure. Hair scraped back in a high ponytail with loose strands feathering her face. Only when Goodrick took the time away from ogling at her body, did he recognise an uneasy, worried expression. She froze standing motionless, didn't even flinch when the door abruptly slammed shut behind her.

"Well, sit down, Allman. We don't have all day for you to stand there looking docile, do we?" A disgruntled Daniel shook his chops in arrogance, looking over at Goodrick for reciprocation or acknowledgement; he got neither. Goodrick pursed his lips at the tone his colleague was greeted with but remained to look at Allman, hoping to reassure her. It only took a few short seconds for her to blink and glance towards him. He pulled a closed smile, nodding towards the chair. Goodrick retook his seat with Allman perching on the edge of hers, appearing uncomfortable.

"Well, we all know why we're here. We have one fucked up body. One bloodied rolled-up magazine used as a sex toy. Correct me if I'm wrong, but no motive, no suspects, no leads?" Daniel asked assertively. He took the role of a mafia boss more literally than Goodrick anticipated. He pressed his fingers so hard against one another, the tips were turning white. He rested his forearms on the table, directing all his attention towards Allman.

Goodrick leant backwards, intently watching their interaction. Allman displayed traits of a battered woman, sheepishly twitching her legs, looking away to avoid any direct eye-contact with fidgeting hands, picking at her nail varnish. He had examined similar behaviour extensively during his time investigating domestic abuse. Puzzled, he maintained his observation

70

of her body language, concentrating on how she spoke rather than what she was saying. A nervous voice crack, broken speech with an impulsive cough; it was obvious. He glanced over at Daniel, who must've recognised the nervousness too. Instead of a concerned expression, he looked like his normal self; arrogant and oblivious. Well, he never was a good enough detective to pick up on these things.

Goodrick found himself lost in speculation of what could be troubling Allman. Sure, it's not nice to have these meetings with a bigoted fool, trying to prove the worth of your wage, whilst they sit behind a desk that'd never seen a hard day's work. Not to mention, Daniel's pompous wall of 'achievements' just to rub salt further into the wound.

"You found that box, didn't you?"

"Box?" Goodrick asked, confused. Engrossed in his new open case: whose fucked with Allman?

"The music box?" Allman stared, with desperation in her eyes.

"Ah yes, the music box! Plays a nice little tune, little cute ballerina in it. Carved with the word 'Ducky'. That's literally only it." Goodrick shrugged his shoulders whilst Daniel held his head in his hands.

"Right, what about that family in Dagenham? They're convinced it's their niece. Why haven't I seen you down there Allman, investigating further?"

"I ruled that as a dead-end. The family-"

"You ruled it as a dead end, did you? Were you notified of this so-called dead end?" Daniel directed the conversation towards Goodrick, snubbing Allman. She didn't seem to have the energy to strike back, she bit her tongue, shaking her head in defiance. Goodrick leaned in towards Allman, forcing Daniel out of the situation.

"Why was it a dead end, Louise?" Goodrick asked calmly.

"The family's black. They sent a picture of a missing black girl." Allman sighed.

Goodrick nodded his head in agreeance before deadly staring back at Daniel.

"A dead end, like she said."

"The thing is, Allman, and I don't want you to take this the wrong way, but you are short-sighted. You have a great detective assigned to this case to help you, and not just any old detective. The best there is, well, besides the obvious." He boasted, pointing to himself before continuing his demoralising speech.

"*The* Gregory Goodrick, offered his assistance on this case, which we're very fortunate to have. The least you could do is appreciate his hard work and inform him of all your decisions."

"With respect, Daniel, Louise has actually done all the grafting. I had a family emergency, and I wasn't even around for a week." Before Goodrick could continue his defensive closing statement, Daniel raised his hand to stop him.

"You haven't even used the team I provided you with; over a thousand lines of enquiry and you've only bothered with thirty or so. What is the point of you being here? Why were you even assigned to this case? You have to tell me because right now, I don't have a fucking clue!"

Goodrick darted concerning looks between both Daniel and Louise in absolute shock at what he was hearing. Anticipating an explosion from Louise to stick it to him, put him in his place. Instead, she sat just there; emotionless. There was no fire in her eyes, no fight in her. Goodrick rubbed his forehead in frustration.

"Daniel, this is all my fault, okay? I disappeared within the first few critical hours of the investigation. I left Louise without explanation, I didn't even attempt to make contact with her."

"But as you said, Greg, a family emergency. Her, on the other hand: complete incompetence."

"My step-mum fell down a little step and was hospitalised, a step-mum I loathe and avoid as much as possible. I didn't need the week off; I wanted it because I was selfish, and for that, I'm extremely sorry, Louise."

He took a deep breath and looked her dead in the eyes as he spoke her name. He needed to say sorry a long time ago and stop pretending he didn't care. She managed to pull a smile together for him, hoping it was reassurance of forgiveness. Rather that then a pitiful smile at his sudden outburst, his realisation he's acted and behaved like a complete twat. The smile soon transcended into a frown when Daniel began barking.

"Well, I'd only need a couple of hours with her to realise I made a big mistake helping the unfortunate office too. But, your hard work hasn't gone unnoticed, Greg. That's why I've spoken to Adriana, and we've both concluded, it's best the case is handed over to yourself without the involvement of one in particular." He nodded in Allman's direction.

"You can't do that." Her voice croaked.

Astonished, he looked at Daniel's lips, reading them to ensure he wasn't mishearing. The upsetting cries from Louise made it all too real.

"You can't do that to me!"

"I'll give Allman until the end of the day to transfer all her notes and evidence to you, and then, we'll strike her name off."

"This isn't fair! All the work's mine, it's my case."

"So, I thank you, Greg, for joining us today, it's been lovely to see you again, and I wish you the very best with it. You'll probably have it closed, boxed off by tomorrow," Daniel said, laughing, extending a hand outwards. Goodrick was in complete shock at the situation he found himself in. Speechless, unable to strum a sentence together. Louise had erupted in a heart-wrenching sob whilst Daniel had the haughtiness to ignore her pleas.

Louise's disappearance knocked Goodrick back into reality after hearing the door creak to an eerie close. Daniel looked unphased by the reaction of a woman leaving his office, sobbing uncontrollably. Goodrick didn't agree with the decision, in disbelief his superintendent was involved. What could he say right now anyway, the damage was done. He stood up nervously and snarled down at Daniels open hand.

He couldn't bring himself to shake on whatever fuckery just transpired. He briskly turned away from Daniel, making his intentions for a sharp exit evident, even to a lousy detective like him.

"Oh, come on, Greg, let's not leave it like this, mate."

Goodrick stopped dead, hearing the scuttering behind him as Daniel frantically tried to stop him.

"We both know she would've slowed you down. Plus, I've had a lot of burglaries in the past week she could do."

"You're going to use a good, no, great homicide detective on some low-case burglaries? Don't you have any nitwits like yourself to do that?"

"Hey, why am I detecting some annoyance from you? You're the one who wanted the case to start off with, not my fault it automatically got filed through my office, and if I hadn't been away, it would've never been given to Louise fucking Allman. That's the only reason you volunteered for the case, to steal it back."

"Oh, absolute bollocks, I was intrigued, that's all. I wanted to help, not steal it for some petty competition between offices."

"What's gotten into you? You were all for the chase to be on top. You finally are, and you don't want to hold onto it?"

"I wanted to help. That's it."

"Oh, come off it. She's done most of the work anyway. She had something good in the magazine, so run with that, and before you know it, you'll be collecting your very own reward at the next police federation ceremony."

"I don't want a fucking irrelevant award for me to hang up in my clammy office to wet wank over whenever I feel inadequate!"

Goodrick shouted in frustration as the realisation of what happened weighed heavily on his shoulders. Maybe if he'd helped Allman from the beginning, which were his intentions, she wouldn't be in this mess now. His devil was on his shoulder however, whispering in his ear. *You have the case now, fuck her.* He shook his head to ignore the thought.

"I don't want to fall out with you, mate. I know emotions are a little high right now. Seeing someone cry, especially a pretty girl, isn't nice, but that's all she is. Don't let her get in the way of your career. This case could be the making of you."

"She's a human being. You shouldn't treat people like they're nothing. She's put her heart and soul into this case. That's why emotions are high. It's not right, and I'll have words with Adriana about this. It's Allman and I together or not at all."

"So, why's that then, you're fucking her, is that it?"

"What? You really are deranged. You know that?" Goodrick curled his top lip and proceeded towards the exit. Trying to move quickly out of the room, knowing nothing had happened between him and Allman, but he couldn't deny his lust for her if asked outright. He was never good at handling his emotions, instead used sarcasm and humour to avoid such conversation, but he wasn't up for making Allman any more of a joke. Goodrick reached the door and swung it open, hitting the cabinet behind it. His last remark about how he felt the meeting went.

Before stepping away, he heard Daniel sniggering behind him. Goodrick closed his eyes and breathed calmly, trying to become placid. If there was one thing he hated more than losing a fight, it was someone laughing at him.

"Something funny, Daniel?" He asked through gritted teeth.

"Oh, nothing, just you and Allman; it makes perfect sense now. No wonder she stopped putting the effort in. The blowjobs were starting to dry up."

CHAPTER 10

The car ride back to her apartment was a haze. Sirens and lights flashed in front of her, but all she could see was a blurred world, distorted road signs from the tears that flooded her vision. Only when she had stopped, did she realise she'd been driving on autopilot. Luckily, natural instincts drove her home safely. She looked around the confinement of the metal frame, confirming she was alone in the underground car park. Dropping her shoulders and sitting back in her seat, she gently wiped away tears that soaked her cheeks using her finger and knuckle.

She looked down at her hand to see a black smudge smeared across her skin, where she had wiped away her self-confidence. She knew lip liner and mascara wouldn't fix all the problems she would've faced today but sometimes, putting on a brave smile just didn't cut it. *Nobody notices if you don't smile, when you look good.*

Pulling the sun visor down, the built-in light illuminated her flaws. Staring back at her were bloodshot eyes, fine black lines running down her rosy cheeks: a visible regret for not wearing waterproof mascara. Just a glimpse was enough for her to tear up again, slamming the visor closed; she couldn't face looking at what that man did to her.

Flinging herself out of the car, she reached the elevator, jabbing the button hastily. It was a long, painful wait until the doors finally opened to her floor. The constant trembling and juddering between floors made her stomach somersault. The anxiety of somebody interrupting her self-loathing, one-way trip troubled her. She was transfixed, watching the orange light behind each number light up as they passed, rejoicing that nobody interrupted her.

Stumbling into her apartment, she was greeted with the mess caused in the early morning rush. There was no way half an hour was enough time to get her ready for that onslaught. Throwing her hands up in the air and smacking the side of her thighs with a heavy blow, frustrated for giving herself more work to do. Pushing the door to her dressing room, she kicked her high heels off, narrowly avoiding the mirror that stood proudly centre-stage. The reflection of her pursuit to make her feel better that morning haunted her. The tightly fitted skirt, the loose, teasingly off-the-shoulders blouse; what was she thinking?

Breathing heavily, she clawed at her clothes, ripping them off her, flinging the blouse over her head before pausing to stare at her reflection. Panting heavily, a new personal record for the quickest time to get undressed. All she wore now was a plain, plunging double d cup bra, beige tights and her signature Bridget knickers. Crumbling to her knees, forcing her head downwards to the soft carpet, luckily soothing the blow. Deep cries of despondency weighed heavily on her chest, rocking her body back and forth.

She tensed her toes to regain some sort of sensitivity to deflect from her pain mentally. Collapsing to her side, she lay there for a few seconds to catch her breath. Studying the side portrait of her shoes, lined up neatly at the foot of the wardrobe. Perfectly placed with precision, none of them had been worn more than once. They looked like they belonged in the extravagant crystal showroom where she bought them from, not collecting dust in an abandoned museum.

The illuminating light from her phone caught her attention. *Fucking Gregory Goodrick.* She watched emotionless, waiting for him to hang up so she could continue her pity party. *What could he possibly have to say for himself?* She knew he was a heartless, self-absorbed man and his stealing her case proved it. That's why he volunteered for it; all the while, she thought he was assigned, that he had no choice in the matter, but no. He left her at the most crucial part of an investigation and made her do all the hard work, just so he could swoop in at the end and take the limelight. The tears began to dry up through the hatred for that man until her mum's sweet smile captivated the screen. She always knew that's what Allman needed to see to calm her. She remembers every sports day, spelling bee and graduations, she'd glance behind to see that big cheeky grin from her mother, always a supporting reassurance for Allman. Even at her mother's funeral, she looked behind her before entering the church: that was the first time she realised she'd never see it again.

Allman couldn't prepare herself for losing, her competitive nature wouldn't allow for it, especially a loss like that. All she had now was a picture taken from her high school prom, proudness with eternal love shimmered in her mother's eyes. Allman began to tear up again, sitting up and leaning her bare back against the cold surface of the mirror, sending chills down her spine. Clinging her phone with both hands, she stared intently at her mother.

Growing up as a single child meant she couldn't offload the burden of losing a parent onto siblings. She never knew her father, nor did she want to. It was his decision to leave and close the door on his family. Allman made sure to bolt and lock it behind him and had never thought of him since. Her only remaining relatives were two cousins who lived out in Canada. If she bumped into them in the street, she wouldn't recognise them, even if their ID fell to the ground. She only met them as a toddler when Allman and her mother flew out after her dad left them high and dry. That's the only time she met her Aunty Melanie and her children, Casie and Rachael. Their surnames always escaped Allman's mind as they didn't bother with them after that. All she ever knew was her mother, and that's all she ever needed, more than ever now.

The screensaver on her phone switched off to a black pit of emptiness. Allman shrieked in a heart-throbbing cry as if she'd lost her all over again, throwing her phone in between her legs. She held her knees close to her chest, crossed her ankles, and wrapped her arms around her legs tightly as she sobbed.

"Please, Mum, help me. I don't know what to do. I thought I had it worked out without you, but it's not working. My fucking plan isn't working! How am I supposed to forget you don't exist anymore? All anybody is on this fucking world is a name, scratched off some bullshit register when you're gone, and just like that, I'm supposed to move on and get over it. How the fuck am I ever going to move on from losing you when I'll always need you?

I can't even cook myself a meal. I only ever baked with you, but even then, all I helped with was licking the spoon: despite your warnings of raw egg. I'm still petrified of the dark. What kind of 32-year-old woman sleeps with a bedside light on? I don't even have children. Christ, I don't even have kids yet. I can't be a mum without you here; you're supposed to teach me how to be one. Isn't that how it's supposed to work? I don't want a family being brought up to look at your pictures, only believing you were good because I tell them so.

I shouldn't have to spend the rest of my life convincing everyone, my mum was the greatest, the funniest, most caring person in the world. I'd want to introduce you and for them to see it for themselves. Not to be some sad myth that the drunken girl in the kitchen talks about at every single fucking party. That's why I don't even go out anymore. What's the fucking point? All I do is end up crying and wishing I was having a glass with you instead.

Do you remember sitting on your sofa and I was trying to show you that new dating site? You laughed so hard at some of the oddballs I spoke to, telling me to be careful. I even miss having you follow me on dates, how you'd caringly sit in your car for hours, so I'd get home safe. I always told you not to do it; you'd be bored, but that grin on your face when I'd climb in, clapping giddily if I said I liked him.

Sorry to have wasted so much of your time, but all of them turned out to be losers, especially that, do you remember him, Dave? When I first kissed him outside that godforsaken run-down pub. You honked your horn, flashed your lights and shouted, that's my girl."

Allman paused, laughing, looking up at the ceiling fan, wiping the wet tears from her face before continuing.

"You were always so proud of me, everything I did, you were always so happy. Even when I came second to last in the cross country race. I would've been last if I hadn't tripped that girl up on the final lap, but you still baked me a cake. Celebrating my achievement by getting a participating medal and a laminated certificate which should have said: 'well done, you suck, but here you go.'

I don't know what to do now though mum. My job's in tatters. That bloody disgusting Flatdick has ruined everything for me. I know you've seen everything that's gone on, but I honestly didn't mean for this to happen. As for the other arsehole, he's welcome to everything he's going to get. You always did say what goes around comes around; I'm just getting sick of being hit in the face with my own karma. If you are here mum, please give me a sign. I promise you won't scare me. I'm begging you. Make the light flicker or something, knock something off, make a noise, anything, please."

Allman slowed her breathing down and listened intently. She unexpectedly jumped at a loud thud coming from outside the bedroom. Sitting in fearful silence, she attempted to listen carefully.

"Hello?" she whispered softly. The eruption of continuous knocking that followed spooked her to her core. She lept up on her feet, running from the enclosed dressing room in fear. Out in the open, she stood in her empty apartment, facing her front door, where the knocking became more persistent. The noise was terrifying; it sounded like two or more people were knocking simultaneously, trying to break into her home. She looked around frantically, to see if there was a weapon to arm herself with. She was sure it had nothing to do with her mother unless she'd find it funny watching a petrified, alone girl scramble around her kitchen wearing only a bra and tights, ready to scar somebody with a butter knife.

She staggered towards her door, armed, the knocking subsided, and strangely she felt more unsettled than before. The silence was broken by what sounded like a muffled argument. Recognising the high-pitch shrieks from Edith, her nosey neighbour, she quickly ran to her door and peered out through the peephole. Seeing the back of Goodrick's head, she could hear him clearly arguing with Edith.

"That doesn't give you the right to bang on that door so loudly, I could hear it over my television!"

"Look, is she in or not? Did you see her?"

"Of course, I saw her. I see everybody that comes down this corridor. I came out to say hello to her, but she walked straight in, didn't even look at me. I was on my way out to the local shop to grab some-"

"Louise!" Goodrick shouted, hitting a closed fist fiercely on the door, cutting Edith halfway through her ranting. Allman could see him clearly now. He stood further back with both hands on his hips, looking down at the floor. He looked conquered, nodding his head to the relentless oration he was receiving from Edith.

"Well, excuse you, sir. I could have you reported, you know! Banging on the door like a bloody bailiff, disrupting my daytime television show! We can't just run around banging on doors without a merited reason. Now, I demand to know what's going on before I need to report this matter further."

"This doesn't involve you. Go back inside." Goodrick ordered.

"It does so when I've had to leave the comforts of my home to investigate a disturbance!"

"Well, maybe, if you spent less time in everybody else's business and stayed in your comfy armchair, you'll be able to catch the end of the Jeremy

Kyle show and find out what sister is fucking which brother, instead of out here, in my business, disrupting me."

"I'll be sure to report this. You won't be allowed back in this building. I'll make sure of it!"

With a slam, Edith scurried back inside her lair and left Goodrick alone in the corridor. Allman stared intently at him, waiting for another outburst of knocks, so she could shout at him to leave. Instead, he looked up with a sad, pessimistic expression. With a shake of his head, he turned and began to walk away. Allman pressed her face against the door, trying to stretch the reach of her sight to see whether or not he'll return. The crashing of the elevator, and the bell chime confirmed he was leaving. Exhaling, she placed her back against the door and slid down, letting gravity take the weight of her consumed body.

"He's a loser and all, mum."

CHAPTER 11

July 22nd, 2015

Checking the hands to his watch impatiently, she was late for work, but this was beginning to look like a no-show. He paced the outskirts of his old familiar office floor, watching the dismay of troubled detectives start their day. He arrogantly found them repulsive, their shocked faces when the workload was piled on their desks, the bitching chit-chat around the coffee machine, moaning about sitting on their arses all day and signing paperwork. A simple task that more than most couldn't get right.

Over at Tannoch, they made a running joke that their office was the elite team of detectives, whilst over here, it seemed everybody smoked spice with the number of troubles they raised. Everyone but a few hand-selected people made the cut, Allman being one of them.

Goodrick followed her work closely; she was his biggest competition, after all. He purposely found himself on most of her crime scenes, but she'd already closed them by the time all the legitimate paperwork was signed to send him. He couldn't believe his luck when she reached out for his help. Out of all the people to ask, she asked the detective who'd been following her all along. He replied to her letter with a sarcastic, flirtatious remark, trying to break down her hard-exterior barrier, but this resulted in her blanking him for the next few years. She must've taken his golden choice of words: 'good looks will get you there,' negatively.

"Greg? Is that you?" A high-pitched voice echoed behind him. The elongated pronunciation of her vowels gave her identity away.

"Jade, how are you?" He turned with a fake smile stretched on his face. The small, wobbly skirt bounced her way towards him and took Goodrick by surprise when she swung her arms around his waist, winding him as her head crushed into his stomach.

"I'm so happy to see you again!"

"Yeah, likewise." Goodrick lied, patting her head like an offspring from a canine family, whilst the other arm remained unmoved by his side. He wasn't exactly a tactile person. Only for the right kind of female would he exhaust himself with a hug, and that would only be to achieve foreplay. Something he very much didn't want to involve himself in with the leech now attached to him. Prising her away, taking a step back to collect himself, he folded his arms across his chest, creating a barrier between them.

"So, whats brought you back here then?"

"I'm waiting to speak to Louise. Have you seen her today?"

"No, I hardly ever see her anymore. Have you tried knocking on her office door?" She points behind Goodrick's shoulder at the door he's standing in front of, which bares the sign: 'Louise Allman.' He mockingly looks over, and with a sarcastic fold of his arm, he points behind him.

"You mean that's her office?" He looked back at her, expecting the acknowledgment of his teasing to become apparent, but instead, she looked at him; concerned.

"Yes, I told them to make those name tags larger. Unless you know where it is, you'll never find anything around here."

Goodrick rubbed his hand behind his neck, grinning. *She's as stupid as I remember.*

"I shall give it a go, then." He smiled as long and as broadly as the Cheshire Cat.

"I'm glad I could help. I tell you, this place would fall apart without me." She patted his chest as she shuffled past him, struggling in her platform shoes that she didn't have the experience of wearing.

"Well, you said it." He encouragingly raised his eyebrows, digging his hands into his trouser pockets as she passed, ending their encounter with a silent 'wow'. With the confirmation of that small talk establishing what the Tannoch office had said all along. He began pacing back and forth, kicking his feet in the air with every gleeful step, glad that he was no longer associated with the rest of the 'spice crew'.

He looked up at the sounds of the doors swinging open, and standing there was Allman. Back in her casual wear with dark circles around her eyes, demonstrating her lack of sleep. She marched towards him, looking down at the floor, avoiding eye-contact with everybody in the office. Goodrick took a strong stance, ready for her to walk into him as she bulldozed through. She took a quick leap backwards, just as they were ready to collide, with a shocked gasp escaping her lips.

She shook her head without saying a word, quickly picking up the belongings she dropped during her fright and continued on her warpath. Goodrick remained puzzled for a second before jumping into action and taking long strides to keep up with her. He knew she was mad at him, ignoring him at her door yesterday, diverting his calls and texts all night, but he hoped being face-to-face would soften her.

"Louise, wait. I've got some explaining to do." He stuttered between his words when the loud crash of the door, hitting the wall, caught him and the rest of the office off-guard. An eerie silence fell over the entire work floor. The buzzing from the office gossip, clicking of keyboards, and the rustling of papers stopped abruptly, and all eyes pinned on them. Allman looked behind herself, past Goodrick, and shouted with an assertive voice.

"Get back to work!"

When she finished delivering her order through gritted teeth, the regular, consistent noises of office life erupted. Allman walked inside, flicking on the light as she passed, and stood with an arm open, inviting Goodrick in. He sheepishly tip-toed through the doorway, avoiding her glare, he could feel her eyes burning into him, and the anger she radiated made him feel cold to the bone. Another smash of the fragile door locked them both inside the confined space.

Goodrick had everything he needed to say rehearsed, but the way she held herself today made him nervous. It was like looking at the old Allman again. She found herself and wasn't the trembling mess she'd been yesterday. He had hoped to work alongside this side of her. Her sharp tongue and her no-nonsense attitude were his favourite attributes; it was what made him most attracted to her.

"I need to let you know, I had no involvement in-"

"Sit down."

As quickly as she demanded, he sat on the edge of the chair like a lap dog hanging on her every demand. She leisurely leaned against her desk in front of him with her hands on either side, looking slightly down in a dominating manner. No matter what hurls of abuse he was about to receive, he'd gladly take it.

"Well, Goodrick, I'm waiting."

Her voice rocketed him away from an anticipating day-dream of what he could do to her on that table.

"I've spoken to Adriana after the meeting with Daniel yesterday, and we've come to a decision."

"You mean the meeting he belittled me in? Are we not going to talk about that?"

"I didn't know if you wanted to or not. I understand why you ran out; I would've as well in-"

"Oh, give-over, Goodrick! You just sat there, didn't say a fucking word in my defence while he was licking your arsehole!"

Goodrick readjusted in his seat with a nervous cough given his recent train of thought.

"I did, believe me, I was in shock when I found out. I can't believe he'd do that to you."

"Is it true you volunteered for my case?"

"Yes, but not for the reasons you're thinking."

"Then what other reason is there other than to take everything that's mine? I'm sick to death of being bent over and fisted by every man in this world!"

Goodrick held his breath. *Something to add onto the fantasy.*

"If you wanted the fucking case so badly, why didn't you say so? You could've taken it. Judging by your relationship with Daniel, he would've given it to you on a silver platter!"

"I didn't want the case, I wanted to help, and it intrigued me."

"Well, it's fucking yours now, isn't it?"

"No, not necessarily-"

"You know what's really fucked me off about the whole thing? How sly you've been. I always thought you were a cock, but then I doubted myself when you actually took the time to care about the case, which by the way, wasn't very much. But I started to think, huh, I had this guy wrong. He's a bit sarcastic and obnoxious most of the time, but maybe that's his front. He's actually quite endearing."

"Louise, just listen to me."

"And you know I actually felt bad when your stepmother fell. I genuinely hated myself for thinking awful of you for an entire week when you told me it was due to family trouble, but no, you wanted an easy week off after all."

"Believe me. It wasn't easy." Goodrick scoffed, shaking his head. Looking in her direction, he was met with a deadly stare; he knew instantly his bad habit of speaking without thinking had caused him more trouble.

"You know what else isn't easy, Goodrick? Filing through thousands of lines of inquiries, multiple people of interest with a disrespectful team of imbeciles. Everyone thinks I'm not good enough because Superintendent Flatdick tells them so! That...that's not easy."

Goodrick peered up at her, as she stared at the wall, crossing her arms to restore some sort of power, but Goodrick could recognise in her face; she's crumbling.

"Ignore Daniel, well I mean Flatdick, whatever you called him. He's exactly that. A narcissistic pig that has no right telling a detective of your calibre you're not good enough. You're one of the best detectives in the district, and you know that."

"You're beginning to sound a lot like him talking to somebody like yourself."

"What do you mean?" Goodrick asked.

"Well, he was blowing so much smoke up your arse, I thought I could hear Dick Van Dyke humming to chim-chim-cher-ee."

Goodrick unexpectedly belly laughed. It wasn't a regular occurrence that he found jokes funny, but with her rigid stance along with her blank expression, he enjoyed the dry humour.

"Sorry, I don't mean to laugh. That's really tickled me."

He said, wiping a tear from his eye. He looked up, thinking he'd be met with the death stare again but instead was greeted with her kind smile. The colour of her cheeks flourished as she let out a chuckle herself.

"I think I've done enough shouting for one day. I'm beginning to get a headache over it all." She hoisted herself up, taking her seat and slumped her feet on the desk.

"It is what it is; I was terrified coming back in today because I haven't signed it over yet."

"Well, that's what I've wanted to speak to you about. Adriana wasn't consulted in the arrangement Daniel made yesterday. He didn't follow protocol, and Adriana isn't accepting the case."

"What do you mean she isn't accepting it? It's the biggest case both offices have. Why wouldn't she want her name on it?"

"If it means scratching yours off without following the rules. She wants no part in it. That's what she said."

Allman snatched her feet from the desk and pushed them under, pressing her chest flat against the surface, giving Goodrick a view.

"So, does that mean it's still my case?"

"Yes."

"But what about Flatdick? Surely, he's going to put somebody else on it from this office. You heard what he thought of me yesterday."

Goodrick leaned forward and crossed his fingers, mirroring Allman, whose hands were now only a short reach away.

"He's wrong about you. And anyway, haven't you heard the news?" Allman looked at him, puzzled.

"He's been suspended. As of yesterday afternoon, Adriana's now acting superintendent for both offices until the mess is sorted."

"What? Why? Surely him throwing her name into the mix isn't enough to cause suspension?" Allman's eyes danced frantically searching for an answer.

"Well, Adriana takes this sort of thing very seriously, as do I. I don't like how he's treated you, and he won't be doing it again." Goodrick glanced up at her and then away. He couldn't hold eye-contact, worried she'd sense he knew more about their relationship than he wanted to let on.

"Well, thanks, I suppose. Look, I'm sorry for what I said earlier. I shouldn't have." Goodrick shook his head.

"No, you're right, it's what I've needed to hear, but nobody dares to tell me. Well, I mean you do, which I'm weirdly grateful for." He grins, locking eyes with her as she reciprocated the smile. Tilting her head, her long ponytail drapes over her shoulder effortlessly. Taking one of her hands away, she pushed her side fringe behind her ear before placing her hand over Goodrick's, squeezing gently. She mouthed the words: 'thank you' so beautifully he had to refrain from leaping over the desk.

He instead continued to smile and nod his head, all the while inside his mind wondering how her soft lips would feel pressed against his. A knock at the door alerted them both and stole their connection away. Allman sat up assertively, snatching her hands back. Goodrick slouched into the chair, and tried to look his casual, relaxed self.

"Come in," Allman instructed.

"Sorry, lovely, it's only me." The voice made Goodrick roll his eyes in despair. *Fucking Jade. Trust it to be her.*

"Grab a seat. Look, we have a visitor." Allman said cheerfully.

"Oh, I know. I grabbed a cheeky cuddle off him when he came in, didn't I, Greg?"

Goodrick raised his eyebrows, demonstrating his reluctance to participate in her propaganda.

"Well, I think calling it a cuddle is a bit farfetched."

"Oh, you!" Jade laughed, hitting him teasingly on his shoulder. Instead of removing her hand, she leaned on him, budging her weight off the ankle-breaking shoes. Goodrick looked horrified as Jade made herself comfy resting on his broad frame. Allman attempted to hide her amused smirk whilst subtly hinting at Goodrick she clocked it.

"What do you need, Jade?" Allman asked softly.

"Well, I only came in to let you know there's a right oddball in reception asking to speak to yourselves."

Goodrick sat up brashly, knocking Jade off balance.

"Me as well? They want to speak to me?" Goodrick asked.

"Well, I think so. I asked him what the matter's concerning, seeing as we can't take personal visits during office hours. So, I tried to give him your number, but he's reluctant to leave. He's demanding all sorts of things."

"What sort of things, Jade? Who is it?" Allman asked.

"Well, firstly, he said I need to speak to Detective Louise Allman in a private room, he doesn't give permission to be videotaped or recorded, and I must let you know, he came of his own accord and that he can leave at any time."

"Who?" Goodrick and Allman asked in sync, both becoming tired of her rambling.

"Well, he wouldn't give me his name."

Allman sighed, rolling her eyes dramatically at Jade's inept ability to do her measly job.

"He told me to tell you the Komodo Dragon was here?" Jade lifted her hand in confusion.

"Komodo Dragon?" Goodrick needed clarification.

"Yes, that's what he said, to call him the Komodo Dragon. I told you, he's a right nutcase, looks like the type that would kill his own mother."

Goodrick drifted away from Jade's dreary voice. He could feel his heartbeat racing and his palms beginning to moisten from sweat. The only real lead they had left was the wildlife magazine centred around a Komodo Dragon, and it looked as if it just strolled right through their doors. He turned in his chair to look at Allman, who had her hands in a tight fist over her mouth, looking equally shocked. Goodrick bit his lip with deep delight and knocked his knuckle on the table to grab Allman's attention.

"The Komodo Dragon's here."

CHAPTER 12

Glaring through the one-way mirror inside an interrogation room, it appeared cold. The bleak grey walls drained colour, manifesting how Allman felt. She stood in the centre whilst Goodrick was on the phone to Adriana, pacing behind her. Allman's stomach knotted, and a gigantic ball of self-doubt squeezed down her throat. Her arms, wrapped around her torso, became increasingly tighter with each passing second. The nervousness of interrogation was getting the better of her. It wasn't her strong suit, especially when so much was riding on it.

Waiting, transfixed on the white door opposite her. She didn't want to take her eyes off the frame, not to miss the first glimpse of whomever was about to walk through. The click of the door behind alerted her. Goodrick had stopped marching, slowly putting his phone back into his pocket. A familiar detective, Paul, extended the door open and, with his tall frame, leaned his upper body inside.

"Louise, he's coming in now." His Brummie accent grated on her. The dreary, snail pace executions of the vowels made anything he said boring and dull. With a nod of her head, he retrieved his body from the room, leaving Goodrick and Allman alone. She watched Goodrick stare intently at the door as it closed shut. She could feel a snarky remark bubbling at his lips. He turned away and smiled at Allman, taking several steps to stand by her side. She was almost disappointed he didn't find anything to say.

"What?" Goodrick asked. Allman's childish smirk must have been printed on her face too long.

"Nothing, I just thought you'd say something." She turned back around, brushing shoulders with him, who was now mimicking her power stance, feet slightly apart and their arms crossing over their bodies.

"Say something about what?"

"Your best mate Paul."

"I don't always have something to say, you know." Goodrick raised his eyebrow. She couldn't recognise if he was being playful but decided to take it as a warning.

An intense, loud siren erupted in the interrogation room. A red light flicked on above the door to announce their arrival. Allman could hear the heavy breathing of Goodrick, who seemed as on edge as she was. Her heart pounded in her chest, excruciatingly feeling like it was ready to rip out from beneath her ribcage.

The two seconds it took for the Komodo Dragon to step out into their scope felt like hours. The red light shined down onto his golden head. He looked like a dead man walking, with his head hung low and shuffling steps. Allman leaned closer to the window, attempting to see more features. He stood motionless, like a statue, as the door began to creak behind him. This gave Allman time to study him from top to bottom, every millimetre.

His trainers lacked any detail; the laces were recently changed, and the immaculate white cotton thread contrasted against the heavily dirtied exterior beneath them. The brown tapered-leg chinos lacked any charisma. The ill-fitting yellow-stained shirt draped off his tiny frame, clearly too big for him to fill. His blonde hair dangled in front, obscuring his face. No jacket, no watch, no personal belongings; nothing seemed to protrude in his pockets.

The crash of the door erupted behind him, shaking the frame. He quickly yanked his head upright to seemingly stare at Allman and Goodrick. The thrash of his sudden movement made Allman jump back. His change of demeanour unnerved her. His hunched shoulders before were now relaxed, broadening his measly chest. Dirty blonde locks casually took their rehearsed place, either side of his face, brushing past his jawline, with a large side fringe scooped over the top of double-bar bridged glasses.

The tiny frame of the glasses secured hefty lenses that ranged from the top of his eyebrow down to his pale white cheeks; parallel to the tip of his red nose. His magnified dark eyes stared deadly at Allman. She began to question if he could actually see her.

She glanced over at Goodrick to read what he was thinking of him, disappointed in his appearance, but then she'd no idea what to expect. Until this moment, they never considered the magazine to relate to a person. It was always 'just a magazine,' a magazine shoved inside the corpse of a dead girl, similar in age to the man who stood in front of them. Goodrick seemed transfixed in his movements. His eyes wandered with him as he took a seat on one side of the table. Allman's palms began to sweat at the eerie glare she was receiving from him. Although his body was sat upright on the chair, sideways on, he twisted his neck to maintain the stare.

"Detective Louise Allman, I'm waiting for you." A sinister smile stretched across his face. Hearing him call for her spooked her. He had an infectious tone to his voice but couldn't quite put her finger on where the accent was from. A posh, elegant kind of flare rolled off his tongue when he spoke, and although his pitch, along with his smile, should have demonstrated kindness, it horrified Allman. There was a malicious tone in his way of demanding her to join him in the room. She turned to look at Goodrick, who was transfixed on watching the man through the window. Obviously thinking of something as he rubbed his palm across his mouth.

"Can you come in with me?" Allman pleaded. She half expected Goodrick to invite himself anyway. They were, after all, sharing the case, although he enjoyed taking the back seat. Something unnerved her going in there alone, they agreed to his terms of no videoing, no recording, only them in the room. But as the moment drew closer for her to deliver her side of the deal, she buckled under the pressure. Goodrick took a deep breath, instantly regretting asking him. He looked over at Allman and said in a mockingly Brummie accent.

"Of course I will, bab." He grew a smile on his face, looking pleased with his Paul impression. Allman tried resisting a smirk at the, somewhat badly, timed remark she'd been anticipating. Oblivious to Goodrick, it was just the thing to ease her anxiety. With one final look behind her at the visitor, who hadn't diverted his stare, she followed Goodrick's lead into the interrogation room.

The man remained looking intently in the mirror away from them, not even phased when the loud siren welcomed the detectives in. Allman stood sheepishly in the doorway whilst Goodrick held the door open for her. With an assertive cough, she scurried inside; Goodrick's way of telling her politely to move her arse. With a thud of the door, The Dragon turned his head casually, with a slight bend of his neck to face them, extending one of his arms across the table.

"Well, please come on in."

Goodrick obliged, demonstrating his casual demeanour; leant back with legs outstretched.

Allman nervously took a seat next to Goodrick, her tightened muscles contrasting against his relaxed state. The man waited until both detectives were sat down before placing his hands in his lap, smiling continuously. Allman knew she'd be the one to start: Goodrick had already got himself comfy for the easy ride. Pulling the chair forward, it scratched the tiled flooring, screeching as she manoeuvred herself closer to the table. Embarrassingly, she could feel both sets of eyes glaring her way. She cleared her throat before looking across the table to begin questioning. As she opened her mouth, she was interrupted.

"So, you're probably wondering who I am. What am I doing here on this fine Wednesday morning in July? I've always hated Wednesdays. Something about them being in the middle of the week really irks me, but today I decided to pay you a visit."

He stretched a smile wide across his face, looking intently between Allman and Goodrick. She recognised his facial expression change when his mind wandered to how he felt about Wednesdays. His face churned into a downward snarl before lifting again into a joyous grin by the time he had finished a sentence. *This is going to be difficult.* She needed to maintain and filter all this information. Without notes or recordings to back up on, she was sure to miss something unintentionally. Before she could think about what to say, he had already continued.

"I'm here because I can help you. I have a magnificent story to tell you both. You'll enjoy it." He nodded enthusiastically, trying to convince himself of the statement. Allman moved quickly, recognising he'd be edging to speak more.

"My name is Louise Allman, and this is Detective Gregory Goodrick. We've fulfilled your requirements of having no recording facilities whilst this little chat takes place, and as you have volunteered to come in today, it's important I let you know that you can leave at any time." She wanted to push the formalities out first before delving into this so-called story he seemed eager to share. While she spoke, his face drained from colour, and he began to shake his head, disapprovingly.

"Well, I know that, Louise. Didn't you hear me call you whilst you stood behind your fancy mirror?" He extended a finger outwards and pointed at the one-way mirror where she and Goodrick stood, protected, minutes earlier.

"I have one just like it; a way to know if it's a secret mirror is to conduct a simple test. When you place your fingernail on a normal mirror, there's a gap between your nail and the image. If I were to go and place my fingernail on yours, it would touch directly. No gap, you see. Luckily, you don't come across many people who fingertip a mirror, now do you?"

He chuckled to himself, excessively breathing out of his nose, almost snorting with his laugh. He amused himself for a couple of seconds before pacing his laugh back down to a satisfied grin. Goodrick and Allman watched on, unamused at his knowledge that almost every interrogation room across the country is fitted with them as standard.

"You say you have a story to tell us? Can you tell me your real name first before we begin?" Allman asked quietly and slowly, like she was addressing a child. For the age of the man, he seemed to behave like one. He sat upright, nodding his head when she began talking about the story but quickly changed his demeanour regarding her question.

"You can use The Dragon. That's who I am, what they called me. That's what you should call me."

"Who's they? Who told you your name was The Komodo Dragon?" Allman pressed. The Dragon appeared irritated, squeezing his eyes shut. He raised a palm upwards in her direction to silently shush her.

"Please, I'm here to tell my story, and then you can ask questions later." He opened one of his eyes to see if she'd behave. Allman sat back in her chair, peering across to Goodrick, who was in a trance. Within a heartbeat when Allman glanced away, The Dragon restored himself in an upright position, hands clasped together and with a nightmarish smile.

"Are we ready to begin then?"

DUCKY

CHAPTER 13

I'm firstly going to tell you about a girl I'll refer to as Ducky. Her and I joined an exclusive group of people to partake in yearly gatherings. What happens in these weeks is directed by a host who is announced by the groups creators; The Network. They had a unique way of secretly communicating to a group of people, subtly providing the whereabouts and whose year it was to plan a week of festivities. The group me and Ducky found ourselves in would communicate through a magazine subscription called Out of Hibernation. Quite a fitting title to The Network's intentions; offering the outcasts of society a way to...mingle, with like minded people.

We were both announced in the same issue, number thirteen, that two new people had joined, Duck and Komodo Dragon were the names assigned to us by The Network. I'd presume some of the other members weren't happy with a fifth and sixth member joining, it meant depending on the roll of the dice, they might have to wait six years for their week to come about.

Within that years magazine, tickets to Portugal were included. I was reluctant, naively believing the yearly gatherings wouldn't consist of boarding a plane, but I had a lot to learn. It wasn't as if you could decide not to go either. If you missed attending a week, you'd loose your place, which wasn't an option. The Network enforced a ruthless contract between themselves and all members of a group. The strict attendance requirement came under the second ruling of the terms and conditions of your membership; join in and participate.

The first ruling was every member was to sign. Ensuring everyone in a group was a fully willing participant for whatever it is you'd plan for your hosted week. The rules of the membership did however have a grey area of what exactly it was you were signing into. It detailed you needed to sign and be one hundred percent willing to participate, but on the other hand, it doesn't explain what with. The only reassurance was because every person had signed, we were all consenting members, regardless of what was in store for us during the different host's weeks. My first week, hosted by Ducky, I was anything other than a happy go-getter. I had to wait out my time and muddle through, knowing my week to host would come around. I guess that's what spurred the group members on, knowing our weeks were coming to entertain in our own…unique ways.

You could say I wasn't exactly eased into my first week, kindly. Shortly after receiving the magazine, my phone automatically downloaded a new app, unaware to me. One I couldn't get rid of, even a factory reset didn't remove the new bloatware. I failed to connect the apps icon, displaying a blue duck, related to Ducky and The Network. It became clearer what the apps intended use was for when the week to Portugal drew closer.

A world map laid beneath my fingertips with scattered lights. I instantly recognised one of them illuminated my location. The only one to be in the centre of the country while the others littered the outskirts. I had used the coordinates to the venue, which were concealed in the magazine, recognising the single red dot signifying the meeting place.

I realised at that moment how presidential The Network was. Their abilities to hack all members phones, presuming that's what the other lights indicated, stunned me. A message was sent through the app from the host, Ducky, explaining her week's first game. From the limited knowledge I'd received regarding The Network's operations, this wasn't the norm. I was led to believe the only contact we'd receive relating to the weeks activities would be detailed from each host's welcome ceremony, officially beginning their week.

Ducky detailed she wanted a cat and mouse chase to the venue in Portugal. The game was a race with one rule, nobody could enter the country until the official first day of her week started. No mention of a winning prize, maybe first dibs on the best room, but she emphasised you didn't want to come last.

I became obsessed with watching the yellow lights dart their way across the country, all of them slowly manoeuvring towards Portugal the day before the intended week was to begin. You could say I was naïve thinking other members wouldn't take Ducky's threats of coming last seriously. I intended to use the plane tickets provided to me by The Network, only flying out on the first day. I accepted that I'd be arriving last whilst waiting in collections at Faro International.

I pushed my passport through the small slit between a bulletproof glass cubicle where I'd observed the man scanning multiple passports, barely turning his neck to identify the person in each picture. He paused abruptly, stopping to study my face intently before whispering to me.

"Bem-vindo ao país, Komodo Dragon."

Pushing my passport back to me without the need to open it. Again, I was horrified the reach The Network had. I became anxious of every camera, cautious of everyone around me. It was a good tactic they used to make me aware to always watch my surroundings, be mindful of what I was now part of. I'm part of the bigger picture now and I needed to respect that in every aspect.

I sat in the back of a shared minibus, hugging my rucksack with the plan to ignore everyone and everything. I hoped when I'd arrive at the venue and be around my own kind, I'd feel more at ease, in a safe zone. A loud man, a Yank, joined me on the bus journey.

"Howdy, what's your story, partner? Where you heading?"

It could have been innocent enough, but I wasn't going to risk talking. I fully believed The Network would test me, especially during my first week. I thought the man could've been planted giving the surprising encounter at the airport. One of their conditions in the contract; strict discretion at all times. I kept silent for the entirety of the ride, actively ignoring him throughout the journey at his measly attempts to entice me into conversation. I sighed with relief once he got off the bus and I wasn't subjected to any other peer pressure.

The journey lasted around an hour before I was dropped in a deserted dusty road that seemed to lead to nowhere. The driver abruptly closed the doors as I stepped out cautiously. Fear began to raise its ugly head now the realisation of what I'd got myself into hit me. Stranded in a foreign country with no sense of direction other than a red light on an intrusive app.

I did eventually come up to a wooden signpost, whacking the sand away, it read 'Imperium', the name of the villa I could now see, sitting isolated at the bottom of a steep sand hill. I made my way to the entrance of the venue, met by cathedral-looking arched wooden doors with ivory columns either side, seemingly looking out of place. The brass knocker was of a duck, confirming I was in the right place.

When there was no answer from my relentless knocking, I checked the app again, sure enough there I was hovering over the red light but a new, flickering purple light appeared. It was difficult to decipher what it meant as the light would glow in multiple places, dotted in all directions. The radius become frighteningly smaller around me until a force propelled me forward and I crushed through the villa's doors. Bracing myself with arms outstretched, I hit the ground painfully with most of the blunt force damaging my knees.

Disorientated, I squinted my eyes tearfully attempting to focus on my surroundings, but my glasses had been ripped from my face during the violent shove. I glanced up to a blurred vision of an exquisitely dressed man standing above me. The burning of his heavily used aftershave wafted up my nostrils when he crouched down to my level.

"Well, well, well, look who's last to show up."

He said whilst staring at me with a gaping smile. I gulped nervously, in shock from the rude welcoming I received. More so frustrated I couldn't see much. Dependant on using my other senses, I began to hear footsteps echoing in the open space. We were being joined by other people, huddled around me where I remained still. Nursing a bruised knee, I attempted to stand up to properly introduce myself. Maybe get a better understanding if tackling me to the ground was really necessary.

I managed to stand shakily and make out the unfocused outline of another three people. They joined the suited man who now stood profoundly in front of the group. Without warning, they swaddled around me like I was a rugby ball in the middle of a scrum. Beating me to the ground, I found myself once more on all fours at their mercy, unable to defend myself as they yanked my trousers down. I attempted to look behind me, but my face was pinned tightly between the suited man's fingers, forcing me to only look into his eyes as he began tutting.

"Now, you are one of us. Welcome, Komodo Dragon."

He stretched his tongue far from his mouth and licked the entire length of my face, from my chin, up and over my sweat-drenched forehead. I froze in fear, stiff from the restraints of the other group members as they pinned me down. A hand stabbed the back of my neck, smashing my face into the tiled floor, excruciatingly twisting my arms tightly behind my back. The weight of one of them sitting on my back crushed my chest, it was becoming increasingly harder to breathe.

A muffled cry distracted me from my own turmoil as it became apparent someone else was also here. I squinted desperately putting the blurred shapes and colours into any vague context. A naked girl, wriggling like a fish out of water to the side of me. She was painfully bounded with all her limbs hog-tied behind her back. I was forced to look in her direction as the suited man walked over to her. Her gagged cries became deafening as she attempted to scream. Helpless, I had no option but to watch the horror unfold as the suited man began stripping. Hearing his satisfying grunting, whilst raping the young girl, dissociated me from any events that happened next.

The only thing I remember was the pain once all the pressure was released. The hand that had clamped my neck was gone, along with the pair of hands that pinned my shins into the floor. I could breathe again now the weight of whoever was sitting on me disappeared, seemingly setting me free as quickly as the attack started.

I consciously became aware of a sickening sensation, a deep throbbing pain inside me. The feeling was as if I'd been struck with an iron rod, and it had impaled me from behind. I was now a lifeless puppet, brain-dead from sheltering myself in the confinements of my mind's subconscious.

Suddenly, the girl turned to face me, her arms and legs extended outwards, dropping the rope that bounded her. Her sinister giggling made me gulp nervously. She gingerly began to crawl towards me, sniggering. I'm haunted reminiscing her broken body creep closer to me, dragging her legs behind her. My instincts were demanding I moved, get up, run...but it was futile, I was mesmerised by her!

I cried out loud from the burning pain erupting again behind me. Thankfully this time, it was over quickly with an instant deflating feeling. I glanced behind me to see the not-so bounded girl, holding a bloodied collapsed magazine, gripping it by one of the corners. They had penetrated me with the recent issue of Out of Hibernation. The girl knelt by my side when I began to cry, now my brain was compiling the events. My heart ached at the sudden realisation we both had been victims of a vicious sexual assault. I felt a bizarre connection to her now, two unfortunate souls now connected through a traumatic life event. I thought she felt it too when she began stroking my head caringly. That was until she softly whispered in my ear.

"I'm Ducky. Welcome to my week."

CHAPTER 14

Goodrick bounced his glare between Allman and The Dragon, feeling very much the third wheel. The Dragon never made eye-contact with him throughout his fanciful story. He was growing concerned with Allman's behaviour, how she leaned in closer to him across the table, her open mouth, astonished with what she was hearing. Goodrick wasn't buying any of it.

The fact about how their corpse was penetrated had already been leaked to the media. Although Goodrick advised against it, they broadcasted the magazine, hoping someone would recognise it. Allman wrote up a report detailing the magazine's origins. No publishing details, no mail footprint, and the barcode, the coordinates, couldn't be scanned obviously.

All the shops and the stockholders she reached out to had never heard of the magazine before. The paper was standard printing quality; anybody with a home office could produce the same prints. There wasn't anything authentic about the magazine physically itself or any clues to know where it came from or who created it.

Allman sent the magazine to a language analyst in Tannoch, Goodrick's office of specialists, where it landed on the lap of Suzanne Darkhorse. She worked on famous cases like the Massey Mauler and The Cleaver killer in Little Lever. Both cases were solved through her analytical mind to decode the ransom notes and spot the hidden context within them. She found nothing in the magazine, just commented that everything was factually correct regarding a Komodo Dragon, and in her humble opinion, it was just that; a factual animal magazine.

Goodrick remembers smirking at his phone when he read Allman's abrupt response, stating she didn't ask for a *humble* opinion, she asked for a professional opinion. In response to that, Suzanne reworded her email, in her professional opinion, the article was factually based around a Komodo Dragon. That was it. Goodrick had fun brainstorming some of Allman's actions after that email. Did she throw her laptop out the window or just slam it shut, he wondered.

Goodrick was caught up with needing to obtain the finer details relating to this so-called organisation The Dragon repeatedly referenced. Highly skeptical, Goodrick wanted to give credit for a thought-out, but far-fetched, ideology that there's a network, for some reason, groups people together, but for what benefit?

The Dragon began painting what seemed any ordinary holiday starts out like. It seemed exciting, a sanctuary for the weird and wonderful. Until the story took an unexpected dark turn. He spoke with a slight curve to his mouth. Either The Dragon was extremely nervous about the subject or found it amusing to share.

Goodrick glanced over at Allman, who turned her feet inwards, pressing her knees together and clenched her hands into fists, gulping heavily, clearly nervous. That end part of the story seemed difficult for her to hear. Goodrick watched on until The Dragon seemed to finish his tale. Instead of jumping in with both feet with The Dragon, Goodrick rewound.

"So, lets recap to the beginning, this so called Network." Goodrick leaned both forearms onto the table and tried to grab his attention. The Dragon reluctantly stopped staring at Allman and engaged with Goodrick.

"A network of people, whom you describe have means to hack into your phone with connections nationally it seems? So, a Government, or like some hidden cult, some would say like the Illuminati."

"I can see the similarities, but don't misinterpret, they are far greater than any Government, and like the Government, they are *very* real." The Komodo

Dragon lowered his face, with his chin brushing against his chest, peeking over his glasses. He didn't seem to have a problem seeing Goodrick clearly from this distance based on the magnification of his eyes behind the thick lenses. *Partially blind for majority of the story, how convenient.*

"Okay, The Network, they group people together, people you said are like-minded?"

"Correct." The Dragon confirmed.

"For what purpose? It doesn't fucking make sense."

"I'm not here to be insulted, Detective Goodrick. I find swearing such a repulsive, derogatory way for people to express their dissatisfaction, bashfully using our beautiful language. You know English is the language of the air. All pilots and workers must speak English whilst flying, regardless of their origin."

Goodrick stared bleakly back at The Dragon, his knowledge of useless facts to deter you from the initial question, a clever interrogation tactic not many can get away with.

"Well, I'll apologise, swearing's my second nature. Let's move on. This group you're assigned to..."

"The Creatures." The Dragon added.

"Okay, The Creatures. Originally four members, now six?"

"Now Five."

Goodrick shook his head and scrunched his nose in confusion. He couldn't understand if The Dragon was forcefully trying to make the details of the story more confusing on purpose or if Goodrick miscounted.

"Sorry, I thought there were six in total? You mentioned a member may need to wait for the sixth year to host?"

"You are correct but now only five Creatures remain."

"So, what..."

Goodrick stopped himself, running through all the logical reasons in his mind. If he was to believe the rulings of The Network, he might as well use it to his advantage.

"Ah, so you're no longer in the group. Is that because you've broken their terms and conditions regarding the policy on strict discretion? Your snitching on them so your out?"

Goodrick asked with an open helping hand, a technique he adapted in many interrogations, befriend them and make helpful suggestions. Simple but effective tactic to find flaws if the interrogator scripts some of the story. If they are lying, it's easier to agree, believing the interrogator is on-side. Unknowingly accepting 'supporting' material they intend to use against you. Many stumble over their own words and soon start contradicting themselves, backing themselves into a corner, by then it's usually too late and the jig is up .

The Dragon rolled his eyes and smirked, pushing his glasses back on his nose using his middle finger.

"That would be impossible Detective Goodrick. There was only one clause on how to terminate your membership."

"And that was?"

"Death."

The Dragon chillingly looked through Goodrick with no hesitation. Goodrick kept his wits about him, avoiding the compelling confidence The Dragon asserted, almost convincing.

"Right, well, so this means you're still in the group, along with four others. What happened to the other one?"

"Like I said, death. That's the only way out, rule five of the contractual agreement got them."

"Like it's going to get you?" Goodrick tensed his eyes, trying to spread fear into The Dragon. If he was that serious about the rules and what The Network's capable of, surely, he must know he's put himself in harm's way coming to speak to them today.

"Well, now I hope you understand why our discussions can't be filmed or recorded. The Network may have their suspicions, but they wouldn't act on anything without unquestionable certainty a rule was broken."

"Unless they approached one of us?"

"It'd be irrational for you to discuss what's said in this room until you know everything because, without me, you'll know nothing."

"I'm not keen on having someone tell me how to do my job." Goodrick sneered.

"I'm not. I'm simply here to tell you my story, and I hope you do the rest."

An eerie silence clouded the room. Goodrick was cut up on the bigger picture of The Network so didn't intend to indulge on the rape scene. If he didn't believe The Network as a whole, he wasn't willing to fuel a sick, perverted encounter either.

For the first time since The Dragon began speaking, Allman rose from her chair and sat upright, clasping both hands together on the table, sucking in her cheeks, and pushing her lips forward. Physically showing them she was thinking out loud.

"So, The Komodo Dragon." Allman smiled his way. He reciprocated the smile looking pleased that she'd used his formal name.

"How did it feel?"

Both Goodrick and The Dragon seemed to shuffle in their seats, both equally unsettled by Allman's question.

"I'm sorry, are you referring to...?"

The Dragon paused, allowing everybody in the room to subconsciously finish it for him. Goodrick's eyes widened when Allman continued.

"The rape. I'm referring to the rape, Dragon."

Goodrick tilted back in his seat, lifting a hand to his mouth glancing away, segregating himself from Allman. He found the toughness in her voice surreal, almost to the point he wanted to let out an unacceptable laugh because she was so blasé. The quietness in both of them granted permission for Allman to continue.

"I thought you wanted to tell us the story? I want to know how it felt."

Goodrick could hear The Dragon breathing heavily from his nose and see him physically shaking. Allman leaned closer towards him and asked him further in a soft, slow tone, almost erotically.

"Tell me, how did it feel Dragon? Feeling that hard, stiff rod squeezed into you. No spit or lube to help ease it in?"

Goodrick coughed, trying to break the tension Allman created. The tale was now spun in a different direction from Allman's perverted tone. Now a story Goodrick found himself enticed with, reminiscing previous encounters with his side-piece Nicole.

A young student turned on by an older man wanting her, eager and hungry for anything Goodrick wanted. Goodrick won the lottery when Nicole messaged him, offering her services, on an online chat room he kept opened on an incognito tab. Their first weekend in a Hilton Hotel always made Goodrick grin with deep seeded lust. *Let's hope they don't always blacklight the rooms.*

"Am I making you nervous?"

Goodrick almost answered for The Dragon, thinking Allman's question was directed to him, able to hear his thoughts. Luckily, he pushed his tongue back in when he saw Allman gazing across the table at the trembling boy.

"I particularly like it that way, behind I mean, wouldn't you agree, Goodrick?"

Allman shot a callous smirk over at him like she knew what he was thinking about. He wished Allman had prepped him on her wayward interrogation tactics before putting him on the spot like this, but he tried to keep up.

"I tend to prefer it, although most women only offer it on special occasions: birthdays; anniversaries; valentines' day, that sort of thing."

"Hm, what a shame. It's every other Sunday for me."

"Remind me to join a church near you then."

Both Allman and Goodrick gleefully looked at each other smirking at their mutual distasteful sense of humour. Goodrick almost forgot a third member was watching the interaction, realising the conversation with Allman was fabricated, although he wouldn't say no to partake in Allman's ritual. He looked over at The Dragon, frozen with a dissatisfied snarl across his face. He looked like a dormant volcano, ready to explode at any given second.

"So please, Dragon, tell me more about Ducky. She was hosting the week so surely she was enjoying herself?" Allman continued.

"She was."

He fidgeted with the end of his shirt, looking down, avoiding eye-contact. It didn't appear like he wanted to engage in a conversation with either detective now.

"But you weren't? Isn't that what you signed up for, to be a fully participating member?"

The Dragon began shaking his head.

"As I said, it was a grey area in the terms and conditions..." He murmured.

"So, what are you asking us to do, arrest somebody on your allegations of rape?"

"I want you to listen."

"I'm listening, but I want to know how it-" Before Allman could finish, The Dragon erupted, leaping out of his chair. The Dragon's pitiful attempt only made the chair wobble, let alone crash and slide against the floor as he perhaps intended to but his fragile frame wouldn't allow it.

"It felt horrible, okay! Horrible! You see people on the news when their house has been burgled, and they say they sleep with one eye open now. How they feel agitated someone had been in their home, their personal space, terrified they will do it again, so they make themselves feel safer. How do they do that? They buy bigger, stronger locks, put cameras up, and obsess with shutting and locking everything. How can you do that when they were inside you, physically inside your body, you can't! You live with it, and so I have. The worse thing about it all is I felt embarrassed, me, the victim! I was the one that felt I needed to crawl into a black hole and disappear. Violated, dirty, unclean, all of the above. Water doesn't run hot enough to burn away those feelings! And let me say it first before you do. Yes, I brought it upon myself because I signed the fucking contract!"

The Dragon slammed both his hands on the table, back hunched and growling through his teeth. Goodrick was taken aback by the eruption of anger, the irony of him swearing at them but it got his point across. He *almost* felt bad for him. Looking across to Allman, she sat unphased, with both arms crossed, staring at The Dragon.

"That's enough for today, I'll be back here tomorrow, same time. I suggest you both get an early night with a big supper this evening. Tomorrow's story will be quite hard to stomach."

He regained his composed posture as he spoke, and by the time he had finished, his breathing regulated, and he looked as if nothing had happened. Allman didn't move, she kept facing forward even when the loud buzzer pinched Goodrick's ears, and The Dragon left. Goodrick stumbled to find his words. So much had been uncovered in the last half-hour he didn't know where to start. He breathed out excessively as if he'd been holding his breath all that time and looked towards Allman. One single tear dripping down her cheek. She pressed her lips together and said with a trembling voice.

"He's telling the truth."

CHAPTER 15

Allman sat back on the chair, running her hand across her tight hair, flicking her ponytail over her shoulder. It's the first time she'd heard out loud how she felt inside. Disheartened, she couldn't come to that conclusion herself. Instead, she heard it from another lost soul's story and felt she was intruding on his misery to understand her own. She didn't know how much Goodrick knew. She clenched her muscles, waiting for his judgement, his questioning. She felt him lean closer to her. All the while, she tried to make herself smaller, pulling her arms closer around her body. She wanted to squeeze so tight she'd disappear.

She flinched when a hand caressed her shoulder; pressure applied when he stood up from his seat. Allman looked up from her pit of uncertainty to see Goodrick with an outstretched hand and a soft smile on his face.

"Come on, love. I'll buy you an early lunch."

Allman stretched a smile back and accepted his offer, wrapping her hand around his, gracefully pulling her up onto her feet. She felt like a child back in school, holding a boy's hand, smirking to herself that he referred to her as: 'love.' Allman felt safe, at ease feeling the warmth of his hand, guiding her away from the cold depths of the room.

Feeling stable, she embraced the loud siren from the door being dragged open. Goodrick dropped his hand and pushed on her lower back, welcoming her back into mayhem with busy detectives racing down the corridors. The Dragon had already scurried away, lost within the herd.

Allman spotted Adriana Cross, arms folded, pursed lips, filling the entire width of the adjoining corridor. The stature of her presence intimidated Allman, from her fiery, chopped red hair, to her seven-inch black, polished heels. Her gigantic arms were squashed into the white, ill-fitting suit blazer she strapped herself into. Tightly wrapped around her waist, with one button missing, presumably catapulted off from her protruding gut. Her skirt would rise to an unflattering length, as she flung her weight side to side.

"Detective Allman, it's great to see you again." Adriana greeted Allman with a firm nod of the head. Before Allman could return any pleasantries, Adriana's attention had already been shifted towards Goodrick.

"Detective Goodrick, you sounded quite excited on the phone earlier. How did the meeting go with this 'Dragon' character then?"

She playfully mimicked The Dragon's name using air quotes and began marching away from them. Goodrick followed her every step naturally like they were attached by a string, talking behind her back. Allman caught up with a couple of quick steps, uncertain about the brash movement. She wasn't fond of talking to a superintendent's back, but office Tannoch must be more fast-paced than she was used to.

"Well, I'll be honest, Adriana, not much to report back on. He seems to know as much as the media at this point, but we will entertain it for bit longer."

"Good. Have you scheduled another talk with him?"

"Yes, same time tomorrow."

"Right. You'll need to go in with a recorder this time."

"I don't think that's a good idea-"

With a crash, Adriana stopped dead on the spot. Allman luckily avoided walking head-first into her cleavage when she turned around to face them.

"Did I ask for your opinion Goodrick?"

Allman squeezed her lips together, avoiding the situation. Her stomach filled with dread, reminiscing the times she'd be present whenever Mike and

Jay got a telling off. She'd never have the confidence to snigger out loud in front of Julie, let alone Adriana Cross.

"No, you didn't, but-"

"No buts. Recorder tomorrow. Is that clear?" Adriana shot Goodrick a scolding look.

"Yes, Adriana."

Allman held her breath, never had she seen Goodrick so well-behaved. This woman was a Goodrick whisperer!

"Good! For the time being, I'll be setting up an office at this godforsaken place." Adriana snarled, looking up and across the ceiling to display her disgust.

"Don't worry; we've terminated the rats now." Allman cheekily smiled at her. Goodrick turned a sterned face towards her, widening his eyes, signalling to Allman she shouldn't have said that. To his surprise, his expression melted when Adriana laughed in a whimsical way.

"I believe so. Well, there's one more to terminate, which reminds me, I'll need to speak to you tomorrow regarding Superintendent Chadwick, Louise."

Allman felt like she'd been shot in the stomach. Even after Adriana turned away and carried on her journey. Allman was transfixed on staring at the empty void Adrianna left. Goodrick skipped in her direction, placing both hands on Allman's shoulders.

"Are you okay?"

Goodrick looking distressed must've signalled she was struggling to keep her emotions contained. With three quick nods of the head, she wasn't quite there yet to talk physically, but that was enough for Goodrick to drop his hands as well as any concern.

"Come on, let's get some food in you."

"Well, where are we going?" Allman quizzed after they made their brisk walk towards the car park.

"There's no point asking a woman what she wants to eat. They can never make their mind up." Goodrick jokingly shouted across the roof of his car.

Allman sniggered, on the contrary, she found herself decisive and independent. Living alone since the age of seventeen meant she had to be, but there was something exciting to be jumping in Goodrick's car. Ready to be driven to a place she'd no say in, it was a comfortable ride she could get used to.

"Very well. I hope you have good taste. No seafood and I'm allergic to mushrooms."

"That's a shame. There's a new crab house in town that specialises in fungus." Goodrick stretched a sarcastic smirk.

The eruption from his car speakers was deafening; his stereo continued playing the last song at the same bellowing volume. He embarrassingly scattered around, hitting his phone repeatedly to stop it.

Allman smiled, watching Goodrick's hopeless attempts to hide what must be his guilty pleasure. She understood what it's like to be confined in your vehicle, a space where you're the greatest singer of all time. After a few seconds of pressing every button, silence descended. Goodrick put his head in his hand, looking embarrassed. Allman cheekily grinned to herself, looking out of the window to spare him. Allman began humming the song, tapping her hand on her knee. She began singing along like she'd do in her own vehicle: no judgement.

"Country roads, take me home, to a place I belong..."

She looked across at Goodrick, who was now smiling widely, showcasing his exquisite white teeth. It was the most attractive he'd looked, Allman thought. Seeing him slightly giggle through his smile, he genuinely looked happy. An unexpected duet broke out when Goodrick began singing alongside her.

"...West Virginia, mountain mama, take me home, country roads."

He pressed a button and the softly sung vocals by John Denver helped to mute their distorted singing capabilities. Allman enthusiastically clapped her hand against her knee to the beat, with Goodrick hitting the steering wheel, creating a loud baseline for the song. Their unexpected duets carried them along their journey before Goodrick pulled into a parking space on a busy main road.

One shop, in particular, caught Allman's attention, recognising it instantly: 'Claire's Bric a Brac'. Saddened at the sudden reminder where Allman and her mum once spent many quality hours, digging through lost treasures with the hopes to make it rich with one of their finds.

"Clod's Café? We're eating here?" Allman asked. The small sign squeaked in the light breeze before them.

"Believe me. This place is a hidden gem."

Allman followed Goodrick inside the quaint café.

"Gregory! I wasn't expecting to see you again." A robust woman eagerly cheered from behind the counter.

"Eileen, please meet my good friend Detective Allman."

The older woman wiped her hands together on her floral apron and looked across with admiration. She had never been greeted with a kinder face before. Stretching her hand across the counter, she began to introduce herself.

"Hi, I'm Louise."

Eileen bounded towards her, ignoring the attempt of a handshake, and flung her arms around Allman with a squeeze.

"We hug in this family, my dear. It's so good to finally meet you."

With a confused expression on her face, Allman leaned downwards and patted Eileen softly on the back, looking over at Goodrick.

"Finally?"

"Oh yes, Gregory mentions-"

"Two menus when your ready Eileen." Goodrick quickly ordered, the woman obliged, hobbling away.

"So, who's Eileen?" Allman asked, intrigued to know who he'd been gossiping about her to.

"She's the owner," he abruptly said, taking a seat at a nearby table.

"Well, I guessed that, but who is she to *you*?"

Goodrick's eyes shifted uncomfortably back and forth until a waiter broke the tension, gracing their table with a saucer of mixed biscuits along with a pot of tea.

"She seems to be struggling, was that caused from the fall?" Allman queried after noticing the poor woman stumbling under herself. Goodrick shot Allman a confused expression.

"Is that not your step-mum, Gregory, who took a fall?"

He quickly stopped chewing, taking a large gulp to finish. He coughed slightly whilst pouring them both a cup of tea.

"No."

Allman sat back, not wanting to interrogate him further. Her eyes pricked up from her lap when he began speaking again.

"My step-mum is a witch. Eileen over there was the closest thing I had to a mothering figure whilst growing up." He took a swig of his tea before voluntarily explaining further.

"My mum left when I was very young. A useless drunk but thankfully I had my dad. He'd bring me here most days, the cakes are the best for miles around. Through the years, Eileen stepped in as a mothering figure. She has a boy, Charlie, who I don't see much anymore but we were like brothers growing up. He didn't know his father, so that's where my dad stepped in. We all fitted together like a dysfunctional jigsaw but it worked. Eileen attempted to teach me how to bake, but I was too impatient. She always hit the back of my hand with a spoon because I'd lick the cake mixture off the whisks.

By the time it came to put it in the oven, the large cake we'd measured for turned out to be a pathetic cupcake."

Allman smiled, admiring how at ease he seemed to be, comfortably opening up to her, a side of him she'd never realised existed. The story of the baking reminisced memories with her own mother, chuckling at both their failed early baking career.

"My mum and I were exactly the same. I can still hear her shouting, you'll get sick with all that raw egg in your stomach." Both chuckling simultaneously.

"So, where does your mother live?" Goodrick asked. Allman almost choked on her gulp of tea, not expecting the depth of their conversation.

"My mum passed away a few years ago," Allman answered quickly.

"I'm so sorry…uh, any siblings?" Goodrick was eager to move the conversation on.

"Nope, only me and her. So, just me. How about you? Do you have any siblings other than Charlie?"

"Nope. Just me, also."

"So, your dad…?" Allman carefully asked, sensing she already knew the answer.

He shook his head, retrieving a hand out of his pocket, and placed a small locket in front of Allman. It was brass, decorated in fine sketched swirls with half a broken chain attached. She delicately picked it up to study it. Inside was an old, frail photograph of a man in military uniform.

"That's the only picture I have left of him. I keep it in my pocket, sometimes squeezing it when I'm nervous." He sounded mournful.

"So, that's why you always have your hands in your pockets?" Allman smiled sweetly, trying to uplift the mood.

"I was hoping you wouldn't have noticed."

"Well, I am a detective, Gregory."

They both grinned at one another as Allman carefully placed the locket within Goodrick's grasp.

"We need to discuss what's happened, don't you think?" Goodrick said, changing the unexpected topic point.

"Not here. I mean, there's a lot of eyes on us." Allman hushed quietly.

"I guess you're right. Can take a doggy bag back to yours?" Goodrick asked, tapping his finger against the table with a raised eyebrow.

"Sounds like a plan. I have been meaning to ask you, but how did you know where I lived? That first time you brought the magazine? You just unexpectedly turned up?"

Goodrick smirked across the rim of his cup.

"You forget Louise..." He paused, swigging the final bit of his tea.

"I'm Detective fucking Goodrick."

CHAPTER 16

He casually walked through Allman's door, flinging his belongings on the nearby sofa, making himself right at home. He relaxed into the corner position, content with the comfiness of the cushion; it made a change from the hard-cutting one he slept on at home. Allman slumped onto the sofa beside him, both turning into one another. She pointed down at his shoes.

"Honestly, get comfy," she insisted.

He happily obliged, placing his shoes under the coffee table, where his favourite coasters resided. He knew they had much to discuss, but it was nice to pretend momentarily, he was there for a social visit.

"Right, where do you want to begin?" Allman asked.

Goodrick shrugged his shoulders, wanting to remain in the fantasy.

"I'll start then. I believe him."

Goodrick squeezed his eyes together and sighed.

"Really? You believe in all of it? The Network, the rules, Portugal, Ducky, rape...all of it?"

"Yes." Allman confidently said.

Goodrick shook his head whilst Allman shuffled herself closer, cornering him.

"He was authentic. I could feel it." Allman pleaded her opinion. Goodrick sat with his head resting against his hand whilst she continued.

"I'm not saying I believe *every* detail yet, but there's no reason not to at this point. I mean, it's possible that this group does exist, and these people are real. It's not that far-fetched."

"So, you really think this governing group of people, The Network, would condone rape?" Goodrick challenged.

"Yes, unfortunately. I believe the higher in power they are, the more control they have to orchestrate such a thing. We should know, the amount of sick bastards we've come across in our careers. To me it seems The Network is acting like a shepherd for society, herding all the wrong'uns and controlling their antics, away from public eyes, hence the secrecy of it all."

Goodrick nodded, it wasn't the most out there conspiracy theory he had heard. The correctional system was under breaking point with a horrifying average ratio of eight prisoners to one guard.

"Hmm. There's just something about him I don't like."

"Well yeah, he's a bit of a weirdo, troubled."

They finally agreed on something. Goodrick stared up at the ceiling with both his arms crossed, contemplating.

"Let's say it's all real. Why would he be speaking to us?" Goodrick asked.

"Well, that's what I'm unsure about. I don't know what his intentions are yet."

"If we believe him, I find it difficult The Network wouldn't know already. What happens if he doesn't turn up tomorrow?"

"I really don't know."

"I'll do some digging, find his real name at least."

"Not much else we can do. Adriana was quite forceful about recording him, wasn't she?"

"Yeah. I'll tuck it into my jacket, he'd be none the wiser."

"Wouldn't Adriana want everything above board, though? As in, we would need to tell him he's being recorded?"

Goodrick shook his head.

"No, he won't agree. Besides, you know it's not illegal to record someone without their permission, *if* it's in the public interest to do so. There's always two ways to skin a cat."

Allman nodded, allowing the weight of her consumed head to hit the back of the sofa: looking exhausted for the day.

"Are you worried about the meeting regarding Flatdick?" Goodrick cautiously looked across at Allman to read her response. It was something he had wanted to discuss since their meeting with him yesterday. He pieced most of the information together himself before Flatdick confirmed it. He spent a joyful ten minutes explaining in great detail his 'relationship' with Allman. Most of it Goodrick felt was exaggerated, so Flatdick felt the bigger man, or somehow had 'one up over him'. He wanted to hear what really happened between Allman and Flatdick in her own words, in her own time. For now, getting him suspended and allowing her to keep her case was the only thing he could do to help Allman.

"Yeah, I'm shitting it in all honesty with what it will entail, I don't know what to tell her."

"You tell her what's been going on. You tell her everything." Goodrick commanded.

"How much do you know, Gregory?" Allman asked in a defeated tone, turning her head to look at him. He could see the pain beneath her eyes. Her deep hazel eyes were watering with her brows creasing inwards: he hated to see her like this.

"I think I know a lot." He nodded gently with a soothing voice, not wanting to cause her more pain by explaining the depth of his knowledge. Her body language when Flatdick was anywhere remotely near her and the reaction to The Dragons story, it was obvious she was experiencing some sort of trauma. The triumph of her questioning techniques with The Dragon surprised Goodrick. He applauded her efforts and capability to keep professional in the face of distress. He reached his hand across to her and cradled her cheek in his hand.

"You're good at your job Louise; don't let anybody ever try to force you to prove that again." He meant what he said, stroking his thumb softly against her.

The look in her eyes suddenly changed. All moisture that was once bubbling above her lash line dried up. Goodrick synchronised with her movements, allowing her to take the lead, closing his eyes and tilting his head slightly. Her lips were tediously stroking against his. He felt the warmth radiating from her flushed cheeks and the smell of peppermint escape her mouth. She pushed further in, locking her lips over his. Goodrick moved his hand to the back of her head, brushing his fingers through her silk-like hair, reciprocating the kiss. She held his face firmly as she manoeuvred, flinging one of her legs across his lap, straddling him. He was happily pinned between her thighs.

As the kiss deepened, he felt Allman's wandering hands teasingly rub between his legs. He reluctantly pushed her away from him, both gasping for air from the intense passion she initiated.

"Are you sure about this?" Goodrick asked. He hoped he hadn't stopped prematurely, gagging for more. She only paused for a couple of seconds, but the wait was torturing. To his delight, she nodded her head confidently smiling, permitting them to resume.

Her perfumed scent of red berries wafted as she began to plant feathering kisses against his neck. He moaned with pleasure when the tickling sensation morphed into small bites of hunger for him. In desperation, he yanked at the bottom of her t-shirt, pulling it upwards over her head and dragging his palms against her delicate body. She broke the connection to his neck, holding her arms upright and throwing her top behind her carelessly. Her affectionate smile before kissing Goodrick again sent shockwaves rushing through his body.

Unable to control his need any longer once gifted the sight of her bare chest. He pushed his weight through his heels, and picked her up in one swift movement. He tensed his arms, stabilising his feet before walking towards the large floor-to-ceiling windows. Pressing her up against the glass as she gasped at the cold surface against her back. His heart raced, feeling the beat through his throat.

Aggressively, he dug his fingertips into her behind. He was sure his hands-on approach might've bruised her. She responded similarly, mauling at his shirt buttons, losing her temper at the last stubborn one, ripping it at the seams.

"Fuck, I'm sorry," she breathed, trembling.

"Don't be." Goodrick shook his head, taking a breather.

He could feel the pain from between his legs where his growing erection ached to be released. He yanked her skirt higher, clawing at her tights, stretching them apart until he tore an inviting hole in them. Looking up at her, he smiled widely.

"Well, we're even now." He said smiling before steadying himself, anticipating the upcoming sensation as he pulled her underwear to one side. Slowly, he thrust his hips forward, pushing inside her. With a final strong thrust, he was fully inserted, feeling the walls of her vagina tense around him, swallowing it whole. He buried his head inside her neck, gasping his hot breath against her skin at the instant pleasure she rewarded him.

She leant her head back against the glass whilst digging her fingernails into his broad shoulders, keeping a tight grip from the quickening pace. Hearing her moaning with pleasure, it egged him on to becoming relentless with the pounding blows. He loved seeing her lips tremble, unable to control the delicate screams of gratification.

"Please, Gregory, I can't take much more."

Feeling her legs begin to shake either side of him, spurred him on to finish. He breathed heavily through gritted teeth, the veins in his neck protruding, ready to explode. Allman erupted with a high-pitched shriek escaping from her lungs. Goodrick swallowed her screams, locking his mouth around her lips as he began to soften his pace. Both of their legs trembling as it became apparent they were both reaching peak satisfaction.

Carefully, he lowered Allman's feet back to the ground. They both chuckled nervously at their intense, unexpected moment.

"I think we both could do with a drink now... after that." Allman said, picking up her blouse from the floor and leisurely walking into the kitchen area. Goodrick nodded, composing himself back together, full of euphoria from what just happened.

A loud vibrating noise alerted them both to look at the coffee table, equally distanced between them. Nothing displayed on Goodrick's phone screen other than a flashing red light, giving the hidden callers ID away. A trick he thought clever at the time, justifying a red notification as low battery, not in fact from his fling, Nicole, requesting a booty call. Goodrick stared at the flashing light that once brought him excitement but now glowed as a gigantic warning. The realisation hit him hard when Allman approached him holding two cups of freshly brewed tea. He buried his phone quickly into his pocket with a frown on his face, rubbing the back of his neck anxiously. With the fresh reminder of the mess he's in, a loveless marriage, meaningless hook-ups with Nicole, where did he see Allman fitting into all this? He had some unfinished business he needed to take care of before he could entertain whatever this was with Allman.

"Is everything okay?" she asked him, looking concerned. His occupied mind didn't remind him to acknowledge her presence.

"Yes, sorry, I was in my own little world. I know this is *really* bad timing, but I need to go and do something." Goodrick reluctantly announced, knowing she'd hate hearing it as much as he did saying it.

"Again? You're just going to leave, again?" Her face churned into an appalled frown, with every good reason. Picking up his jacket and hanging it loosely over his arm, he hopped around the coffee table and attempted to embrace her with a hug. With the use of only one arm and Allman defenceless whilst holding onto the mugs. He tried to soften his brash reactions delicately.

"I'm really sorry Louise but please just trust me. I'll come to pick you up tomorrow morning, be ready for nine." He pressed a closed kiss on her forehead whilst she stood awkwardly. He could hear the disappointment in her sigh when he pulled away.

"Yeah, I suppose. Good job I was planning on staying in to work on the case anyway."

They both pulled an equally dissatisfied smile before he walked away, leaving her alone in the apartment.

A disturbing sensation of worry filled his stomach, he hated to see her so unhappy but knew his mind wasn't in the right place to stay in her presence. Clicking on the familiar profile, he hit the keypad quickly, ignoring the misspelling before pressing send.

'we neec to talk…now.'

CHAPTER 17

July 23rd, 2015

Pacing outside her apartment complex, checking the time repeatedly beginning to fret about Goodrick's timekeeping. Spinning behind her to the sound of tyres screeching, she watched Goodrick's car race up from the entrance of the car park, braking harshly by side of her. The loud, heavy music was switched off as she opened the car door, greeted with his tiresome, weak smile instead. Climbing inside, angrily looking across at him when she wasn't getting much of a welcome .

"Late night?" she sneered.

His groan wasn't the response she was hoping for. The acceleration of him pulling away pinned her against the leather seat uncomfortably.

"Can you slow down?" She begged. He lightened his foot on the accelerator, not saying a word. Allman slumped back, watching the blurred trees zoom past her, wondering what could be wrong. It wasn't like him to act or behave in this way, he could be arrogant but never rude, in this nature.

She stayed up most of the night herself, panicking over their encounter. *What if this implicates the case? What if he's embarrassed...*" She closed her eyes, trying to refocus than panic herself on any what ifs. The second talk with The Dragon excited her but also coming today, a meeting with Adriana, terrified her. *What is she going to ask me about him? What does she know?*

With Goodrick's fast driving, they were in the car park in record time. Leaping out, she slammed the door shut to express her frustrations, marching into the building, leaving Goodrick to catch up.

"You could have waited for me."

Allman turned around with a face like thunder when Goodrick closed shut her office door.

"What the fuck was that about?"

"What?" He shrugged.

"You could barely look at me this morning. What's happened?" Allman demanded answers. Goodrick looked disinterested, rubbing his hands over his dreary eyes.

"Nothing, I just didn't get a good nights sleep."

"Neither did I, but that doesn't give you the right to be an absolute cock to me!"

Goodrick began shaking his head, looking down at the floor with his hands in his pockets; looking unamused.

"I think you're overreacting, Louise."

"I'm overreacting?" She scoffed.

"You're the one who left abruptly again with no explanation, and with what had just happened, yeah, I'm a little on edge. I tried calling and you just ignored me."

"I think you're being a little needy. I was just busy." He said with a stern face across at her. Allman took a step back, hurt deeply. *Needy?* She couldn't say anything, astonished at what she'd heard. He took a step forward, taking his hands out of his pocket with a concerned look on his face. He must've realised what he'd said before thinking of any consequences.

"Look, Louise, I'm sorry for saying that. That isn't what I meant." He opened his arms around her, trying to look at her face. Allman gawked down at the floor, open-mouthed, speechless.

"I really didn't mean that. I… I've just had a very, *very* bad night, I can't get into it right now, but I'll tell you about it when the time's right okay?" She looked up at him, hearing the sincerity in his voice.

"Don't make me beg, Louise," he whispered in her ear.

She really wanted to be mad at him for longer. Wanted to slap him across the face, but she couldn't. Not that she couldn't only in a professional manner but she'd melt when looking into those deep blue eyes. She didn't know why or what it was, but after any argument following with the littlest of compliments, she was always drawn back into him. Was Goodrick's chillingly, charmful spell working or was she in that much desperation for any affection, she was indeed how he described; needy.

Slouching her shoulders with a roll of her eyes, she at least made him sweat a little but needed to get on with their day regardless.

"Let's just concentrate right now on The Dragon, he'll be here soon." She said, pushing Goodrick softly on his chest to create distance between them. Goodrick stood back respectively.

"You take the lead on it, you were impressive yesterday."

"You are referring to the interrogation I hope Gregory? Goodrick grinned, tapping his jacket pocket, whispering in hushed breaths to her.

"It might already be on."

Allman smirked walking over to him with her arms assertively crossed. She leant forward seductively looking up at him as she spoke directly into the pocket that hid the recorder.

"For the record, Gregory Goodrick's a total dick, speaking of which his-"

Before she could finish, Goodrick childishly grabbed her from behind as they both erupted into laughing. Goodrick covered her mouth with his hand, playfully stopping her from speaking, before whispering in her ear.

"Are you going to behave?"

Allman submissively nodded her head, spinning around within his arms to face him. Goodrick leaned slowly inwards to embrace her which Allman gleefully dodged.

"It won't be that easy, Goodrick." She smirked tutting at his futile attempts to 'kiss and make-up'. A sudden knock at the door alerted them both to stand for attention. With her assertive voice, Allman granted them access to enter.

To Allman's surprise, Adriana strolled in. A gulp of sick was in Allman's mouth, horrified she'd heard them giggling and messing around like school children.

"Morning, you two," Adriana said cheerfully closing the door behind her.

"Good morning Adriana." They both said simultaneously, *just like school children.*

"Are we all ready for The Dragon? He's arrived, waiting for you both in room three."

Goodrick patted his pocket, indicating his plans to record the conversation as she instructed.

"Yup, we're all set."

"Perfect. Allman, I've arranged for us both to have our meeting at three here. Believe it or not, this is the nicest office." Adriana said with a frown.

Allman nodded with fear beginning to creep up again. She could only speculate on the reasons behind Flatdick's suspension, whether that included their relationship or not, she had no idea. Knowing she signed a contract with internal relationships forbidden, would they even care if it transpired into non-consensual? What she did yesterday with Goodrick would give Adriana reason to take her off the case at best. Allman's guilt began to weigh heavily on her shoulders. She hadn't taken her livelihood of maintaining her career into perspective when she jumped on Goodrick.

The men always seem to come out fine, but the women are seen as weak and unpredictable; a liability. It had been initial attraction and lust that kept her consumed by Goodrick but in recent days, found to appreciate his company. His sarcastic humour would always put a smile on her face, even when she didn't want it to. The sex was a spur-of-the-moment, a hot fifteen-minute release of sexual tension that had built up between them that neither wanted to contain anymore. She wanted him, and she got him. *But for what price?*

"Excellent, see you then." With a nod, Adriana left them alone. Goodrick nodded back whilst Allman, away with the fairies, curtsied. The horror of what she'd done registered in her brain after Adriana shut the door, hoping she hadn't stayed long enough to see her execute the noble goodbye. Goodrick erupted in a fit of laughter, wiping a tear from his eye.

"What the fuck was that?"

"Shut up!" Allman demanded, hitting him harmlessly in the arm. *He definitely won't let that go.* She began to walk out of her office with a much-detested smile on her face, hearing Goodrick chuckling behind her. Both seemingly gleeful to be back in their wayward tit-for-tat relationship.

"You about done, Detective Goodrick?" Allman's asked, checking he could control his giggling fit before starting the interrogation.

"Yeah, yeah, I promise, yeah, I'm done." He said in between broken laughs, contradicting himself.

"Is it recording?" She asked quietly as they both got themselves comfy in the room. Goodrick pulled his jacket to the side, poking his hand inside. The siren of the door opening made him jump; quickly restoring into a neutral position, giving Allman a wink.

The Dragon tediously walked into the room, thanking the policeman who held the door open for him. He shuffled his steps, finding trouble to pick his feet up off the ground. He stood sheepishly behind the chair, looking across at both detectives.

"Good morning, Detective Goodrick." Goodrick raised his eyebrows and gestured with his hand as a response, not saying a word. The Dragon waited for a moment before kinking his neck to look directly at Allman.

"Good morning, Detective Allman. May I say, you look absolutely radiant this morning."

Allman pulled an uncertain smile making brief eye-contact with Goodrick with the unusual remark.

"Please, take a seat. Thank you for coming back in." Allman's gestured.

The Dragon didn't move, he maintained an awkwardly kinked neck darting a deathly stare at Allman.

"Erm, you can sit down now... Dragon." She tried using formalities, maybe he took offence as he referred to them politely enough. Allman looked desperately over to Goodrick when it failed to have any impact.

"What gives, mate?" Goodrick cockingly asked.

The Dragon creepily turned his gaze towards him, without so much as blinking. His movements made Allman feel uneasy. The Dragon lifted the same oversized yellow shirt he wore yesterday upwards. Allman shuddered, every muscle in her body tensed, expecting to see him packing a loaded gun. She sighed deeply when it was only a rolled up envelope concealed in his waist band. He smacked it down on the table in front of him. It reminded Allman of how the magazine at the crime scene was found, tightly rolled, but inserted into a corpse. Taking a large gulp, she felt frightened at the realisation.

"What did I ask you not to do?" The Dragon asked softly.

Allman looked across at Goodrick with a confused expression who hinted down at his pocket with a quick glance.

"I came here to help you, all I asked for in return is your word, Detective Allman." His eyes gunned on her. She felt her heart beginning to race quickly. *It's impossible for him to know.*

"Now, I'll give you one chance so I can sit down and share more of my story. But if you don't obey, the contents of this envelope will be distributed."

Both detectives didn't say a word, equally compelled at what The Dragon could be referring to. Allman couldn't admit they planned to record him, adamant he couldn't be referring to that, she wasn't willing to gamble with it. With both of them refusing to speak first, The Dragon rolled his eyes in frustration.

"You agreed not to record me, Louise."

Allman turned her neck quickly towards him that she could feel herself becoming dizzy. *No, what, but how did he know?* Her eyes squinted, she wasn't sure if to dispute the accusation she was guilty of or to admit. The Dragon bent his fingers towards them, beckoning her to come clean and pass it over. Goodrick reached his hand inside his jacket pocket, looking at Allman. She knew Adriana would be furious they disobeyed her orders, but they were being left with no other option, they needed The Dragon's cooperation.

Goodrick pulled the recorder out, revealing their not-so-secret device, before sliding it across the table. The Dragon whacked his hand downwards without moving his glare from them; stopping the recorder in its path. He held it upwards towards the light, inspecting it. Allman and Goodrick passed concerned looks between one another. To Allman's relief, he dragged his chair outwards and took his seat, smiling widely at them with his hands together over the envelope.

"Right, now that's sorted, we may begin."

Allman tucked her chair inwards and cleared her throat.

"Oh Louise, you best get yourself some water. You'll have plenty of questions to ask after I'm finished."

LIZARD

CHAPTER 18

Now then, this one's a little bizarre, so I hope you keep up. That years magazine arrived by post on the same day I received Ducky's, exactly a year prior on 12th January. It involved a small paragraph about lizards, precisely the anolis-carolinensis. Did you know when they're caught by a predator, they can lose their tail and grow it back? Each magazine is supposed to give you a hint about what that week will consist of, not always obvious however. I understood now why the previous magazine issue mentioned ducks having a rape culture, who knew?

A new ruling became part of the already complex agreement between ourself and The Network, strictly no phones allowed. I believe Ducky was on thin ice with The Network for pulling her stunt. They didn't appreciate the bending of the rules, travelling before and after the seven days, enticing the Creatures to communicate before attending the week. The Network's intended purpose is bringing people together for a reason, to engross with one another for only seven days once a year. We aren't even allowed to speak to one another until the host has welcomed us formally into their week. The Network found Ducky's relaxed approach untasteful so I believe she was given a slap on wrist as it was her first year and no formal rules had been broken.

Thankfully, this years venue was only a direct train journey away. Being stripped from a mobile was unnerving for the first time, felt I had lost a limb. For entertainment purposes for the travel, I took my iPod to pass the three hour train journey from Buxton. I was happily listening to my usual playlist until a song I'd never heard before repeatedly played. I questioned if it was a corrupt file, maybe I shouldn't admit this to yourselves, but I'd torrent my music. So it wouldn't have striked me as odd if one of the pirated files wasn't the song I believed it to be. Unable to control the device however, the screen began to flicker with an image of a Lizard before deafening me with the relentless song on full volume. I resorted to placing the iPod and earphones in my pocket but the muffled tune provoked unsatisfied glares from other passengers. I still hadn't become familiar with The Network's tactics but I was at least a little less spooked than previous year, but annoyingly embarrassed. I'd spent the previous year keeping myself to myself, treating everyone as a suspect in case I ran into an informant for The Network. Now, they purposely drew the attention on me, another test I presumed on how I'd react.

The train tickets specified where I should wait to be collected. By now I had learnt the song by heart as it continued to play in my pocket. Only eerily stopping when I heard a rattling of an exhaust from a beaten-up car speeding down the road. I was apprehensive as it walloped up the kerb next to me. The driver lowered the passenger's window when a couple of unsettling seconds passed.

"Oi mate, Dragon, you getting in or what?"

A real cockney accent was pushed out, alongside a lollypop that he twirled around his mouth. Reggie was his name. He was what The Network refer to as Runts. Disposable people they use from time to time but aren't assigned to a specific group. They are signed into a contract, like we all are, but some rules didn't apply to them as it did for me. Only difference between a Creature and a Runt was a Creature attended every year and they hosted a week themselves. Runts were called upon when and if needed, but must attend if instructed to do so and of course, strict discretion with no refusal of what was needed of them, along with their statutory ruling of being over the age of eighteen.

He seemed enthusiastic about what was to come, more in the know than I was. An experienced Runt who had his 'expertise' called upon regularly from The Network. I attempted to prise any information from him as the magazines only give a vague idea of the host's personality. I didn't make it obvious I was fishing for clues, knowing The Network would disapprove. Although the fact Reggie was clearly on something made me doubt how much of what he told me was true.

He explained I'd be with the other Creatures and their Runts momentarily at a derelict, abandoned school as this years venue. The building formally known as Fingask: The School Of Science. Apparently closed down in the fifties following a fire but now was a popular venue choice used by The Network. Reggie informed me I needed to be blindfolded from this point onwards for the remainder of the car ride, he suddenly became anxious he might have shared too much with me. I obliged of course, not wanting to agitate a drugged up tearaway who was behind a wheel.

Reggie led me blindly to where I trusted him I needed to be. I became disoriented from being thrashed around in the car to now being led to some unknown destination on foot. Reggie pushed on my lower back with a hissing laugh until stopping me, guiding me up a small set of steps. The blindfold was ripped from my head, blinded by bright flood lights. Me, along with the other Creatures found ourselves in a 19th century looking operating theatre. Staggered platforms wrapped around the walls, centralising on an empty operating table.

Shuffled amongst the other Creatures, I adapted to their behaviour, eyes in front, waiting for the host's arrival. We didn't wait long until The Lizard walked through the door wearing clinical PPE head to toe. Myself and the fellow Creatures watched on whilst the Runts were gathered by The Lizard, joining him at the epicentre. Reggie wasn't the only one with the shakes, all the Runts demonstrated drug withdrawal symptoms. Diluted pupils along with the occasional neck cracks and gurning suggested they were all victims from some sort of substance abuse.

"With the welcoming of the two new members, I took the opportunity to recreate my first week for you all." The Lizard announced in a bellowing voice, beginning his welcome ceremony.

"Firstly, let's choose our Runt! With a round of applause, please make as much noise as possible for your favourite."

Unlike being chucked into my first week with a shove, this felt like a fun, interactive game show where I was part of a paying audience. Funnily enough, that's exactly what it was, The Creatures acted as an audience, watching from the first levelled platform and the Runts were given the opportunity to be contestants. Reggie caught my attention by rigorously stretching his head high, tensing his jaw, and mouthing the words: 'me, pick me.' The Lizard started, hovering his hand over the first quivering Runt; a blonde, flimsy woman who was biting flesh from her finger beds.

"Any votes for Jayne?" The Lizard shouted. The only noise came from Ducky, excitedly howling, clapping her hands frantically together. The Lizard quickly moved down the line, we all remained silent until his hand hovered over Reggie. I didn't know what we were voting for but it was easy to get caught up in the upbeat atmosphere as me and the other Creatures cheered loudly. Weirdly feeling proud that Reggie was my Runt, the obvious favourite within the group. Reggie punched the air, leaping upwards to celebrate with the rest of us. I smiled widely at the evident happiness he displayed, his excitement was efficacious.

"Well, Reggie boy, it looks like it's finally your time." The Lizard smiled warmly at the ecstatic Runt. He tore a smile from ear to ear, beginning to remove his clothes before jumping onto the table, wearing only his underpants. He was certainly no David Beckham; new day, new briefs. Yellow stained with brown smears, hole ridden and most probably yanked up days ago. The sight of it almost deterred from the upbeat atmosphere created in the room. A song suddenly erupted from a surround system with The Lizard beginning to clap above his head. He enticed us, the crowd, to join in. We all matched his showman energy and happily clapped along to the beat. My eardrums channelled in with the music. It was that song. That bloody song that blared repeatedly from my iPod.

'*I've been grinding so long, been trying this shit for years, uh-huh.*'

Reggie gave me a satisfying thumbs up as he shook excitedly on the metal table. The Lizard pushed softly on his head so he lay flat.

'*And I got nothing to show, just climbing this rope right here, uh-huh*'

The Lizard began wiping down Reggie's leg with some substance, iodine I believe? The sticky, you know, brown stuff you normally see used in theatres.

'*And if there's a man upstairs, he kept bringing me rain, uh-huh,*'

I slowed down my clapping, now out of sync with the rest of The Creatures who kept up with the pace of the happy song. Harrowingly, the drip fed clues that had been there all along, stared me in the face.

'*But I've been sending up prayers, and something's changed.*'

The plastic lined flooring, the theatrics of the white gown with green latex gloves and protective boots…

'*I think I finally found my hallelujah.*'

The operating table, the theatre lights, the medical instruments…

'*I've been waiting for this moment all my life, and now all my dreams are coming true.*'

The Lizard held up his chosen surgery tool…

'*Yeah, I've been waiting for this moment.*'

The realisation of what I'd clapped for, sunk in…

'*Feels good to be alive right about now.*'

The disturbing echo from a chainsaw's clattering blades silenced the song. The Lizard began to dig his bloodied chainsaw into the left leg of Reggie, below his knee. Reggie gripped onto the side of the table, screaming hysterically, but then laughing, then back to bellowing. The juxtaposition between hearing Reggie cheerfully cackle to watching him be torn apart still horrifies me today.

The blades measly shredded through his flesh, like a sharpened knife slipping through butter. His tainted blood began sprinkling up over The Lizard, showering him. He leant his flabby body over the chainsaw, desperately forcing the torture device down, I heard the cracking through Reggie's tibia and fibula bones. The Lizard tugged at Reggie's almost detached leg, stretching and snapping the final ligaments from the limb. Blood began to pour and spool onto the plastic sheets below.

The Lizard held his trophy up towards myself and the rest of The Creatures, looking ecstatic at his achievement. The rest of the Creatures erupted in an applause, wolf-whistling and cheering. The Lizard was gleaming, embracing the audience as he took a bow. He held onto Reggie's hairy dismembered calf, shaking it gleefully like a captain of a winning football team shakes the premier league trophy.

I desperately tried to look at Reggie, to confirm what state he was in. The other Creatures jumped from the platform and huddled around The Lizard, congratulating him on the hashed job. I shook Reggie rigorously, desperate to hear his weasel laugh or see his blackened gums, but nothing. Tears began to bubble in my eyes, I didn't know the man but I felt deep sorrow. Who was he really, where was his family, how did he end up here? The metal trolley began to be dragged away as I stood questioning myself. It was at that moment I felt the gravity of the situation I was involved in. Reggie might have been a discarded piece of rubbish to society, littering the streets with needles but he was somebodies son. Saying that, I guess he might've always felt discarded, unloved, perhaps even rejected by his own mother. That's what some animals and us creatures do right? Kill the runt.

CHAPTER 19

Goodrick tried reassuring himself as he reluctantly continued listening to The Dragon's story. He began feeling queasy himself, tightening his eyes shut, although he wished he could do the same for his ears. The picture imprinted in his mind of a man, blood-soaked, waving around an amputated leg. It was too much this time. *Why did it have to include blood?* Every now and again, he'd look towards Allman for guidance. Her concentrating frown didn't offer much. He felt relieved when the story came to an end, pushing out an appreciating exhale of hot air.

Both he and Allman remained silent, staring across the wooden table at The Dragon's senseless grin. He sat poised, with his fingers locked, looking back and forth between Goodrick and Allman, waiting for their reactions. Allman shuffled in her seat before leaning forward and tapping the table with her finger.

"Why should we believe you?" Allman opened with.

"Well, Detective Allman, I'm not here to convince you. I'm simply here to tell you my story." The Dragon replied.

"Why, though?"

"You'll understand after it's all been told; I'm not even halfway through yet."

"I don't want to hear any more until I see any relevance between what you are telling me and what that means to my case."

"Oh, so you haven't worked that out yet?" The Dragon asked with his hands open. Allman looked behind at Goodrick over her shoulder, shrugging back at her. He was none the wiser about what any of this had to do with their case either. The only details he had picked up on was the insertion of the magazine, which was public knowledge, and the mention of Buxton train station being close to the crime scene, again, public knowledge. Nothing else remotely stood out to him, besides the obvious. When Allman returned her glare towards The Dragon, his clap pierced through the tension building in the room, and his nasal laugh echoed.

"Oh, here I am, thinking I'm within the company of the two best detectives this district has to offer." The Dragon chuckled.

"Very well. I guess I'll need to be more obvious in the storytelling. Your body, the young girl whose death you're investigating, well, I've already told you about her."

"You know who our victim is?" Goodrick's ears pricked up, The Dragon's voice pulling him from his slouched demeanour to sit upright next to Allman.

"Victim? I suppose that's what you can call her." The Dragon rolled his eyes looking across to the mirror whilst shaking his head.

"Who is she?" Allman demanded. They waited patiently for a couple of seconds until Allman smacked her hand flat on the table.

"Tell me who she is!" Allman's voice roared. Goodrick was taken aback whilst The Dragon casually sat across from her, gazing into his reflection; unnerved.

"I need a name Dragon." Allman's voice began to sound shaky, and the desperation in her tone became obvious. Ignorantly, The Dragon removed his glasses and began rubbing them against the bottom of his shirt tediously. He pulled his glasses up towards the narrow fluorescent light beam that hung directly above him. Allman patiently waited until he pushed his glasses back on his face and turned towards her.

"Ducky."

Goodrick frowned, his eyebrows pushing against each other. The Dragon resumed to his original position of forearms on the table, fingers linked with a punchable smirk.

"Ducky?" Allman asked to confirm. The Dragon nodded confidently.

"Your victim's Ducky."

Allman looked across at Goodrick for backup. He struggled to comprehend what The Dragon was saying without knowing more.

"What's her real name?" Goodrick asked.

The Dragon flicked his eyes over at him with a snarl.

"You know we only go by the names assigned by The Network, therefore, her name's Ducky. The Duck, if you want to be pretentious." The Dragon smirked.

"The girl who incited your rape?" Goodrick delivered brutally.

"The very same." He nodded firmly.

Surprisingly to Goodrick, The Dragon didn't flinch at the mention of the previous day's story. He hoped for more of a raw reaction like Allman received yesterday but instead was given a cold, blank stare as if it never happened. Goodrick studied his behaviour more closely, recognising the discrepancies in his body language. Yesterday he was twitching with the bottom of his shirt; keeping his head down whilst telling the majority of the story. Contrasting todays performance; a more assertive, professional demeanour. Goodrick coughed, unnerved at the sudden realisation.

"What else can you tell us about her?" Allman asked softly.

"There's nothing else to be said about her, for now." The Dragon remained staring at Goodrick whilst answering Allman's question. He pushed upwards unexpectedly from the table, pushing his chair backwards as he rose. Allman and Goodrick quickly followed his action, standing up with him. Goodrick tried to hold himself more assertively, broadening his chest with both hands on his hips.

"Would tomorrow same time suit you both?" The Dragon openly asked. Without hesitation, Goodrick and Allman both nodded.

"You do know, however, if I wanted to, I could have you arrested for withholding information relating to a crime scene? Especially now if you are wanting us to believe you are a witness to a grisly murder? You'll have no option but to stay here, handcuffed, and tell us what you know." Allman threatened. It was wasted on him, childishly smiling as he shook his head slowly.

"You won't arrest me, Detective Allman, not yet. Whilst I'm a free man, I'll speak freely, but the day you put me in handcuffs..." The Dragon tutted softly, "...that's the day I stop talking." The Dragon began walking away from the table, heading towards the exit, clearly done with his story telling for the day.

"Are you not going to take your envelope?" Allman shouted at his back. The Dragon had already alerted the policeman waiting behind the door to open it. The red-light siren flashed above his head as he chillingly turned around to face them.

"I think it's for the best you keep hold of it. Hopefully, I won't need to use it. See you both tomorrow".

With a grin, The Dragon casually walked out of the room, leaving both the detectives clueless. Goodrick waited for the slam of the door to reach across the table and without haste, retrieved the unravelled brown envelope. Pressing it firmly down, he pushed his weight through his hands as he attempted to flatten it. Allman moved closer to him, eagerly waiting. Reaching his hand inside, he pulled out a series of photographs. Mostly dark, negative spaces of nothing but a series of windows lit on what was the top floor of an apartment block.

Pushing the first picture under the pack, the same image repeated. Goodrick frantically kept replacing the top image. Closer and closer, the image zoomed into the windows. When the next photograph was exposed,

Allman gasped, snatching the photograph from Goodrick's grip. The image of Allman's bare back became visible, capturing their sudden burst of passion from day before. Goodrick shook his head, dropping the series of photographs on the floor in frustration. *That fucking dirty bastard.* Goodrick paced behind Allman in circles as anger boiled within him.

"How fucking dare he?" Goodrick shouted out loud.

"The low life must have been tugging himself off in the bushes…"

"Gregory." Allman quietly said.

"…he sat there with a stupid fucking grin on his face like he has something on us."

"Gregory!" Allman shouted, turning around, to stop Goodrick in his pacing. She was shaking slightly with a stutter whilst she spoke.

"We don't mention this to anybody, especially him. As far as we're concerned, we didn't see them, okay?"

"Yeah… I guess, but I-"

"Am I clear, Gregory?" Allman asked assertively.

He could sense the anguish in her demand. She wasn't upset or angry; she was ashamed.

"Are you embarrassed by this?" Goodrick probed, taking a step further towards her, who seemed hesitant to answer.

"Well, of course I am! He has pictures of us fucking!"

"That could be anyone in those photos." Goodrick tried defusing the situation by wafting his hand to the side, rolling his eyes.

"Oh yeah, and how many people do you know, living on the top floor of an apartment building with what's clearly my horrendous dolphin tattoo on their lower back!" Allman shouted, pushing the picture into Goodrick's chest and walking past him, running her hands through her hair. Goodrick studied the up-close photograph that he hadn't seen yet. Pinned behind the glass was indeed a poorly tattooed dolphin. A small grin stretched on his face.

"Well, that's interesting." He said, turning towards Allman, who was now pacing herself, biting on her nails.

"What is?" she snapped back.

"I didn't take you for a girl who'd have a tramp stamp." Goodrick smiled jokingly but realised very quickly his big mouth had landed him in trouble yet again.

"What did you just say?" Allman asked with an open mouth, shaking her head slightly.

"Oh, come on, lighten up. I'm obviously joking, Jesus." Goodrick huffed, picking up the photographs he dropped on the floor and began to shove them back into the envelope.

"No, I won't 'lighten up.' Apologise right now." Allman demanded.

"I'm not a child Louise."

"Well, sometimes you could fool me."

"I don't have to take this." Goodrick shook his head in disgust and made his way to the door, smacking his entire hand over the exit button.

"Where the fuck do you think you're going?" Allman called after him, quickly leaping to his side. The door unhatched but was quickly slammed shut again by Allman. Goodrick could feel his hand shaking, clutching onto the handle.

"You're not leaving again! You haven't told me where you went last night!"

Goodrick looked down at Allman. There was the look he was so used to seeing; desperation. Her eyes flickered with doubt as she gazed up at him. He hated the situation himself, but he wasn't going to let her make him feel any worse about it. When his anxiety would begin to bubble inside him, like it was yesterday, he's learnt it's best he remove himself, as quickly as possible, from the situation. Sadly, it took the multiple replacement doors at his dads old house to teach him he's better off being alone.

"Let go of the door, Allman," he instructed firmly.

"But where are you going?" She pleaded.

"To do some real detective work! I know how much you'd rather sit in here, listening to a madman's fairy tales, but I can't anymore. Now move out of my way!"

Goodrick wasn't sure if Allman released her pressure from the door or if his sudden rage ripped it free. His anger was boiling within him, and he needed to get out. He bulldozed through the building, ignoring everybody in sight as he headed to his car for a way of an escape.

Smacking his hand relentlessly against his steering wheel, he exhausted some of the built up tension. Once his hand had become to throb, he stopped briefly, closing his eyes now finding unknown pleasure in the silence. Unwelcoming thoughts flooded through his mind, mostly the ones he tried burying deep inside his conscious vault, along with any guilt. The constant gulp in his throat made his mouth water with words that couldn't be spoken. The ache in his bones meant he had finally given up. Maybe when the voice inside your head tells you, you've fucked up, it's time to stop and listen.

He wrestled with the image of Nicole standing in her apartment last night when he left Allman's apartment. She'd poured him and herself a glass of wine, she must've gone out and bought it, especially knowing he was coming over, but it wasn't the taste of Tesco's finest red that left him with a dry throat.

"You're breaking up with me?" Nicole asked.

"It's not like we were together in the first place. I just don't want this carrying on further."

"Since when? What did I do? I mean… get out! I can't even bare to look at you. Just fucking get out!"

Goodrick clasped his face in his hands. It wasn't going to be easy, he knew that much but underestimated the strength some women have. He expected Nicole to crumble into a pile like her many dirty laundry clusters. He could feel the heat from the bruises that throbbed beneath the surface of his back, where Nicole repeatedly hit him, forcing him down the stairs and out onto the open street.

He turned around to be greeted by her pointing at him with a fiery, intense look in her eyes. He was shunned by the flaky, red door being slammed in his face. A group of teenagers that were standing outside the chip-shop, laughed out loud and continued to share their satisfied smiles as Goodrick embarrassingly walked past them. Shockingly, that was the worse he felt that evening; being mocked by nameless, unimportant people.

The shock of Nicole's rage unphased him. If anything, she did him a favour by reacting like that. It meant fewer echoes of sobbing to pull on his heartstrings. Now all that was on his mind was Allman, her blank stare when she stood holding onto the mugs in her apartment yesterday, when he suddenly needed to leave, and just now, the same bleak expression when she tried to shut him in the interrogation room. He felt he couldn't possibly begin to explain his actions, but he couldn't comprehend the thought of her being embarrassed by what they did.

After everything he's done in his past, he'd never regret their fifteen minutes of weakness for one another. He could still feel the passion radiating off her soft skin. He began to grin when he remembered feeling her smile through his kiss and hearing her softly gasp and whimper. The reminiscing of the moment, that was photographed, began to pump blood through his dormant heart.

Opening his eyes quickly and forcing himself upright, he felt a newfound surge of energy to sort this out. His outburst minutes earlier was completely uncalled for. His breathing techniques and the grasp of dad's locket would normally have helped to control his feelings but being around Allman intensified everything inside him.

He knew he needed to make things right between them, but apologising wasn't part of his strong suit, knowing she deserved more than an already too late I'm sorry. He will help her, making it up to her in his own unique way by doing the only good thing he knew he could do well; playing detective.

CHAPTER 20

Allman sat frigidly, glaring down at her phone, being bounced by her relentless, shaking legs. She was sitting outside her office whilst members of her team darted concerning looks her way. Allman rolled her eyes and attempted to block them out. She almost resented Adriana being here, scuttering and riffling through her office rather than using another for this meeting. Forcing Allman to wait outside, like she was waiting for detention, it didn't sit right with her. Nor did the feeling of being ignored by Goodrick. Looking down at her phone, she could see the list of unanswered messages she'd sent him. She continuously flicked her thumb up and down the messages, repeatedly reading over them.

'Come back to the office. I didn't mean I was embarrassed by you, just the situation.'

'Gregory, we really don't have the time to waste on this. Stop proving a point and get your arse back here!'

'Look, even if it's going to be a long night, I'll order us food. Just get back here now! I need your help!'

She cringed, seeing how pathetic she sounded. She missed the days she could stand on her own two feet and had no need for assistance on her cases. This one, however, truly baffled her. She was in split minds if Goodrick was right about The Dragon and if he really was a psychotic lunatic who was taking them for a ride. She tensed her jaw at the thought all that he had said thus far was fiction. Her gut feeling was telling her there was more to it, a much bigger picture than she or Goodrick could presume, and her gut feeling had never been wrong. Her thoughts were ripped away from her at the click of her office door swinging inwards. Adriana's stern face appeared to the side of her.

"Okay, in you come, Louise."

Allman looked around her bleak office, realisation of what it looks like for visitors sunk in; dark and murky. Adriana sat directly in front, in her chair, making Allman feel inadequate. Allman stood by the desk and waited until Adriana was firmly seated in the high-back leather seat, then shot her a scolding look. It may be the anger she was harvesting for Goodrick that made her feel annoyed with Adrianna's behaviour, but she wasn't going to start this meeting already feeling like she was losing.

"Hope you don't mind, but I'd like to sit in *my* chair. It is my office, after all."

Adriana looked surprised at her request, but with a nervous cough, she pushed the chair backwards and began walking around the perimeter of the desk.

"Of course, where are my manners? Please sit."

Allman was relatively shocked; she did as commanded and moved to the smaller bucket seat opposite. Allman took her throne, lowering her body with grace, embracing the wave of empowerment that washed over her. While she sat back leisurely, Adriana struggled in the seat Allman assigned her, trying to adjust her robust frame within the width restricted chair. With a good balance, she sat sidewards towards Allman and placed pieces of paper on the desk facing her. She reached forward and retrieved the pile of paperwork whilst Adriana began reciting in the background.

"There's nothing to worry about, just a little discussion, off the record, about the relationship between you and Superintendent Chadwick."

Allman glanced at Adriana from the top of the papers. She could see her with her hands on her knees, smiling kindly. Seemingly genuine and trustworthy, but Allman knew better than to put faith in anybody, especially superintendents, so quickly.

"What do you want to know?" Allman asked assertively whilst scanning the paperwork. Reading a transcript between Superintendent Flatdick and presumably someone from Internal Affairs.

"Well, people talk Louise. I, for one, don't listen to hearsay, I prefer to hear it from the horse's mouth, but I know from what Detective Goodrick told me there's a lot more to it than meets the eye."

Allman froze; a hot flash of fury shot through her body, and before she could stop and compose herself, she blurted.

"Why, what did Goodrick say?" As the words escaped her chapped mouth, she wished she'd taken another second to ask it more slowly and professionally. Adriana must know there's truth in whatever Goodrick reported, and at this stage, Allman doubted herself if he really knew the whole story or had he came to assumptions on his own. She tensed her eyes, remembering the chance she had to ask Goodrick exactly what he knew, but instead, she pounced on him like an unstroked kitten because she was finally getting shown a glimpse of affection by someone.

"I think it's best if you told me, in your own words first, what's been happening," Adriana instructed.

Of course, she'd say that. Allman was mentally battering herself with what she'd say. What if Goodrick didn't say all that much or anything at all, and this was all a ploy to make her speak? What if Adriana and Goodrick already know the full extent, and anything Allman tries concealing or denying could potentially damage her image and reputation? How would a superintendent ever take her seriously again if she blatantly lied to them directly? She took a deep breath, channelling into Goodrick's advice that moment before she kissed him: *'you tell her what's happened. Tell her everything.'* Allman flicked her eyes open with her gut insisting her to trust Goodrick and tell Adriana.

"You want to know from the very beginning?" Allman asked with an uncertain sigh. Adriana nodded quickly, waiting for her next words.

"As you know, Flatdick," Allman stuttered, shocked, quickly trying to regain her words.

"Sorry, I mean Superintendent Chadwick." She was going to continue until she heard the hushed chuckling from Adriana. When she looked up, she saw her covering her mouth with her shoulders shaking. Allman felt eased when she noticed Adriana laughing softly to herself.

"I'm sorry, Flatdick?" Adriana asked with a tear in her eye.

"Yeah, sorry, it's just a stupid nickname I came up with. I promise I won't reference it again." Allman said quickly, trying to prove she could be respectful, even given the circumstances.

"Oh no, please. If it's easier, use it." With Adriana's blessing, she continued.

"Well, like I was saying, when Flatdick joined our office, there were rumours Internal Affairs were investigating him, hence why he was transferred quickly. I don't know exactly because, like yourself, I prefer to wait to be told than listen to office gossip. He did, however, really struggle when he got here. He never fitted in. In my opinion, he came in too hard, expecting his reputation – which I wasn't aware off – to exceed him.

He started changing protocols, demoting good detectives, and placing people where he thought they belonged. The morale dropped rapidly. People started doing the bare minimum. He had no idea how to run a successful task force or how to make people work well under his leadership. Whereas I've always taken great pride in the work I do, I've never needed somebody to pat me on the back and tell me I'm doing a good job because, well, it shows. But I was aching for a promotion, something new, something to keep my mind occupied.

When it was announced your office was looking to expand and take a new homicide lead, well, I thought that was my calling. I don't mean to sound big-headed or full of myself, but I know my track record speaks for itself. I single-handedly closed down fifteen hundred open cases in my first two years. I mean, that took a lot of sleepless nights and energy drinks."

Adriana nodded, "I'll be honest with you now. I was surprised your name wasn't called. Although I'm very, very happy with Detective Goodrick, and he's been a real credit to my team, I was expecting you, in all honesty."

"Yeah, well, that makes two of us." Allman sighed, lowering her head with the disappointment swaying heavily around her neck. She looked down at the papers, reading one of the lines Flatdick had said.

'The woman was obsessed with me. She inappropriately touched me on more than one occasion.'

"Do you know why you weren't referred to me by Superintendent Chadwick?"

Allman nodded her head before looking back up and rubbing the entire length of her face already feeling mentally drained.

"Yeah, I know exactly why."

She glared blankly across at Adriana, who nodded her head, wanting to soak up the much-wanted information.

"I felt, after years of hard work and never getting anywhere with it, I'd try something else, a different approach to get what I wanted. The rumours started out that Flatdick was having an affair with somebody from his task force, so I already knew there would be a chance for the same thing to happen here, so I thought, why not me?"

Allman looked down and across at the floor to the dismal blue carpet, zoning out of the situation. She kept talking without a thought of how it sounded or the repercussions.

"The first time I tried my new, at the time, brilliant idea, it was a Friday night, and I only had to come into the office to sign some papers. I strutted in after main office hours wearing my best high heel shoes, an open blouse, my hair was down and curled, red lipstick, the whole lot. I intentionally didn't knock on his door, just made enough noise in here so he knew somebody was around. It took him a few minutes to come and investigate, and he walked in to see me on all fours picking up piles of photocopies from a box I knocked down from that top shelf."

Allman paused momentarily, pointing to the top shelf that housed three dusty cardboard boxes. Adriana followed her fingertip and then returned her gaze to Allman, which she avoided again, looking in a different direction in the room feeling embarrassed to admit her actions.

"He must've had a shock when he walked in to be greeted with my arse in the air, but it worked how I intended. He dropped to the floor like a sack of spuds and helped me clean up. That was the first time we had sex, it was completely consensual, and I did it hoping it would give me a better chance of being promoted. I know how stupid that sounds now. Hearing it out loud like that, I'm embarrassed to say it but I was just so desperate."

"Am I right in thinking at this time, Superintendent Chadwick had been here no longer than six months?"

"Yes, about that sort of time, I think."

"And you had the horrible ordeal of losing your mother around that time too?"

Allman shot a look at Adriana with dread filling her stomach. She couldn't muster the words but nodded her head firmly. She hated the thought of bringing her sweet mother into the same conversation relating to her shameless act.

"That must've been tough on you, losing your mother, then trying to come to terms with working with a new superintendent with new protocols. How did you handle it all?" Adriana shook her head, displaying sympathy. Allman almost laughed,

"Well, I didn't, not very well, obviously."

"But I'm right in saying you weren't in the right frame of mind when all this began. Personal problems may have clouded your judgement?"

Allman nodded intensely.

"Absolutely. I mean, I'll never use my mother's death as an excuse for my actions or try to confuse the feelings I felt as justification for what happened. But I wasn't myself because of that, and I only have myself to blame for not seeking help earlier."

"Do you feel you have the help and support now that you lacked back then?"

"I guess, I mean, nothing or nobody will ever be able to make me feel better about losing my mum, but I've come to terms with it now, although I don't want to."

Allman sniffled, looking down at her hands that were now tearing little pieces of strands of the paper away from the sheet of lies.

"How long did your relationship with Superintendent Chadwick last? What stopped it?" Adriana asked mercilessly. Allman was fighting back the tears from the brief reminder that her mother was no longer here. Her only coping mechanism was to completely blank the pain out and act as if she never existed. The agony of losing that unbreakable love she'd only ever known was far greater than pretending she never had it in the first place.

"I, erm, I think it lasted a while." Allman speech was broken up, like how she felt inside.

"Was it a few weeks, months, years?" Adriana probed.

"It ended exactly the same day he told you over the phone that Goodrick was transferring to Tannoch."

"November 1st, 2013?"

Allman was taken aback; she didn't expect Adriana to know what felt like a minimal interaction, a passing conversation on the phone. Even Allman didn't relive that day if she could help it but she must've been right.

"You sound certain," Allman said, shrugging her shoulders.

"Well, if it was the very first time I was told, that was it. How did you know about that phone conversation? Were you with him at the time?"

Allman shuddered. How could she put it in a competent way of telling her she was indeed there, under the table, sucking his dick.

"Yeah, I was there."

Allman felt she didn't need to know every little piece of information. If she did, she almost felt mean for sitting Adriana on that chair.

"And did he tell you beforehand that Goodrick would be transferring rather than yourself?"

"Nope, I found out the exact same time as you did."

"So, were you as speechless as I was?"

"You could say that." *I was speechless because I had a mouthful of knob cheese if that's what you mean.*

"I'm sorry you found out that way. He should've known better than to do that."

"Oh no, I think he knew *exactly* what he was doing."

Allman shook her head assertively, feeling her deep hatred for the man.

"So, did everything end right there and then with you two? Or did things get a little more, complicated?" Adriana tensed her eyes, tilting her head slowly. *She knows.* Allman remained silent, chewing on her bottom lip, unsure what to say.

"When did it become non-consensual, Louise?"

With a great sigh, Allman put her feet securely on the ground to stop herself rocking, placing both arms on the table for stability, she glanced down at the paperwork once more.

'I called it off with Detective Allman, but she was persistent. What was a man to do in my position, say no?'

"The same week." Allman admitted delicately.

"What happened?" Adriana probed further.

"I was here, sat right here, finishing some work. Time got away from me. It was only when I finished the paperwork I realised I hadn't heard chatter or anything really for quite some time. It was past six o'clock, and I instantly had a gut feeling to get out quickly before he knew I was here alone. I grabbed my things and jolted out the door, but he was already standing there. He'd been waiting outside that door for god knows how long. I was pushed back inside, and at that moment in time, he stupidly thought we were still on, but he'd known all along what I'd wanted. I only mentioned it every other day about moving across, and he promised me the transfer, if not, his position at the very least, as he was hoping to move back to his original office once the 'drama' had been smoothed over. I obviously got neither, and it was very apparent I'd get nothing. He was using me as much as I tried to use him, so I gave him the benefit of the doubt. Explained to him that I didn't want it to continue. He took offence and didn't take too kindly to being told no. I repeatedly said no...I kept saying no."

Allman struggled to carry on. The first time she was raped by him was like a scene from a film. She could explain what happened, but only because she never realised it was happening to her. When the awareness sank in, she felt her legs shake and a ball of sick levitate up her throat. Both her hands were squeezed tight into white knuckle fists. Adriana leaned forward and placed her dry hand over one of Allman's.

"It happened more than once, didn't it?" Adriana gingerly asked.

Allman nodded her head, the movement shook the tears that clung to her eyelashes free and trickled down her cheeks.

"You're not the only one, you know?"

Allman scrunched her nose with confusion as Adriana continued.

"A few girls from his previous office came forward after he left with newfound courage to say a similar thing."

Allman shook her head angrily.

"You mean to tell me he was being investigated for rape allegations all this time?" Allman almost spat when she asked the question. Adriana must've picked up on the outrage in her tone and let go of her hand quickly. She looked away from Allman, looking slightly embarrassed now herself.

"It appears so, although they never had any proof, it was all kept under wraps."

"So, they let a man carry on working here for almost two years and sat back whilst he did the very same to me?"

"They initially moved him because of an affair that later turned out to be a rape allegation. At the time of his transfer, they thought the only risk he could inflict was on himself and his reputation. In this office, there are only four women accounted for throughout the building. The board thought it was the ideal place for him to avoid any… trouble."

Allman shook her head, baffled at what she was hearing. She could understand their way of thinking. *Less woman for him to force his dick into they mean.* She couldn't help feel let down, even by the same system she dedicated most of her life for. She sniffled her nose and blinked frantically, trying to stop the tears from flowing further whilst leaning her head backwards.

"Louise, I'm sorry this happened to you and that unknowingly, the board and I allowed it to continue."

"It's only him to blame for all this."

"Would you want to make a statement about it? Although I'll say, we do have enough evidence already."

Allman wasn't sure what to do, of course Adriana would tell her it'd be kept confidential, but as she said, she was only one of four women here and it wasn't as if people didn't have their suspicions already. Would it make her look weak to her fellow colleagues if she admitted to it, or would she look a coward if she didn't?

"Can I have time to think about this, please?" Allman asked calmly, lifting her head back down to face Adriana.

"Of course, there's not a lot of time however, I'll be moving on this first thing Monday morning, but my phone be on from now until then."

Allman nodded her head. She felt deflated from a whirlwind of emotions, coming in strong, then weak, then trying to be strong again. Sometimes she was happier being nothing. Adriana retrieved the now chewed-at pieces of paper from in front of Allman and turned towards the door.

"You get yourself a deserved break. You should thank Detective Goodrick next time you see him." Adriana said, turning around with one hand on the handle.

"Oh yeah, why's that?" Allman asked sarcastically pulling her mouth to the side. If it wasn't for Goodrick, she might not had to admit to all this to begin with.

"Well, he got you that worthy promotion. As of the 3rd August, I expect to see you at office Tannoch, 8am sharp for debriefing." With a satisfied look on her face, Adriana pulled the handle and walked out, leaving Allman alone in her wake. She should've been happy, ecstatic, it was exactly what she wanted, but the realisation sunk in. She got the promotion exactly the same way she intended to but no longer wanted it was only manifested from one thing; dick!

CHAPTER 21

D riving through a gravel car park, the rocks under his BMW scattered away from the weight of its presence. He creased his face at the occasional clicks from the loose stones hitting his polished black paintwork. He lowered his head, looking in both directions through the perfectly lined trees that framed the narrow track. He was slowly approaching a sign, strangled in overgrown ivy. It stood profoundly in a flower bed, a tombstone for all the dead and withered plants that once flourished here. Goodrick softly pressed on his brakes and leaned over to read the sign clearly.

'FINGASK: SCHOOL OF SCIENCE.'

Surprisingly to him, there may have been truth in the The Dragons's story, but how difficult would it have been to google this place? He pulled up to an impressive water fountain depicting two dolphins jumping through waves. He couldn't help smirking, thinking about Allman and her god-awful tattoo. With Allman presently on his mind, he began to read the highly anticipated text messages. The despair in her messages smacked him across the face.

He shook his head, feeling irritated with himself that he didn't swallow his pride and tell her where he was going. Now that he was here, he knew he had made an even bigger mistake by not bringing her. She would've been more appreciative of being involved rather than him storming off and delivering his findings afterwards.

The thought of the lonely four, possibly five-hour drive home made him shudder. Checking the time on his phone, 15:35, he figured she must still be with Adriana regarding Flatdick. He hoped she'd taken his advice and told her everything: Adriana wouldn't care for being lied to. He put a lot of faith in Adriana to sort this mess out, if he wanted to sort it out himself, Flatdick would already be eating out of a tube, but luckily for him, Goodrick liked his job and wouldn't risk losing it over a maggot.

Jumping out of his car and slamming the door shut, he bounded up the concrete steps, ready for whatever was waiting for him. He came face-to-face with how he remembered The Dragon describing the doors were like at the villa. Big, wooden, cathedral-looking, with two ivory columns on either side. Goodrick remembered The Dragon saying the doors looked out of place at the villa, but these looked just right for what you'd expect by the grand exterior of the building. The school's exterior walls were decorated with granite stone, exquisitely carved with scrolls, topped with gargoyles on every corner.

Goodrick looked up, impressed with the significance and presence the building had over the wasteland it sat on. He stretched an arm outwards, expecting the door to be shut, but to his surprise, it creaked open. He stood patiently waiting whilst the aged hinges groaned until the door came to an abrupt stop, hitting an object behind with an echoing thud. Goodrick leaned in closer to try to outline anything inside the building. The sun positioned itself conveniently behind, offering no assistance to Goodrick to help illuminate inside. Huffing, he retrieved his phone and flicked through his options, locating the torch setting.

A muffled, scuttling noise distracted him away from the tapping on his screen, and he turned his attention back towards the open crevice. He positioned himself a foot away and listened intensely, tilting his head to one side, trying to tune in to what he could vaguely hear. The noise became more apparent and louder. He turned his head again and stared into the abyss, frantically moving his eyes from one side to the other. The noise became heavier, faster, approaching him, closer and closer.

He squeezed his eyes shut, expecting a waft from a disturbed animal. He presumed a bat from the sounds he heard or maybe a rat. When it became apparent whatever was making the noise came to an abrupt stop, he began to open his eyes slowly. An obscure outline of a girl shook him to his core, making him leap backwards. He frantically threw his arms outwards for balance and luckily stopped his heel on the top step, narrowly avoiding a nasty fall. He breathed heavily, clasping at his chest and staring at the frigid girl who stood in the doorway. Pale, white hair clinging onto her sunken cheekbones with dark circles stamped around her eyes. Her small frame was drowning in an oversized, torn purple hoody. Nothing on her legs except dirty hockey socks that were pulled up above her knobbly knees.

"Sorry, love, you scared the absolute shit out of me then."

He stretched his back upright and took a step towards her, expecting a gesture back. Instead, the frail girl looked behind her briefly as if somebody was talking to her and then back again towards Goodrick. He stood with both hands on his hips, pushing his jacket out to the sides, broadcasting his police tag that dangled around his neck. The girl studied the tag and turned her head back behind her. Goodrick smacked his lips apart, licking tediously on his bottom lip, trying to look in the same direction as she was. Her neck quickly snapped back around, and a fierce, stabbing expression intensified in her eyes. Goodrick smiled awkwardly, becoming uneasy with the awkward situation.

"I should introduce myself, I'm Detective Goodrick, and you are?"

He waited patiently for a name, but she remained harvesting the same unwelcome glare.

"Right, so I don't necessarily need your name, but I'd like to ask you some questions if that's alright?"

He opened his hands in an inviting motion before pulling out his small notepad and flipping it open.

"How familiar are you with this building?" He pressed his lips together with anticipation she'd respond, but she didn't.

"There's a particular room I'm interested in. Perhaps you can show it to me, an operating theatre?"

Her eyes deepened at the mention of the theatre. For a brief second, she broke her eye-contact with Goodrick and looked down at the floor before peering up at him again.

"You know what room I'm talking about, don't you?" Goodrick pressed. Her eyes now wildly shook. He took a step closer.

"Can you show me?" Her smothered chest began pulsating under the feeble material of the hoody as she began to breathe uncontrollably.

"Take me to it." Her sharp cheekbones became wet from unprovoked tears as she struggled to maintain herself under his scrutiny. Goodrick shuffled himself slowly towards her like a lion prowling towards its prey. When he was closer, he extended his hand outwards.

"Take me." He instructed.

An ear-piercing scream sent Goodrick flying backwards again in fear, but this time knocked him down to his back. The heavy crack from the concrete hitting his tailbone sent lightning strikes of agony through his legs. His ears were being deafened by the relentless scream of the girl who remained looking down at him, mouth gaping, displaying no teeth, whilst she eye-wateringly stretched and bulged her eyes from their sockets. Goodrick stared up at her in his dismay.

He watched hopelessly as she stepped backwards into the darkness and slammed the door shut on him. Through gritted teeth, he yanked himself up and soldiered through the intense pain in his back. He punched his fists repeatedly into the wood, one blow after another until he was forced to stop to catch a breath. Resting his head on the surface of the door, he felt the stinging of the wood splinters cut deep into the sides of his hands, where his delicate skin battered against the spikes.

He pressed himself away and began walking backwards, looking up at the three levels. All the windows seemed to be boarded up, and the odd two or three that weren't were smashed through. He turned around, reluctantly, to watch his feet down the stairs. Shaking his head, he couldn't comprehend what had happened. The girl, thought to be homeless and severely undernourished, alone perhaps in that vast, empty place?

A fluttering noise, generated by the soothing sweep of the wind, captured his attention. Goodrick turned around to look at the back of the fountain that he'd walked straight past moments earlier. A piece of paper was flapping in the breeze, attached to a dolphin's fin. Squatting lower, he pressed his hand against the paper and read the contents.

'I hereby give notice that Farnham Town Council is the owner of 103 Cinnamon Lane North, Fingask: School of Science and that you are occupying the said property without the council's licence of consent. Unless you vacate the property within seven days of this notice, then Farnham Town Council will seek, without further notice, to obtain a court order to evict you.

10th October 2011.'

Goodrick desperately tried reading the bottom of the laminated paper and got half a name for who was ordering the eviction: 'RICH'. The address was smudged, but he could read the number clearly. Punching the digits into his phone, he anxiously climbed back into the comfort of his car and let his bruised back be cradled in the seat. The ringing intensified as the phone connected through his speakers, and a chirpy lady answered the phone.

"Hello, Farnham Council. My name is Sophie. How can I help you today?"

"Hi, yes, Gregory Goodrick. I'm a homicide detective for Tannoch, I'm looking for some information regarding the building at 103 Cinnamon Lane North."

"You said 103 Cinnamon Lane North, sir?"

"Yes, Fingask: School of Science, to be exact."

Goodrick waited patiently, listening to hushed background chatter from the other end of the phone.

"I'm sorry, sir, but the Fingask school closed down in 1952 due to a fire and then demolished in 1986."

Goodrick looked through his windscreen at the building that stood in front of him. Sure the building was derelict with broken windows, but he couldn't see any fire damage. It might have been at the rear of the building, but it was too overgrown to climb through. One thing he was certain about; it definitely was not demolished.

"Demolished as in flattened?" he asked.

"Yes, sir."

"Can't be, I'm staring at it right now, and there are squatters living here. Are you sure we're talking about the same school?"

"Oh yes, there has only ever been one Fingask. You must be lost, sir."

"There's an eviction letter placed on the water fountain outside with this telephone number and part of a name, Rich, maybe a Richard, who sanctioned it on the 10th October 2011."

"I'm really sorry, sir, but I'm unfamiliar with a gentleman by that name, and I've worked here for almost thirty years. I'm sure if you do a quick internet search on the school, you'll find what you are looking for."

"I need to speak to somebody right now! There's a young girl living in this building who requires help."

"As I said, the school was demolished in 1986-"

"Let me speak to your supervisor!" Goodrick became impatient with the tedious jobs-worth he was inflicted to deal with.

"Okay, sir, hold the line and I'll transfer you."

All background noise was muted. He looked down at his steering wheel, rubbing his finger and thumb in between his eyes, pinching at the bridge of his nose. Hold music started to play, and a cheerful, lively song erupted through the speakers that alerted him upright. As the song played, a deep, concerning feeling fluttered in his stomach. The words, where did he know those words from? He looked down again, a crease developing in his brow, trying to concentrate on the lyrics of the song he was certain he'd heard before, but the music behind the track didn't hold any recollection. He started repeating the lyrics in hopes it would jog his memory.

"I've been waiting for this moment all my life. Now all my dreams are coming true. Yeah, I've been waiting for this moment..."

He started racking his brain, trying to find the source of the information he desperately knew.

"Feels good to be alive right about now."

He flicked his eyes up frantically, looking at the building as the Cathedral door swung open with what he thought was a horrifying noise of a chainsaw. The Komodo Dragon's voice chillingly whispered through his mind: '*he chainsawed Reggie's leg off*.' Goodrick quickly fastened his seat-belt. Looking behind him, he pulled his car into reverse and pressed his foot down on the pedal. The car tyres circled, struggling to gain friction over the loose pebbles.

"Fucking come on!" He shouted desperately, glancing backwards to the building where the sickening noise of the machine blades was becoming more dominant in his mind. He was flung forward, hitting his chest against the steering wheel as his tyres shuddered and found traction beneath the gravel. Peering over his shoulder, he maneuvered the vehicle, reversing rapidly down the cramped road.

The bumps in the dirt track jerked his car in all directions. The song relentlessly became louder as Goodrick speedily tried to exit the concrete compounds of the school. Darting his fingers over his dials, failing at all attempts to stop the music playing.

"Fucking stop!" Goodrick roared, beginning to thump the vehicles dashboard screen as it reached an unbearable volume. An image of a Lizard flicked under one of his punches. Diverting his attention temporarily, he froze, stunned.

"What the-"

CHAPTER 22

Allman breathed heavily, looking between the two boards that were dotted with miscellaneous pictures: snapshots of the decapitated hand; the body laid on the rug and the picturesque surroundings of the crime scene. From each photograph was a string connecting the information the task force knew thus far.

Due to her meetings with The Komodo Dragon being off the record, she hadn't involved her team, but now felt it was necessary. She dragged another board across the room to adjoin the two already at the front of a bank of lined desks. She snatched a red marker and began writing at the top of the board. 'THE CREATURES.'

Underneath, she wrote the name given to their body, 'DUCKY', before drawing a line, connecting it to a picture that captured the mangled corpse. She began writing the second name they knew, 'LIZARD', as an eruption of chatter piled through the door. A team of four trusted detectives filtered through and took their assigned seats.

Twirling around on her heel, she was pleased to see them all arrive on the dot, 17:05. It was the perfect time for a briefing as they wouldn't be disturbed by anyone. Her team was handpicked, all dedicated, and enthusiastic like herself. After-hours meetings were on everybody's agenda as none of them clocked out early.

The first detective to her left was Paul, the boring Brummie who didn't have much to say. He was a computer whiz, a tech geek who could about hack any electrical device. She took pity on him, being Jade's cousin, and gave him his chance to prove himself through the ranks, but his skills nor his devilishly good looks, couldn't help him find a personality. One up from him was Benjamin, a loud, happy-chappy scouser who had enough personality to give Paul a hall pass. His bald head and large gut wouldn't phase you when you'd hear his deep belly laugh after he delivered one of his many one-liners.

Directly across from Benjamin was Sam, a frigid, awkward soul who over-analyses. Sometimes his theories were so bizarre that annoyingly, most of the time, he was right. His obscure obsession with serial killers would be troubling if he wasn't on the crime fighting side. Lastly, at the end on the right was Dave. The calm, collective detective. He reminded her of a young Goodrick but with a little less arrogance.

"Right then, boys. Has anybody got anything new for me before I begin?" Allman asked, snapping the red lid back on the marker and placing it down on the table. Back-and-forth glances were made between the team besides Paul, who sat looking down, fidgeting with his hands. Benjamin was first to speak, like always.

"The girl in the CCTV footage at the train station has been found. Not a lead, not a girl. Just a very feminine man who booked the wrong ticket. An absolute waste of time."

Allman rolled her eyes, arming herself with the marker. She turned back around to their sparse lines of enquiry and striked off - train ticket. She knew it wasn't related with her case but was box-ticking to keep Flatdick happy. That was the last line of enquiry that was marked on the board. All of them ended the same way: dead-end.

"So, what's this about then, The Creatures?" Dave asked.

Allman glanced to the new board, taking a sidestep towards it and knocked her pen against the name Ducky.

"Our victim went by this name. She's thought to have been part of a secret network that goes by the name Out of Hibernation, hence the name for the magazine that was inserted in her. The particular group she was assigned to called themselves The Creatures. There were six members in total, and so far, we know about Ducky, Lizard, and The Komodo Dragon."

Allman wrote The Dragon's name in the middle of the board and circled it a couple of times, displaying the importance of that particular member.

"And how do you know this from the magazine?" Dave probed further, recognisably the most intrusive of the team.

"There's more we understand now about the magazine, but everything we're being told is by The Dragon in his own recollection of events. He seems eager to help tell us about this group and The Network."

"What's he said so far?" Sam included himself.

"Well, The Network offers its members a week to host, let's say, activities once a year where all members participate. It seems each week consists of sexual fetishes, but I'm not talking about swinging conventions, this group of people are into some real disturbing taboo shit."

"Like what?" Surprisingly, Paul whimpered, looking upwards.

"So far, we've been told about rape and body mutilation, and I believe it's going to get worse." Allman peered round at the small task force who darted concerning looks back and forth.

"We don't know everything yet; it seems The Dragon likes to keep Detective Goodrick and me guessing and stringing the story along. We've heard two of the week's stories so far, and I'm sure we will follow up with the further four. But this was to make you all aware of staying vigilant and open your minds, as I believe this is going to open a whole can of worms when we bring this Network down."

"How many do you think there are?" Sam questioned with a puzzled face, leaning his face on his fist. Allman looked back baffled, and shrugged her shoulders. She wasn't sure in what context he was referring.

"You know, like, how many groups do you think this Network has if this is the only one that's been discovered? I mean, what if The Creatures is only the beginning? There could be hundreds, thousands of these groups worldwide, we all know about sex-rings and trafficking gangs being uncovered every day. What if this is the same? Maybe we should start asking around-"

"This doesn't leave the room. It's strictly confidential. I'm trusting you guys to keep this between us because until I know the full scope of this Network. I don't want anybody else interfering and possibly getting hurt. If The Dragon so much thinks I've breathed a word, he'll keep his mouth shut. I want you guys to keep an eye out and report anything suspicious."

Allman nodded her head firmly but inside she was a trembling mess. The Dragon knew where she lived, he somehow knew. She flinched at the flashback of how he rolled those images so tightly around, like the magazine inside the victim. She was terrified for her safety was the honest truth why she was only now involving her trusted four. Every time she'd say his name aloud, she was burdened with his mouth-tearing smile. Beginning to think the killer had been sitting across her all this time; mocking her. Knowing her curiosity wouldn't allow her to jump the gun, arrest him only for him to remain silent, she'd be no closer to the truth.

"And what sort of things would you consider suspicious?" Dave asked with a snarl across his face. He was the youngest in the team, but he made up for it with smugness.

"If someone so much as farts near my car, you report it, is that understood?" Allman said with a stern face. All the detectives, besides Dave, quickly nodded their heads at her command. She felt relieved that some of the pressure was lifted off her shoulders. It was consuming her energy to store all this information without giving her a chance to speak freely about it. She could feel her thoughts wrestling with themselves at what could happen next, and without the constant help of Goodrick, the only other soul who could ease her of this strain, it was impossible for her to keep quiet now.

"I do believe this Network exists, and that's why I cannot stress enough to only talk about this here. Under no circumstances does anybody try anything without my backing. For now, we continue as we are and keep filtering the lines of enquiry. I want the house to be swept again. Three names that have been given relating to this Network were depicted on the doors upstairs, and I want to know why these carvings or the conditions of the rooms were never reported in the first instance." She continued with her long list of demands.

"I want to collect any DNA with another team. Once they've done their checks, use another team. Send the results to a lab. Once we have the results, use a different lab. I won't be satisfied until I'm sure the forensics haven't been tampered with. I need at least three individual reports. The house has been on lockdown since. Only me and Detective Goodrick have had access to it, so we shouldn't find any inconsistencies, but I want to make sure for peace of mind that we did everything thoroughly and correctly the first time round. Is that clear?"

It'd been a while since she felt this empowered again without faking it. She never had any reason to doubt her competence; that was all Flatdick's fault. Months of belittling her took a toll on her capabilities. Since her meeting with Adriana, which ended over an hour ago, she began to have a better understanding of the circumstances.

She felt stronger knowing she wasn't the only one he manipulated, avoiding being individually shamed. She'd rather be in a lineup of sobbing women rather than try to stand on her own. That's where she always got things wrong; wasting energy to look independent and rise above others. Whereas, if she stood humbly, with both feet grounded, she'd find more people to walk alongside, rather than swinging her legs and sitting alone on the highest pedestal.

"Why is The Komodo Dragon helping us?" Dave queried.

"I don't know yet. I'm none the wiser about what his gain would be from telling us. Detective Goodrick seems to think he's making it up as he goes. The Dragon has been careful not to relate anything to the crime scene directly that hasn't already been public knowledge except the names. He's hinted that he's local to the area surrounding the crime scene. There's a chance he knows the house well and knew what the room doors depicted before speaking to us."

"You don't think a person with an overactive imagination could come up with something like this?" With a dissatisfied look on Dave's face, Allman knew he'd be the difficult one to persuade.

"I'd love that because the thought of this Network, those people living amongst us, truly terrifies me. Like Sam said, who knows how many more there could be?"

"I don't think it's wise to cross the lone-ranger theory out just yet," Dave said in a self-righteous way.

"Look, I'm telling you now. The Dragon's telling me the truth, I can feel it. This Network exists, these people are real, one of which is now dead, and it's our job to find out who killed her."

"If you say it's real, then it's real, boss." Benjamin spread his hands in the air, trying to defuse the tension building between Allman's authority being wasted on the freckled, baby-faced Dave. Benjamin was a lot older than Allman but respected her greatly; her most loyal servant.

"Can we discuss this with Detective Goodrick?" Sam asked.

"Not for now. I don't want another word said on the matter until I know more. Goodrick and I seem to be going down two separate paths with this, and I wanted to make sure my team, all of my team…" She darted a concerning look over to Dave.

"…Is on board with me in case things get complicated. As you know, office Tannoch works for no district, no council, so they can't be told no. They have the power to overrule and take any case up and down across the country with no questions asked. They answer to nobody but the Supreme Court, and I'd like to keep Goodrick and Adriana on our side."

All members of Allman's task force nodded their heads. As much as she dreamed of working at office Tannoch, many people resented their power. Everyone, besides Dave, would voice their concerns daily about the office and how neighbouring districts would resent Tannoch. Avoiding asking for help from the know-it-alls. Allman knew there'd be a better time to tell her team that as of August 3rd, she'd be leaving to become one of those know-it-alls.

CHAPTER 23

"Louise!" Goodrick slammed his white-knuckled fist against her apartment door. He hit it so hard that one of the gold plated digits from the door number unhinged itself and swung loosely. The nosey neighbour, Edith, creaked her door open behind him. Her voice shrieked, making Goodrick shudder.

"Do you mind? It's ten o'clock at night!"

"Shut up! Fucking shut up!" Goodrick shouted, facing her. She took a step back, pulling her grey cardigan over her shoulder, clinging it close to her chest with another hand beginning to close her door.

"I reported you once, and I'll do it again!" She threatened.

"Always in everyone's business, aren't you? Every single fucking time I come here, you're here. I told you last time to mind your business, and you still won't fucking listen!"

Goodrick began walking towards her. He could feel bits of spit escaping from his mouth and flicking towards her appalled expression. As he got closer, unknowing what his intentions were, he felt a hard pull from his shoulder. He spun quickly, facing the open door to Allman's apartment.

Piecing together the blurred colours, he construed it was Allman who dragged him away as she attempted to defuse the resentful tension caused by his temper. He pitied himself as he dragged himself inside Allman's darkly lit apartment. All the windows that allowed the lights of the city to shine through were shadowed by newly hung curtains.

He crumbled into a cushion on the sofa, dropping his head into his hands. Rocking back and forth, listening at Allman's attempts to recover any of his dignity.

"I'll talk to him, don't worry, Edith, I'll sort it."

He dazed out of the conversation and started rattling his brain with the last thing he remembered. He was back in his car, steering frantically to manoeuvre backwards through the gates.

BANG.

He looked up from his dismay to Allman storming in from her hallway.

"What the fuck was that all about, Goodrick? You frightened her to death!"

Goodrick stared up at her with little to no expression. She continued flapping, waving her arms in all directions. It reminded him of their first real encounter when she was expressing what they knew at the crime scene as she hovered around Ducky's body.

"I know she's a nosey nobody, but you can't speak to her like that. I could hear you all the way from the bedroom! You need to apologise, and no, you-"

"Okay." Goodrick interrupted her, nodding his head slowly; he was exhausted. It was time to swallow his pride and try doing the right thing, for once.

"I was out of order, I'm sorry. I'll straighten everything out with Edith, I promise."

Breathing heavily, he slumped his head back down, looking between his legs as his elbows wobbled on either knee. He felt the presence of Allman to his right from the dip in the cushion. The absence of talk would've normally been awkward, but he was thankful to be with her, to be with anybody. The song played in his mind persistently, torturing his thoughts. *Did I really hear a chainsaw? Could The Lizard have been there? Fuck, is The Dragon telling the truth?* He felt a tight sick knot in the pit of his stomach as he questioned himself. Did he really see an image of a Lizard, or was this a side effect from whiplash? He rubbed his heavy head painfully slow, recollecting the thud from crashing into an iron gate when he tried to hastily escape the grounds.

"I visited the school, Fingask. I saw it." He broke the silence, looking across the table that had two recently used coffee mugs. One he recognised now as Allman's favourite, a large white mug with pink and blue polka dots, stained green inside. The other was black with a faded emblem. *Whose mug is that?*

"That's where you stormed off too? Without checking with me first?" Allman began her inquest.

"Anything could have happened!" She screeched, sounding genuinely troubled for Goodrick's wellbeing. He remained silent, pursing his lips.

"Something did happen, didn't it?" Allman spun off the sofa onto her knees and sat in front of Goodrick. Looking slightly down at her in a dominant manner. She sat back on her heels, wearing loose-fitting pyjama trousers and a skimpy vest top. Without even trying, she had him like putty in her hands. He began talking, traumatised to think of anything other.

"Yeah, the schools there. It was off a country track, ten miles in. I didn't see another building or car around, so it's pretty remote."

"What did it look like? Did it have fire damage, as The Dragon said? Was it unlocked? Could you get inside?"

Goodrick scrunched his face at the relentless questioning. He couldn't blame her; they were all questions he was asking himself. On the journey back, he was trying to find the words to describe what had happened.

"I couldn't see any fire damage. It's overgrown and derelict like he described, but someone was there."

"The door was open, and it was a young girl, looked like she hadn't ate a meal for weeks. She didn't say anything, nor did it look like she wanted to. Someone was inside, whispering to her because she kept looking behind for guidance. I don't know if they were telling her not to speak. But she did start fretting when I asked her about an operating theatre. Like violently shaking and screaming, as if she knew exactly what I was talking about."

"You didn't see it? Did you not go in?"

"No, she slammed the door when I was approaching her. But I thought somebody else might have came out if I didn't leave."

"Who? Did they say anything?" Allman leaned closer into his space, now with both her hands on his knees, separating his legs to make more room for the inquisitive questions.

Goodrick shook his head. He could feel his palms beginning to sweat as he rubbed his hands together, starting to feel uneasy. It only hit him now that he could have been seriously hurt. His foolish, spontaneous tactics of handling everything have put him in danger in the past, but he's always been lucky to get out of it unscathed. This time he was very lucky the only damage was to the rear of his car and pride.

The thought of his cars condition made him queasy. With the force he reversed into the iron gate; it must've left something far nastier than a surface scratch.

"No, but I thought I did hear something," Goodrick said.

"What was it?" He looked at Allman, her eyes glistening, hungry for the information.

"I thought I heard a chainsaw." Goodrick looked at her dead in the eye, hoping she'd make the connection without more to give. She seemed unsatisfied, looking away, before sitting back on the sofa. Goodrick had his stare stitched to her, following her every move, anticipating a more flamboyant reaction, but she slinked away, pressing her body into the crevice of the sofa, almost sulking. He pivoted, resting his knee against hers, and continued to read her expression.

He knew she understood. Maybe it sunk in that maybe The Dragon was telling the truth, although Goodrick recognised inconsistencies. The door, although vaguely described, matched a different Creature's week. No evidence of fire damage unless it was in the Council's records, the same records stating the building as demolished however.

Goodrick shook his head, trying to gather his thoughts about the story. Without seeing the theatre with his own eyes, he could never truly know if it existed at all. The shaking and the obvious distress the girl displayed when questioned about it couldn't sway him enough to separate fact from fiction.

"You could've been hurt, Gregory," Allman said caringly. Goodrick nodded, fully agreeing with her.

"I know. I'm sorry I stormed off, I shouldn't have, and it was silly of me to go with no backup. In all honesty, I didn't know what I was walking into. I half expected a derelict, fire-damaged building crumbling to the ground that may have had evidence of the theatre existing."

"We can get all that information from here. I did do a quick search on it myself, Farnham, is that where you went? Fuck, you must be exhausted."

Goodrick flung himself backwards; hearing her say it made him realise he was indeed, exhausted. Sleepless night due to the needed argument with Nicole, trying to stomach The Dragons tale of The Lizard's week, and then the regretted argument with Louise; he was drained.

"Four hours, thirty-six minutes' drive there, and five hours forty-two back due to rush-hour." Goodrick said, rubbing his closed eyes.

"So, what does this mean? Is it true? The school's real at least. The Creatures could exist as well then." Allman said whilst Goodrick rolled his eyes.

"I'm not 100%. There was an eviction notice at the property dated October 2011, threatening to evict the squatters. The girl I saw must've been one of them. When I called to inquire, they said fire damage, and then it was demolished. I know my eyes can play tricks on me but it most certainly isn't gone, like they want us to believe."

Goodrick found the energy to mutter. The song replayed on his mind, he couldn't be sure anymore what he really heard or saw moments before the bump.

"The Dragon hinted The Network is their own form of government; they can manipulate things in the public eye. What if that's the reason the council believes it's demolished because The Network made it so?"

Allman's adventurous mind started spinning as she prompted herself higher on the sofa as Goodrick slinked further back.

"This could have been a setup; this could be The Dragon telling us who the killer is. The Lizard might have been there. I mean, think about it, the victim's hand was chainsawed off, we know that, and we now know about The Lizard's week."

Goodrick started to drift out of consciousness, hearing her voice become hurried with excitement. She was like a dog with a bone when she felt she was on a line of enquiry, and all he could think about now was how comfy the sofa felt. He didn't have the strength or patience to tell her anymore of the ordeal, yet.

"Do we tell The Dragon tomorrow you visited Fingask? We can make arrangements to drive there together with my team." Goodrick shook his head, prising his tiresome eyes open, hearing enough for the night.

"We can't jump the gun on this, Louise, I'll file for reports tomorrow morning regarding the building and all records, but for now, we need to listen to him. He hasn't given us anything concrete yet."

"So, you agree, we hear him out?" Allman chirped.

"Yes, I do. But right now, all I need is sleep."

"Here?" Allman sounded surprised. It wasn't like Goodrick to prompt an uninvited sleepover, but he felt so weak he wouldn't be able to lift his feet to take his shoes off, let alone think about driving in his already battered vehicle to get an even bigger headache when he got home.

"If that's okay, I'm so tired, Louise. I'd really appreciate it, although I know I don't deserve the hospitality."

"It's fine. After all, it would make me feel safer, you know, after the pictures."

Goodrick glanced over at Allman, who was now fidgeting with her hands. It was a coping mechanism he'd noticed she did at times of distress. He reached over and softly cradled her hands in his, feeling his troubles dispersing. She seemed grateful for the touch as she smiled placidly. Now the drawn curtains made sense. He felt pleased he decided to come, although he was expecting to feel unwelcome with how he childishly left their last conversation.

"I'm sorry about before, I was frustrated about the pictures, and I don't cope very well with controlling myself at times."

"Yeah, I can tell," Allman smirked, leaning her head to the right, hinting at his brief encounter with Edith in the hallway."

"I'll apologise to her in the morning, but I'm more concerned about how you're feeling. I shouldn't have walked off, but I needed some air, and the grand idea I had to visit the school sprung into my mind. Before I could stop and think, I was already on the slip road, joining the motorway."

"It's fine, Gregory. I wish I could've been there with you, but I had that meeting, so even if you suggested, you'd have gone alone."

Goodrick sat upright. He felt ashamed that he forgot about her meeting with Adriana regarding Superintendent Chadwick.

"Fuck! With what happened, it didn't cross my mind; how did it go? Did you tell her everything?" Goodrick asked, spinning to face her with his new founded energy. As his attitude perked up, he felt Allman's disappear.

"That's a conversation for another time. I have a heavy night of evaluating ahead of me before I can even approach that subject." Allman said sheepishly.

Goodrick nodded intensely, acknowledging it was a very personal matter. He was left alone with his thoughts as Allman shuffled behind the wall, a sound of a cabinet unhitching clicked behind him, and before too long, Allman returned with a thin pillow and a heavy duvet. Slumping it over the sofa, she gave him a half-hearted smile before raising her hand.

"Well, goodnight then, Gregory." Allman softly spoke.

Her smile weakened Goodrick, he couldn't help but look away before returning the smile himself, but she was already gone. The darkness that filled the hallway she disappeared into now crept inside the open room. The only light source was the touch lamp positioned on the coffee table in front of him. Leaning slightly, he retrieved his phone. Two missed calls and one text message from Bernice.

'Are you going to come home tonight or stay out with your whore again?'

Goodrick rolled his eyes, ignoring the message from his estranged wife, and swiped up to begin a new message to an unknown contact.

'Who was at Dolphin View today?'

'Louise Allman returned in her vehicle at 17:54 with an unknown male.'

'Unknown male?'

'6'6 male wearing a long oversized beige coat. The surveillance crew inside the car park couldn't confirm his identity either.'

'Get me surveillance footage from the lobby. As of tomorrow morning, operate Dolphin View 24 hours a day until further notice.'

'Understood GG'

CHAPTER 24

July 24ᵗʰ, 2015

"Car sharing?" Goodrick beamed from the side of his BMW. Allman paced herself behind the vehicle to behold the crumpled boot. A sharp indentation, from the impact, scrunched the car like foil.

"My god, what happened?"

"Yesterday, I was reversing, trying to exit the school grounds. I didn't judge my speed or the tiny gap. I went straight into the gate didn't I."

Allman smirked, beholding his poor judgement; Gregory Goodrick was good at *almost* everything. He was kneeling down, delicately tracing his fingers over his beloved's injuries.

"I can recommend a good body repair shop if you like?" Allman graciously offered.

"It's alright. I have an old friend, Gav, coming over to pick her up."

"Her?" Allman quizzed with both arms crossed, watching Goodrick as he threw a bag of the previous day's clothes in the back. She intently looked inside, but the blacked-out windows were difficult to identify anything. She found it odd he announced before that morning shower he was grabbing spare clothes from his car. She remembered asking herself, who packs for an unexpected stay, but it was Goodrick after all. Always seen in a prestigious showroom manner, it wouldn't startle her if she found a butler hiding in there, ready to slave on him day and night.

"Yeah, Betty." Goodrick said proudly, patting the roof of his car. Allman sniggered; he didn't strike her as a car-naming fool.

"How original. Did you come up with that all by yourself?"

"I did, actually."

They both smiled at one another as they walked together, making their way to the underground car park. The morning had been quiet thus far. She spent most of it staggering around in her bedroom, unable to do her normal morning ritual. Get naked, put the kettle on, round of toast, shower, change, and out. The first step she did confidently, launching her vest top over her head as she rose from her slumber. It was only when she was about to kick her trousers off at her ankles, with her hand on the handle, that she remembered Goodrick stayed over.

She'd spent the previous evening anticipating a sleepless night, rolling and turning with the fear that somebody was watching her apartment. Flinching, she yanked her pants back up, thinking of all the times she felt safe and would float around her apartment naked with no care in the world. *How long has somebody been watching me?*

She launched herself out of her bedroom after finding a suitable top to throw over her shoulders. The gloomy shadow that was cast over the living area and kitchen saddened her. It was normally a light, golden start in the mornings, especially in the prime of summer. The feel of the sun's heat radiating over her bare skin was the perfect way to wake herself up. Now walking into her kitchen, she felt it could be 06:15pm, not in fact AM.

Looking up and down the length of the windows, she couldn't see the regular reflection she was used to seeing, but saw something nonetheless. The once open, bright outlook that the windows gifted her was now dark and dismal. Layers of heavy fabric draped over them, masking the beautiful scenery they portrayed beneath.

Allman picked a loose thread of fabric from her oversized top and couldn't help sense a familiar feeling. Her bravery and confidence felt hidden now beneath the flimsy material, shadowing it, protecting it, but hopefully never taking it.

She breathed heavily, regretting her decision to hang them, as if The Dragon had won. Paul was the tallest person she could find at short notice, and with him only living in the next apartment block, it made perfect sense to ask for his help. He seemed happy for a lift home for once rather than using the train. After her prompt, unscheduled meeting finished, it would mean he missed his regular stop. His usual twenty-minute commute easily transpired to fifty due to Allman. To repay him the favour, she offered to cook his tea and, for a short while, genuinely enjoyed his company.

She found it difficult to begin with to see him more than Jade's older, hot but dense, cousin. Since working with her team, he may not hold a conversation longer than two minutes, but he could hack you into any database within that time, and that was all she looked to him for, before now. Last night was an eye-opener for her, he expressed himself so openly, and they talked for hours. Starting with their mutual interest – Jade. It was the perfect distraction to stop her mind racing as to where Goodrick was and the debate of should she, shouldn't she report Flatdick.

Allman felt the conversation would turn naturally towards work; it's easy to talk about something they both equally know about without there being any awkwardness, but it didn't. He cherished her with memories of his childhood with Jade, growing up in Birmingham centre together, how she helped him secure his flat here and how he first got into computer science. It wasn't before long that Allman began opening up too, something she tended to keep sheltered, especially when work was involved.

She never liked the two mixing from her experiences, but there was something inviting about Paul. He wasn't so tense to be around as she felt with others. It was due to their conversation she realised how difficult it could sometimes be to talk to Goodrick. His excessive eye-contact, at first is mesmerising, but she was thankful for Paul's deep brown eyes to be diverted elsewhere. It felt easier to talk openly rather than feeling interviewed by Goodrick's stare.

The gentle, delicate touch of Paul's hand on her elbow felt familiar. It didn't feel like an electric shock like when Goodrick would slightly brush past her. It felt nice and, well, normal to have a conversation with somebody without any underlying intentions she felt from Goodrick. Allman thought about her interaction with Paul and found herself biting on her finger, smiling to herself out of her car window when they pulled up at traffic lights.

"Louise, it's on green," Goodrick's voice rocketed her back into the present.

"Shit, sorry." She apologised, lifting her foot from the brake pedal and continued on their morning journey. All the while, she could feel Goodrick's glare burning through the side of her head as if he knew what she was thinking about.

"So, did you want to talk about Adriana's meeting now?" Goodrick carefully asked. Allman shook her head; she'd already prepared to give herself the weekend to think about Adriana's offer. As soon as she'd think out loud about the matter, she was stuck in two minds about what to do. Knowing Goodrick could persuade her to do almost anything, she thought it best to make her mind up first, and then it would be her decision to tell him or not.

She felt disheartened tackling it this way, he was, after all, only trying to help her, but she needed to do this herself; for herself. They spent the rest of their journey in silence, both within their own thoughts. Allman hoped today would go by quickly. She was hesitant to see The Dragon again with her growing concerning fear of him. At the same time, though, she felt engulfed in The Creatures' stories so far and anticipated what today's story could bring.

Allman could feel judgement and accusations as both she and Goodrick made their way to her office. Although she couldn't hear anybody gossiping, the look in their eyes told her everything they were thinking; *look at them two, coming in together now.*

Allman tried to convince herself that nobody saw them both getting out of her car together, which she knew there was zero chance of that happening with the eagle eyes surrounding her. For a team of detectives, nothing and everything meant something to them, and with Allman being the only female lead detective, she was hawked on the most. She felt overwhelmed when she finally stepped into her office, a chance to finally relax.

"They aren't forgiving, are they?" Goodrick commented. Allman huffed, draping her coat over the back of her chair, thankful he felt the same.

"You can say that again. They will be at it all day now. Allman and Goodrick sitting in a tree…"

"K-I-S-S-I-N-G," Goodrick mimicked.

"First comes Ducky…"

"Then comes Lizard…"

"And I wonder who comes next?" Allman shrugged, ending their sing-song. Goodrick looked almost saddened she didn't finish the tune with an epic freestyle of her own before dragging them both into reality.

"Who knows?"

A knock on the door caught her off guard, Allman's heart skipped slightly, and her startling jump was captured by Goodrick, who now had a smirk stretched across his face.

"Come in!" Allman ordered.

"Sorry, only me."

Goodrick creased his face hearing the voice. With his back turned against the door, it was only Allman who witnessed his disgust.

"Paul, come on in!" Allman gladly instructed, waving her hand over to beckon him into the room. A small smile pushed its way through her lips that she couldn't resist.

"Oh, good morning Detective Goodrick. I didn't see you there."

Paul said as he walked closer to Allman's desk with a brown envelope in his grip. Allman focused on what Paul held. The smile soon disappeared, remembering the contents of the last envelope Goodrick opened.

"Really, you couldn't see me?" Goodrick sarcastically asked, looking up at Paul, who was towering above him. Allman knew he was being his usual Goodrick self, but his sense of humour went straight over Paul's skyscraper head.

"No, I didn't. Eh, anyway, it was to give you these. I filed for them first thing, I should have more for this afternoon."

Allman leaned over her table to retrieve the reports from his hands. She noted that Goodrick hadn't replaced his stare anywhere other than on Paul. Feeling awkward, Allman didn't want Paul to catch up on the tension Goodrick was radiating and cleared her throat abruptly as she opened its contents.

"Thanks, Paul. If I need anything else…" She smiled sweetly up at him. Paul understood quickly before she needed to say anymore. With a nod of his head, he was gone before Allman glanced back down. Goodrick's glare followed him out of the room and seemingly slammed the door shut behind him.

"Do you need to?" Allman asked as she flicked through the papers.

"Do I need to do what?" Goodrick asked, pulling his face and snapping his neck back towards Allman.

"You know… it doesn't matter." Allman sighed. There's no point trying to explain sometimes how he'd come across to others. He either wanted it like that or was arrogant enough that their opinions didn't matter anyway. With them only just getting past one of their arguments, she didn't have the energy to start a new one.

Her eyes gleamed downwards at the report Paul handed her. He'd done exactly what she asked them to do, all new forensic results from another laboratory to test the initial swabs at the crime scene.

"So, what's that then?" Goodrick asked. Allman shuffled the papers back into the envelope and placed them in her top drawer where they would be safe.

"I've asked for forensics to be rerun with a different lab."

"Oh? Why don't you ask for Tannoch to do their independent search? I can call it in now?" Goodrick waffled on whilst retrieving his phone out of his pocket.

"Because, believe it or not, we don't always need office Tannoch, especially for things like this." Allman sounded as smug as Goodrick looked as she leaned back in her armchair. She was beginning to feel numb towards him, the charismatic charm that normally bewitched her was diluting, and she couldn't figure out why. Was it due to Paul, or maybe she'd subconsciously thought of all the times Goodrick had been letting her down? They had only worked closely together for over two weeks, with one of those weeks Goodrick abandoning his post and her. But she couldn't resist the intense feelings she felt for him. It wasn't like what other people describe, how they feel they've known someone all their life. It felt she needed him all her life, not knowing why or how he would fit into it, but she needed him to.

"Are you excited about the 3rd August, then?" Goodrick grinned, raising his eyebrows. Just like that, whenever he would show the smallest slither of interest, she would be reeled back into him.

"What did you say to get me in?" She asked naively.

"Well…" Goodrick breathed in before moving himself closer to her, with his arms crossed, leaning against the table.

"I said something along the lines of, I knew a really, *really*, good detective who would absolutely love to represent our office…" Goodrick childishly began walking two fingers towards Allman's rested hand.

"She's clever, ambitious, funny…"

Allman opened her hand to invite his fingers to prance around her palm. He knew exactly what she wanted to hear. She hated to admit it, but she fished for compliments, always needing reassurance for facts she already knew, but she liked to hear it nonetheless. *Tell me how amazing I am.*

"...And tight." Goodrick stopped moving and looked at her dead in the eyes. Allman squinted hers, she felt she knew where he was going with this. Her leg that was happily rocking from the appraisal suddenly stopped. A short tense duration passed with Goodrick staring at her with those dazzling, deep blue stained glass windows that she couldn't help peer through.

"W-what?" Allman attempted to break the spell, but the stutter wasn't convincing either of them. A sudden knock on her door alerted them both towards it as it creaked open.

"Only me! Just to let you both know, The Chameleon Dragon's here." Jade's mistake loosened Allman as she exhaled in a chuckle, stopping her from ogling at Goodrick.

"Thanks, Jade." Allman sounded exhausted, raising her hand to order her to leave. Allman didn't look back up until she heard the click of the office door and watched as Goodrick seemed unpleased with her disturbing them as he rose from his chair.

"Perfect timing." He said half-heartedly.

Both Allman and Goodrick made their way to the familiar meeting place with The Dragon, avoiding to carry on their conversation from the prying eyes of the office. They waited patiently in the room until the buzzer announced his arrival.

The Dragon slowly walked in, this time calm, cool, and cocky demeanour sprung to mind. Nodding hello to them both before taking his seat, he carried a certain charisma and self-importance around himself that he'd not portrayed before. Allman had noted it seemed The Dragon was growing in confidence.

"Hello, hello, hello. Did you miss me?" The Dragon gleamed at them, kicking his feet up on the table and leaning back, tilting the front legs of his chair off the ground. With neither of them interacting with him, The Dragon stopped swinging on his chair and linked his fingers across his stomach against a neatly ironed, fitted navy shirt.

"Have I missed something?" The Dragon asked, rolling his tongue against the rough edges of his mouth, glaring between them both.

"No, not at all." Allman broke the tension by speaking first.

"So, you're here to continue telling us your story?" Allman asked.

"Not my story, *our* story." The Dragon added with his index fingers touching softly, exaggerating the term 'our', inviting both detectives into the freak show.

"Apologies, *The Creatures* story," Allman said, separating herself.

"Precisely." The Dragon stretched a closed grin towards them as Goodrick shuffled back in his seat awkwardly.

"Right, no time to waste!" The Dragon clapped loudly

"Let's get stuck in."

SQUIRREL

CHAPTER 25

The date was 17th May 2012, the year of the Squirrel. With this being my third year, I knew what to look out for. Like the years prior, a magazine slipped through my door. It talked about nonsense, how squirrels liked to masturbate and whatnot, along with an atlas map book. We went old-school, from the directions to the ride. I woke up that day to a 1966 MG Midget parked outside waiting for me. I thought maybe I was the only one to receive a ride, but we all turned up minutes apart from one another, all travelling in the same pale blue car. We drove onto a black gravel car park and reluctantly ditched the rides there amongst other abandoned rusted cars.

A barbed wire fence encased us as far as the eye could see, deserted by the forgotten B road that led us here. Scrapped cars littered your sight, heaped in metal mountains, way into the distance. The sun's light was blocked by a towering shipping container that stood in front, casting a cold chill. Along with the mountains of cars to your right and skyscrapers made from containers to the left, we appeared as tiny nuts in an overgrown tin town. Our wait came to an end when the suit stepped out of the tallest, grandest tower and greeted us with open arms. Even in this weather, he was wearing the famous suit he had the past two occasions, blue pinstriped with a pink tie tucked in.

"Welcome, welcome all," he cheered with a psychotic tear across his face, a smile some would say. We clasped hands with one another, formally greeting each other as we walked through the gaping entrance of one of the containers. The stench of the aftershave he bathed himself in was overpowering as he guided us through what became a maze of heavily dirtied tarpaulin.

The Squirrel stopped abruptly and turned slowly to watch us all gathered, anticipating the end of the maze. He raised his perfectly groomed, manicured hand up to his face, extended a finger over his lips, and with a hushed whisper.

"We're only as powerful as we believe we are, we're as weak as we tell ourselves, but we together, whatever we are, will be magnificent."

He pierced his eyes through each of us to ensure we acknowledged what he had said, although I wondered if it made no sense to the others as it did to me.

With a waft of his arm, he pulled the final sheet of the tarpaulin away, and a classroom was revealed. An echoing click of a switch bounced from the tinned surface and we were embraced by industrial lights. Flooding the gigantic space, exposing five blue plastic chairs, all attached with writing tables. It took a couple of seconds for my eyes to adjust from the poorly strung lights that led me into the container to now being overexposed by stadium lights. I raised my forearm to shield the sensitivity of my eyes and focused on the chairs in front of me.

On top of each of the tables was a standard flip note pad, filled with lined paper, and a sleek black ballpoint pen delicately placed above it. Each table and chair had been precisely laid out identically with absolute precision. There seemed to be no order as to who sat where. We each took the next available chair that was in our way with absolute silence. The only thing you could hear was the scratching of chalk against a blackboard. The Squirrels weight shifted from left to right as he wrote, taking the white chalk from his left hand over to his right at the beginning of each line without any pause or discontinuation of his impeccable, cursive handwriting.

It read lesson one: 'true power is to learn to look in front of you, to the side of you, behind you but never below you.'

The Squirrel enjoyed filling our days with intellectual speeches, engulfing us in what his whole week was about. It was essentially like being in a school, a cult, in the army, or in a church. I guess it depended on what you thought the Squirrel was, a teacher, a leader, a drill sergeant, or a priest. He was, in fact, all of the above with a sprinkle of psychopathic tendencies.

His aim was to teach us how to be his idea of perfection, meaning we were to become him. One exercise he taught us was how to speak like him. Five adults, all from different corners of the country with distinctive accents, were now glaring at themselves into a handheld mirror, repeating words and phrases over and over again, concentrating on how our mouths would move, how the flick of our tongues created different sounds. For hours we would watch ourselves repeat, "we are one. We are the same."

All were attempting to capture his signature cockney accent. The smell of his aftershave hit you before his self-importance grin was reflected over your shoulder as he criticised your attempts. Unsatisfied with my progress, his polished fingernails dug into either side of my cheek, forcing my lips to separate with my tongue wobbling between in limbo.

"Say it again!" he ordered. Any attempt with his fingers jammed between my jaw bones was futile, so I was forced to observe my pitiful attempts in the mirror. I watched as uncontained saliva began seeping from my gaping mouth, trickling down his moisturised hand and soaking his cuff.

"Is this what I sound like to you?" The Squirrel shouted, becoming angrier with my pathetic attempts.

"We are one. We are the same," I repeated with painful tears running down my swollen cheeks as his grip became unbearable. The bellowing of his chant still rang through my ears. I could no longer hear what my dismal attempts sounded like anymore. I began choking on my tongue as my throat seized up. I couldn't allow myself to think rationally, with his anger vibrating and piercing my ear drum.

He released me finally, and my head was thrown to the side, where I began revoltingly coughing for air. Black suede shoes appeared under me with a similar voice above me.

"Remember, Dragon, never look below you." It was at that moment I realised we would become him using force and with punishment.

We learnt almost every characteristic about him from the way he talked and how he walked. We would only drink and eat what he did and learn how apparently there's an improper way to peel bananas. It would infuriate him if we did it wrong. He'd crack his neck to anything that dissatisfied him, so we also learnt how to do that. He had a weasel-like, aspirated laugh when he was pleased, which we all had to adapt as our own for the week. Everything he was, he wanted us to become without any explanation of why or how, and it didn't matter how long it took us to get it.

The lecturing and the teaching filled six whole days. Our only reward if we succeeded him that day was to sleep. The Squirrel believed the brain only needs six hours of rest, so that was the maximum you were gifted if you were lucky. The container was pumped with some sort of gas and The Squirrel kept us stimulated with unfiltered coffee's and mixture of tablets so it was almost impossible to rest even if we needed to. With no natural light either, it only took the first adrenaline fuelled day for you to completely lose track of time and the days merged into one. The Squirrel was the only one who wore a watch throughout the ordeal and the only one wielding the power to determine when we would eat or defecate. He was a regular man, once a day, so we would be punished if we didn't sync our own bloody fluids to his schedule.

The Squirrel was always in immaculate condition whereas the rest of us lived in squalor. One of our final lessons was him teaching us how to shower properly. On what I know now was our final night, The Squirrel ordered us to remove all our clothing. We all stood naked a metre from one another in a straight line as The Squirrel walked back and forth in front of us, spouting his final heart-shattering speech.

"Can you smell that? Something is lingering around us all. Each one of you have your own distinctive body odour that has been wrenching my senses for the past few days. You may have learnt to talk like me and behave like me, but you most certainly don't smell like me."

Beacons suddenly began flashing above us with an ear-splitting siren, startling us all. The first drop of fresh water from the sprinkler system that hit my body felt like acid, hissing off my radiated, overworked skin. It numbed my senses as freezing cold water rained down on us all. The initial shock of the freshness of the water began to make me laugh hysterically.

I threw my glasses off, leaned my head backwards, with a gaping mouth and extended arms. I remembered feeling thankful for every single droplet that seeped into my skin, washing away days of dried sweat. I could see the blurred outline of The Squirrel walking towards me. The fall of the water sounded heavier as it hit the thick fabric of his suit. He stood in front of me, fully clothed, whilst the other Creatures splashed with excitement in the growing puddle that was gathering at our feet.

"Sleep tonight Dragon, for tomorrow is your final test."

I woke with a daze, feeling like my whole body was suffocating. My vision was slightly disorientated, I wasn't wearing my glasses, but that wasn't causing the obstruction. I lifted my hands to my face and felt the static between the fabrics that stretched across my entire body. I sat up, facing an erect dildo that was strapped around my waist. A shadow lurked above me as three sets of feet walked towards me. I looked up to the three bodies who were wearing the same white morph suit, two with the exact same fleshly, veined strap-on but, more creepily, had The Squirrel's grinning face printed on them all.

From their height and body shape, I knew I was in the room with The Squirrel, Ducky, and the second youngest female of the group. The Lizard and the older, plump woman were nowhere to be seen. I recognised the room as being the same classroom I'd spent the last six days being tortured in. However, the dirtied tarpaulin was now beautiful, pure white, with drapes of silk that covered the entire space. Ornate mirrors of all different sizes and shapes were scattered around the room, some free-standing whilst others were suspended from the ceiling, all focusing on a pretty, presentable, laid-out four poster bed with white furnishings in the middle of the room. In unison, all three extended their hands out towards me, and we all walked hand in hand towards the bed.

The Squirrel took a step in front of us; time for his final speech.

"It's difficult for lower beings to pull themselves from their hovel and believe they have the power for greatness. The persons in this room have demonstrated they can transcend from their wretched selves and become this – perfection."

He flounced his arms around himself, portraying his self-importance, before laying himself down on the mattress with all his limbs extended. His suit had a perfectly cut-out hole, strangling his real erection. Only when I looked down at the one I was wearing, I realised the strap-on had been cloned from his. Without hesitation, the other two Creatures began to please The Squirrel.

I had to become The Squirrel, and what would The Squirrel be doing, watching another two Squirrels, fuck another Squirrel. So, I masturbated. I stood there, watching this whole fuck fest transpire, without knowing what to do, so I felt I played it safe as I rigorously yanked at the rubbery piece attached to a belt around my hips. Ducky looked across at me, waving her hand behind her back covertly from the others until I realised she was signalling to tell me to use my left hand. From days spent learning everything there was to know about one person, and what they like, I must've forgotten the lesson in left-hand wanking. As silly as it seemed, I was still petrified to be seen doing something wrong, so I quickly changed hands to comply.

The build-up of the past few days, training people to kiss like him and to touch like him, must have exceeded his expectations because as long and anticipated this finale was, it began to quickly unravel.

He jolted everybody up after a few minutes, and the two women carried his signature, calm and collective walk towards me. We all kneeled as The Squirrel mirrored the same walk until he stood in front of all three of us. Although we all wore the same faces, I could tell his eyes were primarily on me beneath the mask. He grunted with his legs quivering as he pleased himself, with his left hand, looking at himself with me beneath it.

"Remember, if you do look below, you should only see yourself." That was his last quote to teach us before he released himself all over, well, himself.

CHAPTER 26

Goodrick tilted his head towards Allman with an open mouth. He had contemplated believing The Lizard may have some truth in it but now this? Allman stared slightly down at the table, pursing her lips with her arms crossed. He couldn't begin to guess where her mind was.

"Do squirrels really masturbate?" Even before Goodrick finished the question, he knew it was the wrong thing to begin with. A hissing, weasel laugh bellowed from the other side of the table, just how it was described in the story, with both Goodrick and Allman gingerly looking that way.

"Well, apparently only with their left hands." The Dragon made himself hysterically laugh until he was choking on his tongue and began to breathe with difficulty. Goodrick leaped from his chair and heavily hit The Dragon's back until he was able to compose himself again.

"Please help yourself to some water," Allman offered, raising her open hand to the jug that was placed in the middle of the table with a stack of plastic cups. The Dragon shrugged to assert he was fine whilst Goodrick took his seat. Goodrick kept his eyes towards Allman, whose eyes were shifting between the two of them. It seemed they were all choked up.

"Well, am I going to sit here all day-"

"You can leave," Allman instructed, cutting The Dragon's question. With uncertainty, The Dragon pushed his tongue into the side of his mouth and cracked his neck to the side.

"You don't want to ask me any questions, detective?"

"No. Unless you have any, Detective Goodrick?" Goodrick watched as Allman and The Dragon stared at each other, not aware of what was happening or why Allman wouldn't be questioning further.

"I, eh, I've never heard of a gang bang like that. I'm not too sure-"

"We're done here." Allman interrupted, standing up. Both Goodrick and The Dragon shot up in disbelief as Allman pressed the buzzer and invitingly held the door open for The Dragon to leave. Goodrick was hesitant to let The Dragon walk out,

"I mean, are we not going to question further into the newest piece of the puzzle?" he sheepishly asked her.

"Another member of this group, The Network named The Creatures, likes to get off torturing people to become his deranged, perverted sex tools to essentially fuck himself. Thus giving him the name Squirrel because I mean it's very common knowledge squirrels like to masturbate… with their left hand." Allman comically waffled before looking down at The Dragon, who was as astonished as Goodrick.

"Now, be on your way," Allman instructed. The Dragon reluctantly began to walk to the open door, only to be welcomed by the police officer on the other side who'd escort him out of the building.

"Well, I must let you know, Detective Allman, we're yet to finish our story. I have another two Creatures to discuss with you."

"I know. I've been counting myself, "Allman smugly said with her hand now balancing on her hip.

"Will tomorrow same time suit you both?" The Dragon asked.

"Sunday's better."

The Dragon agreed, sulking it seemed.

"Sunday it is, well until then, detectives," he nodded his head towards Goodrick, who was standing a few metres behind him.

"And to you, Detective Allman," turning his gaze back to her before leaving them both in the room. Allman pushed the door, following The Dragon out until it came to an abrupt stop.

"And why is Sunday better?" Goodrick began to ask the real questions.

"I have a thing on tomorrow."

"Sorry, a thing? We're missing an interrogation for a thing?"

"Well, you can hardly call it an interrogation, Gregory, but yes, I need a break too. We all can't fuck of and get a week unscheduled absence like some,"

Goodrick smirked, knowing she had him there and realised he may have been a bit too brash with her. He'd known she hadn't had a proper break in the case for weeks and indeed deserved one. He began to become concerned about what this 'thing' would be, who would she be with, who was the man seen at her apartment, and why was he becoming overwhelmed with jealousy.

"So, this thing, are you going to share what it is?" He sheepishly asked, knowing it wasn't his place. Hopefully, he carried it off as a genuine interest of one colleague to another, but Allman was beginning to see right through him.

"You'd really like to know, huh?"

"Of course, we're partners. I need to know everything you're doing, where you are, and who with." Goodrick realised the desperation in his voice before Allman's eyes widened at his statement.

"Well, I meant to say to a certain degree, yes, I'd very much like to know." He tried reassuring her.

"Well, if you must know, it's a very close family friend's 60th birthday party. Nothing too fancy, a garden party with some people I consider family who I've been detached from for some time. I think it will do me a world of good to reconnect, and who knows, maybe have fun for one night without this case on my mind."

"I couldn't agree more. You deserve a break, Louise."

They both slightly smiled at one another, although more questions were deafening Goodrick's thoughts. *Who'll be there, will that man be there, and is she staying the night? Will she be staying the night with that man?*

"You can come along with me?" Allman's sweet voice ripped him from the unnecessary probing questions he was giving himself.

"I mean, only if you want to. I know it's a Saturday night, you probably have better plans than to come with me to a garden party where you won't know anyone. I can't imagine you ever feel socially awkward around people you don't know. I mean, you are so confident in every scenario. I thought maybe you just wouldn't. It might not be your sort of thing".

By the time Allman had finished tripping over herself from her anxious rambling, Goodrick had walked up to her, being reeled in by every stumble.

"It most definitely sounds like my sort of thing. I'd love to come along, Louise. Does this mean your asking me out on a date?"

Goodrick smiled, seeing the tension lift from her shoulders.

"Don't push it Goodrick, it's only a garden party." Both smirking to one another, equally pleased for an excuse to spend time together.

The loud siren of the interrogation room's door alerted them both to look that way to see who was joining them.

"Hello, only me again." Paul's wide grin lurked from around the corner. *Oh, for fuck sake, him again.* Goodrick thought as he stood back to watch Paul slink his way into the room.

"I have some further reports I need your signature for, and also, Detective Goodrick, a message by a Gavin was left for you, he advised your car was ready?"

"Surely not." Allman looked over at Goodrick in disbelief. Goodrick, too, was surprised by the news, he knew his friend was good, but he couldn't have had the vehicle for more than two hours.

"Well, that's Gavin for you. I'll call a taxi and come straight back." Goodrick smiled over at Allman.

"Get through as much as we can today because I have a hot date tomorrow." Goodrick said cheekily, tapping Paul on his broad chest as he past them. Allman grinned to herself whilst signing the papers Paul had given her. Goodrick was within an earshot when he heard Paul begin to make small talk, abruptly stopping Goodrick in his haste to listen.

"I didn't get a chance to thank you properly for last night. Your spag-bol was incredible, even if you did serve it with naan bread."

"Hey! You said garlic naan would be fine."

The door slammed shut with their echoing giggles tormenting Goodrick's confidence. He stood tediously for a couple of seconds, rolling his tongue against his lip becoming increasingly jealous.

So, that's the mysterious man.

CHAPTER 27

July 25ᵗʰ, 2015

Allman was scanning the contents of a report Paul had provided her the evening before whilst waves of airplanes flew above her car. The knock on her apartment door at nine o'clock startled her. The only few people who knocked on her door recently have been Edith – who would normally be telling her not to breathe so loudly – or Goodrick.

She'd learnt Goodrick would become too impatient if she failed to open the door within a second of him gracing her, so when the other knock didn't come quite as quick, she knew it was somebody else. Arming herself with the closest weapon she could grasp, the tv remote, she shuffled her way to peer through the peephole. Paul's warm eyes were welcoming, sighing with relief, she ripped the door open. Paul left her disappointed when he advised her he couldn't come in.

A handsome young man was ready to party himself into the weekend, and all Allman would be doing with her Friday evening was now engrossing herself with the contents of the reports. She felt she concealed her disappointment well enough to be thrilled with her plans, although there was nothing she'd love more than throw on a strappy dress and join Paul, drinking into the night. *You need to make tomorrow count, that's all.*

She'd minimally explained to her team what The Dragon was telling them, only the bare basics to understand The Network and what they provided their members. That's why she was shocked when the first report was a picture depicting a crumbled building on the ground – Fingask was demolished in 1986. She'd already enquired with the police department of that county to hold their own independent research following Goodrick's visit. The reports would file to her office through Jade first, then Allman with a guaranteed delay and no real sense of urgency.

All of them thus far had advised there was no such building with people like Goodrick had described, and their independent investigation was ongoing as everyone was adamant it had been demolished. With them having such a small department, she was trying to be patient, not to mention office Tannoch was involved. Every report had to be submitted through them also. She missed the days when real police work mattered, and they could take Goodrick's word for what he'd seen as gospel, but now most of her work's admin based. They didn't consider anything proof until it was written down somewhere, and at least four people bore witness to it. It reminded her that she hadn't been provided a copy of his statement for the visit. She was sure him being a high-profile detective, he would've done it by now and didn't need reminding.

The bulk of the report Paul handed her had been his own personal research. She could tell because it hadn't been stamped by office Tannoch and the only signature was Jade's. She didn't mind when some of her team would undermine the system. The overall importance was to catch the bad guys, although it did mean harder work when the time came to prove anything if the reports hadn't been submitted following protocol. Jade must have told him about the recent Fingask speculation, and this armoured Paul to go down the rabbit hole.

As much as it frustrated her, Jade couldn't keep her mouth shut, especially to Paul, who Allman already anticipated had reciprocated information back to his cousin regarding their pleasant night together – no doubt Jade was already choosing her bridesmaid dress after four years of trying to get Allman and him closer.

Allman kept glancing up from her car at the sound of the planes deafening her reading. She must've read the contents over fifty times last night, but her head was swarmed with unanswered questions. She was trying to piece together as much as she could before Jay made his appearance, it was after all, her day off, but reluctantly, Allman never truly gave herself a holiday.

'Fingask: School of Science – Demolished. Speculation has arisen that a professor of the school was using mentally challenged young adults and sometimes children as young as three, for off-the-books scientific research. Many reported it included sleep deprivation and unauthorised amputations'

"Mate!" A familiar voice screeched into the open window of her passenger car door, abruptly stopping her.

"Oh my god, Jay!" His heartwarming smile caressed the atmosphere that was suffocating Allman from the confines of her car. She quickly dropped the newspaper article as if it suddenly meant nothing to her. When she opened her door, she felt the gloom from the reports spilled out onto the hot tarmac and felt the warmth of the sun that day. All that filled her now was pure happiness.

Jay's athletic legs ran him towards her, scooping Allman up in a gigantic bear hug. His unrestricted, ripped biceps from the tank top he wore lifted Allman off her feet with ease as he spun her around. Allman giggled like a schoolgirl. It had always been their big hello for every gathering. She stood back in awe of her best friend, his mousy brunette curls of hair were pushed back with a backwards beaten-up baseball cap, the one she remembered him winning in a bet at college. His arms seemed to grow with each meeting through hard months of grafting from the manual labour of working on an oil rig.

She was always so proud of what he'd accomplished. Through school, it never made sense why they were best friends to others, he was the naughty school boy selling packets of foreign cigarettes with a markup price of 30% and she was the book nerd studying in the library through lunch breaks. She knew her school life could have been so different if she didn't have Jay's protection. She was, after all, the ideal target to bully with her jam-jar glasses and the dot-to-dot game of acne on her face. Jay always saw past that, but she did wonder if their mothers hadn't been friends, where would they be now?

"Mate, you look incredible!" Jay gleamed down at her brushing her tangled hair from her face. Allman was always happy to hear the compliments, forgetting she probably had darkened circles wrapped around her eyes from all the late night. It didn't bother her too much; he'd seen her in every state. From the spotty nerdy kid, stressed-out college student, a professional detective to a nervous wreck when her Mother passed; he'd seen it all.

"You flatter me too much. Are you sure you don't want a piece of this?" Allman humoured him, swinging her hips side to side to over-sexualise her assets. Jay left her and her pursing lips in his shadow as he made his way to the passenger seat, laughing comically.

"I've said it once, and I'll say it again, if you had a cock, you'd be all I needed."

He threw his backpack into the car and looked across from her over the roof with his toned forearms now resting on the arch of his door. It was difficult for her to look across at somebody she admired in every way and feel she needed to say something, the dread of him not knowing how much she appreciated him haunted her. Just when her face was cleared of any tangling hair from the breeze, she opened her mouth, but the air was filled with Jay's soothing, hushed voice.

"I know you've missed me. You don't have to say anything. I've really missed you too, Lou."

Her heart dropped, knowing he always knew what to say, so she didn't feel the need to. Even now, as two highly skilled professional adults, he was still looking out for that nerdy, friendless little girl he'd taken under his wing all those years ago. With a thankful smile, Allman opened her car and leaned inside, naturally gazing across where the Fingask file was sprawled out.

Jay had already began collecting the contents and forming them neatly back into the folder as Allman awkwardly tried to help but kept shuffling them the wrong way.

"I thought you said today was your day off?" Jay, inquisitive asked before locking the file away in her glove compartment and taking his pride and place in the passenger seat.

"Yeah, well, you know what I'm like, but I promise from this moment now, no more work." She half-heartedly smiled, knowing full well she wanted answers to her questions as she indicated her way out of the airport.

"Hmm." Jay said in a displeasing manner as he wiggled around in his seat. Stretching his legs as far as he could, looking to his right where the controls were, pulling the bar up and shuffling the seat forwards and backwards.

"What are you doing?" Allman asked, with his twitching arse becoming distracting.

"Somebodies been in my seat." Jay darted a cheeky grin over to Allman, knowing full well the stretched smirk on her face gave something away.

"Tell me who!" Jay demanded excitedly.

"You know that show-off detective we don't like?"

"Yeah, the 'Gregory – I'm good at everything – dick' who did the Houdini disappearing act on you?"

"Yeah…him." Allman stopped at a set of red lights and took her chance to read her friend's expression, who looked back at her, stunned.

"Him? He's the one who's been sat in my seat and adjusted my settings?" Sounding offended. Allman chuckled at the childishness of it all.

"Well, he's my partner. Of course, he's been in the car." A good alibi, Allman thought.

"And just so you know, I invited him tonight to the party."

"Are you out of your mind?" Jay scoffed.

Allman knew Jay would take the news badly. It was better he knew now and ripped the band-aid off rather than find out later.

"Look, you have seen one side of him, from what I've told you, and yes, most of the time, it's been bad, but honestly, he's growing on me. I really think you two will hit it off," Allman said, defending her actions.

"Are you trying to convince yourself or me? Hit it off? That sounds like you want him around longer, and you need your best friend's approval. Is that why he's coming, for me to give you the go-ahead?"

"Jay, I hardly need your input on who I so wish to 'go ahead' with, but yes, a little validation from my best friend would be appreciated. Just try to forget everything I've told you about him and treat him as you see him tonight."

"I already don't like him."

"Don't be so childish. You don't know the poor guy, and it's not as if I'm asking you to shack up with him and be back-to-back wanking buddies. I'd appreciate it if you gave him a chance before ruling him out."

"Hm, well, if it matters that much to you."

"It does."

"Fine, I promise not to spit in his drink."

"Is that the best offer I'm going to get?" Allman asked, glancing over to Jay, who was now glaring out the window, avoiding her.

"It's far more than he deserves." Jay spitefully said.

Allman sighed, knowing her stubborn friend won't budge on the matter. She was reluctant at times to tell him anything remotely negative about anyone because that'd be it for them. Soon as they would upset her, they were on Jay's hit list for life. They had a better chance of Santa Claus being real and making his nice list before they could convince Jay Anderson otherwise.

At times it would frustrate Allman, but she knew it was how he showed he cared for her. He couldn't help being protective over her, more so after her mother's passing. It took her four solid weeks of convincing him she'll be fine on her own and he needed to return to his job, not become her shadow to make sure the sun didn't burn her that day.

"I mean, hypothetically speaking...." Jay piped up. Allman sighed and rolled her eyes, for in the brief silence (that was three whole seconds) she'd now be teleported into some make-believe world that mainly dominated her and Jay's conversations. 20% would be real life, whereas the other eighty would be fuelled by both their anxiety, over-thinking, 'what if' scenarios.

"What would happen if he was a cock to me, disrespected me at my own mother's surprise birthday party, and I hit him?"

"For god sake, Jay." Allman huffed, growing tiresome of the game.

"No, really, what would happen? If I hit him on private land, would I be arrested for assaulting a policeman, or do you reckon he's up for getting roughed up and lay one on me?"

"He's not a policeman for a start, and regardless if an assault is caused on private land or in public, it's always a chargeable offence. You can use reasonable force to eject someone from trespassing on private land but seeing as he'll be invited as my guest, no, you may use no force to remove him whatsoever." Allman said smugly.

"But what if I hit him? Would he hit me back?"

"My god Jay, no, you won't hit him."

"But hypothetically speaking, what if I did?"

Allman could feel Jay's persistent eyes. She knew better than to play along but knew he wouldn't drop it.

"Okay, hypothetically speaking. If you hit Detective Goodrick, for whatever reason, he'd absolutely fuck you up."

Jay began laughing and throwing his head side to side in disbelief.

"No, I mean it Jay. Detective Goodrick's well known for being a bad boy, and from what I've seen, he'd beat you hands down. In fact, I put money on it."

Allman jokingly reached into her side jeans pocket and pulled out a scrunched five-pound note, wafting it in Jay's face gleefully. She began laughing herself when he snatched it out of her hands.

"Take that as peace money to keep your hands to yourself tonight, promise me?"

She glanced over quickly for confirmation as Jay began delicately unravelling the note.

"I promise. But I'm going to need a lot more of these." He joked back at her with a huge grin. Allman felt a nervous sick butterfly feeling in the pit of her stomach. She felt concealing any information from her friend was as worse as lying to their face.

"Goodrick and I are sleeping together." Allman blurted out unexpectedly. She could feel the heat of embarrassment radiate through her cheeks.

"Are we talking real life now or hypothetically?" Jay asked, sounding genuinely confused. Allman let out a laugh that their conversations can sometimes be so made-up that from time to time, they needed reassurance.

"Real life now."

"So, are you and him a thing?" Jay turned in his seat, fully engaged.

"No, we are, erm, complicated. We're colleagues, both working on this case together. I mean, we've known each other for years, of course, but only recently have I learnt more about him and got to know him better."

"And? Does he spend all his time telling you how great he is? He's done a good job of doing that over the years and belittling people from what you've told me."

"No, I genuinely think he's misconstrued, that's all. He's at times, well, most of the time, bigoted, but he has reason to be, you know? Like, he doesn't seem to control his emotions that well, so at times he seems rash. At other times, he can be gentle and, well, kinda sweet." Allman nodded her head. She wasn't sure if she was trying to convince herself as well as Jay.

"So, he's good in bed, that's what you mean?"

Both Allman and Jay erupted in laughter, with Allman teasingly hitting his arm.

"Well, there's only been the once- "

"Once? You've only slept with him once. So you aren't sleeping with him. You *slept* with him."

"Well, I mean, there's always tonight." Allman giggled, raising her eyebrows towards Jay.

"Oh, for fuck sake, and there I was thinking you couldn't wait for a night with your second family but all the while, you're going to be imagining sucking his dick."

"And now, so will you." Allman teased.

Jay shook his head with a smile on his face. As much as he wanted to hate the guy, he'd always keep Allman's best interest at heart.

"He does have some nerve, though. I mean, it's the first case he gets assigned with you, and he's already got into your pants."

"Hey! Is that a blow at me?" Allman shouted, taking offence.

"No, of course not. What I mean is, it seems very obvious he tried it on with you after he volunteered himself for the case, stole the case-"

"He didn't steal it. He actually stuck up for me in more ways you couldn't possibly know."

"Well, he has a set of bollocks, I give him that. I couldn't work alongside someone, knowing they did all the hard work, fuck them over, and then, amazingly, literally fuck them, all within a week." Jay clapped his hands together sarcastically.

"He didn't fuck me over. He sometimes goes around things the wrong way."

"Well, who the fuck just disappears for an entire week anyway?"

"I told you he had a family emergency. His stepmother had a fall."

"For a whole week, though?"

"Well, it was more than a week, give or take a couple of days, but he was apparently by her bedside in the hospital the whole time."

"And the guy doesn't have a phone? Not a text to say sorry, but I'm going to drop from the face of the earth. You keep up the hard work until I get back, yeah?"

Allman shook her head. As much as she wanted to believe the good in Goodrick, Jay did make an arguable case, and he wasn't finished.

"I mean, who does that? Who can just disappear, like that." Jay loudly clicked his fingers, startling Allman.

"Who do you know that ups and leaves for an entire week with no communication with anybody? Like nobody does that."

Jay continued looking into the far distance as he played judge and jury with himself, leaving Allman alone with her over-imaginative mind standing on the witness stand.

A Creature would.

CHAPTER 28

This one won't do, Goodrick thought to himself as he kept pressing neatly ironed shirts against his chest one after another. First, his favourite salmon shirt, he turned on his heel back and forth, smouldering in the floor-length mirror that stood in what was once called his bedroom. Five sets of mirrored doors encased his impeccable collection of designer suits. Drawers could be pulled out to showcase a vast amount of collectable watches and neatly folded ties that were housed in perfect square cut-outs, all kept in complete unison with one another.

This part of the bedroom had been kept exactly how he liked things, neat and tidy. The rest of the bombshell was not his responsibility as he grudgingly looked at the littered floor of unwashed laundry behind him. He began to frown, thinking back to the days the only bit of unwashed laundry were from his female companions, they'd quickly be picked up and thrown out along with their owners, sharpish. He'd never pass up, if he could help it, having a full English served with conversation with Eileen.

"Dad!" A little voice screamed behind him. Automatically a smile tore through Goodrick's face as he saw the reflection of his little boy jump into the room.

"Get over here, champ," Goodrick cheered as his little boy ran as quickly as his little legs could carry him. The feeling of hugging your child couldn't compete with anything Goodrick had ever felt. Feeling their full stomachs pressed against yours, their warm clothes fitting comfortably around their backs, the giggling from being a happy, content child; nothing came close.

He held onto his son, Gregory Junior, as tightly as he could. It was times like this he regretted the job he did, the hours the office stole from his time with him. He was sure the stress of the job had already claimed years from his life.

However, his child would never have the worry about where his next meal was coming from or not having a warm roof over his head. It was a far cry away from the daily struggles he faced as a child watching his single father struggling to make ends meet. Sometimes the only meal he'd be guaranteed was from Eileen. She was horrified when his dad confessed to her he'd go without eating so Goodrick could. Since that moment, every morning Eileen would make sure he was well-fed, something she remains to do.

He wonders if that was the reason why he married Ida; her money ensured that somewhere down the line, Goodrick would be financially secure. He wished his father married with his heart and not strategically, with Goodrick's livelihood being the deciding factor. Otherwise, he could be calling Eileen mum.

"Oh, so you've decided to show your face?" The smacking of an angry piece of chewing gum being tossed between somebodies cheeks echoed from the hallway. Goodrick reluctantly looked up to see the stern look from his estranged wife, Bernice.

"Come on, G. Time to get bathed and changed," she ordered a disgruntled mini Goodrick, who was now kicking his feet in defiance, to be released from his dad's grip. Goodrick reluctantly held his son down to the floor as the toddler dangled like a monkey wrapping his arms around his neck.

"Come on, son. You heard what your Mum said."

"Will you still be here when I get out?" Little Gregory's eyes glistened with hope. Goodrick felt a sick blow hit his stomach as he hated the feeling of letting him down.

"I won't be tonight. I have a work thing, but I'll be back in the morning bright and early to take us for breakfast at-"

"Eileen's!" Both Gregory's cheered in unison.

"Will she let me have a cupcake?" Little Gregory sneakily asked his dad under a hushed whisper as he released Goodrick from his grasp.

"Only if you finish eating all your beans, you know the rules," Goodrick said proudly with a smile on his face, stretching his back upwards and ruffling his son's hair.

His little bundle of joy bounced himself out of the room, so Goodrick was left with Bernice. Turning back around to face himself in the mirror, he finished buttoning his top button and then undid it again immediately, pondering to himself how formal will he need to dress. The only information Allman provided him with was the address. It was a surprise 60th birthday party, and to dress smart.

Of course, Goodrick took it upon himself to research the hosts of tonight's party himself. Julie and Neil Anderson married straight from school, eloping to Gretna Green, happily married, if that's possible, with two children, James Anderson and Michael Anderson – both educated from prestigious colleges, the same Allman graduated from.

He put two and two together and realised James and Allman were the same age and followed each other in their school years before Allman graduated with criminology and James with engineering. That's where the link of their shared accommodation blurred for a few years before James reappeared at an address in Australia and Allman at the apartment she's in now.

He questioned during his research if Allman and James were together, but after a few minutes of stalking James's (referred to now as Jay) social media accounts, past history of boyfriends, and the weekly reference to his "best friend" with a selfie of him and Allman forced him to put his macho caveman instincts away; he wasn't a threat.

"A work thing?" He could hear the judgement in Bernice's question as he turned around after finally deciding on wearing a couple of buttons undone.

"Well, sort of, a social gathering but with a work colleague," Goodrick explained as he began his ritual of packing an overnight bag; he was doing it with wishful thinking but mainly out of habit.

"Look, I know you think you're this big, amazing, clever detective, but I've been doing some detective work myself."

"Oh, have you?" Goodrick humoured her.

"Yeah, I have, actually! Jenna, you remember Jenna, the girl who gets her nails done wearing-"

"The pink and blue sports bra." Goodrick finished the sentence with an exhausted monotone; he'd heard it a thousand times.

"Yeah, that's her. She texted me the other night and asked what you were doing by that run-down chippy off Kingsway bridge. And I sat here and thought hmm to myself, ain't been no murders round there."

"Just because I'm a lead detective in homicide doesn't mean I only follow the dead bodies, you know. There are witnesses and leads to follow, and I could be placed anywhere at any time."

"Well, how convenient!" Bernice spat.

Goodrick exhaled deeply, trying not to become irritated. She was, after all, correct. He wouldn't class somebody texting her as detective work, but he was there a few nights ago, breaking up with Nicole. It exhausted him to go through the same rigorous arguments knowing he made his intentions clear years ago; he wasn't happy and wanted to finalise the divorce. Bernice, being as stubborn, refused to grant it and, from then, made it her goal to try to guilt trip him into falling back in love with her. Truth being, he never loved her to begin with.

He only agreed to marry the one-night stand he got pregnant because he was spoon-fed her family would disown her and the child if out of wedlock. His promises to support her meant nothing if it weren't signed on a piece of paper. Goodrick was under the influence they both had the understanding it was a marriage of convenience. He was naive to believe he could carry out the fake marriage and do as he pleased with others. He failed to foresee the string of women that would come afterwards could never be more than occasional hookups.

Distancing himself from any genuine emotion, too scared to have feelings grow, and becoming attached to somebody he'll never be able to truly have. When his son arrived, he gave everything he could to become a real husband and flattered her with gifts, and played the perfect family man believing that's what he was destined to be. The novelty quickly wore off, and soon enough, the pictures and memories were only of him and little Gregory on days out. Looting pirate's treasure and hunting monsters in the woods, with Bernice becoming white noise in the background.

He thought she'd grow tired of a burdened, sexless, emotionless marriage as quickly as he did and find someone else to move on with. However, it seemed it was Goodrick's money and the security of living in a nice apartment. Having nice cars and expensive purses meant more to her than trying to revive her dormant sex drive. Goodrick chuckled to himself, thinking he must have found her on a good night, or he needed to learn to stop flashing the pound signs to score.

"Well, I'll be off if that's everything," Goodrick said, giving himself the once over in the mirror. Dark navy suit tailored pants with a black leather belt, a blue tucked-in -slightly unbuttoned- shirt supporting his father's handed down silver knotted cufflinks, and the matching jacket draped over his arm. His hair was fashioned how it always is, slinked back with minimal gel and freshly groomed stubble.

"So that's it then, I'm supposed to give up my life to look after your child whilst you go out gallivanting!" Bernice shrieked, stretching her arm across his pathway, blocking him from leaving the room.

"Bernice, this is becoming exhausting now. Just sign the damn papers, and you'll be a lot happier a lot sooner. I'm divorcing you one way or another, so how about you try to make things peaceful for a change?" Goodrick quietly asked her, aware not to raise his voice due to little Gregory in the next room.

"You won't see him. You know that, don't you? I won't allow it." Bernice threatened in desperation.

"You go ahead and try to stop me from seeing my son because believe me, it'll be the last thing you do."

"Oh! Is that a threat? Are you threatening me, Gregory? Mr. I'm above the law and have friends in really high places!"

"I don't need to threaten you, Bernice. We both know what I'm capable of. Now, please remove your arm." Goodrick felt he asked as nicely as he could, pointing at her forearm that barricaded his exit.

After a few seconds of neither of them moving, he attempted to crouch below her elbow before being jolted backwards by a hard shove to the face. It hadn't been the first time she used her hands, elbows, even feet, in violence towards him. She was a huge fan of using a remote control to attempt to batter him whenever she didn't get things her way.

Goodrick wiggled backwards at the inconvenience of her attempt to hurt him. Taking punches in the face since a young lad through boxing and learning to talk with your fists in his neighbourhood, her attempts felt like tickles, although he'd never give her the encouragement to try harder.

"Really, Bernice? Gregory is in the next room, you complete psychopath, now out of my way." Goodrick barged through her defences and shot a quick wave to Gregory, who he could see was completely transfixed, playing on his bedroom floor with a train running it along a city rug.

"I'll see you in the morning, champ!" Goodrick shouted through the open door.

"See you tomorrow Dad!" Little Gregory cheered, thankful his playing kept him distracted.

He was quick to leave the apartment before Bernice would cause a scene in front of him, so far, their arguments have always been behind closed doors, and as far as little Gregory was aware, his parents were nothing more than loving partners. With the exception, his father would work around the clock, so time spent as father and son was limited.

It was in that instance Goodrick realised he was doing exactly what his father did for him. Becoming miserable for the sake of his child's happiness, believing you are doing what was right by them, but Goodrick didn't have it in him to play happy families much longer and keep up the appearance of having one. Just because two people have a baby together doesn't necessarily mean they will be the best parents together. Goodrick knew he'd be a better parent separately, and in time, Bernice would be a better person too.

A familiar buzzing vibration rippled in his trouser pants. Retrieving his phone, he knew the flashing blue light was from Allman.

'Hey, just letting you know I'm leaving in a taxi to the Andersons now, be there in about 23 minutes.'

He smirked down at his phone at how precise her timings were from time to time. Everything around her life she dispatched to perfection, something Goodrick admired.

'I'm setting off soon myself. Just need to do some things first, and then I'll be there shortly after.'

'Oh, what things?'

'Just things.'

'Well, aren't you a man of mystery?'

'You have no idea.'

CHAPTER 29

The sweet fragrance of roses heightened Allman's senses as she stumbled through a driveway of overgrown ivy with pink rose bushes. She could see in the far distance, through the metal gate, an enormous marquee tent assembled in the orchard behind the impressive four-bedroom home. She gazed up at the 16th-century-built farmhouse in awe of its stature. Painted white with black rock-faced stone sills and turning pieces with cambered arches, it was a magnificent building.

Allman vividly remembered the house inside out. Each room held a piece of history, her favourite being inside the kitchen. Jay's mother, Julie, once told her there was a secret well hidden beneath the tiles, right in the heart of the home. Due to superstition, she placed a solid oak table over it so nobody could walk directly above it.

The surrounding orchard and field made the perfect venue for any social gathering. It was frequently rented out as a wedding venue where history buffs would walk down and tie the knot.

Allman sensed a feeling of belonging as she took a moment to embrace the house she spent the majority of her childhood running through, playing hide and seek in the surrounding woods that lined the outskirts of the plot. She smiled at the memories other children shared, all the ghost stories about the house, the hauntings, and not to visit at Halloween.

Allman was grateful for the last one; with every 31st October, Jay's grandmother would make the most incredible treacle and toffee apples that could still make Allman's mouth water today. In the absence of all other surrounding children, Jay, Allman, and Mike filled their boots. There's no such thing as door-knocking because everything they needed was right there. That didn't stop them from creating their own outfits from black bin bags, however.

The stretch of the pitch-black driveway was enough to scare people away. If they made it to the brittle white fence that Allman now placed her hand on, they'd be celebrated for their bravery. Allman only ever felt love in that building. It wasn't only from Neil and Julie's obvious warmth and affection. Decades of laughter echoed through the hallways. It felt, at times, the only place Allman truly called home.

"Here she is!" A familiar voice rippled from the open door that hadn't been locked for years. The sweet grin from Jay captured her gazing eyes as he outstretched his arms, ready for her embrace. Allman pushed the rickety fence and hugged Jay tightly. She'd only left him for two hours that day to get ready but being apart for five months warranted another hug.

"You look incredible!" Jay flattered her.

"Oh, this?" Allman joked, looking down at the purple, floral, fitting dress with a seductive slit up the thigh.

"I wish these would stay in place," Allman stated whilst dragging the thin pieces of fabric, that made the nuisance straps, draping over her bare shoulders.

"I have some sellotape knocking about. I bet that would do the trick." Jay graciously offered. Allman couldn't read from her friend's expression if he was genuinely offering a solution.

"I'm sure after a couple of these..." Allman outstretched her hand and retrieved a tall glass of pink, bubbling complementary drinks that were floating on a silver platter in the arms of a well-dressed server. She took an enormous gulp of the drink and beckoned the female server to stay put whilst the very last drop soaked through Allman's throat.

"Ah, as I was saying, after a couple of these, I won't care that much what I look like." She joked, retrieving another glass before letting the server carry on her route.

"Well, you kinda look like an alcoholic." Jay joked as Allman teasingly hit him with her silver clutch bag.

"Well, it's my first day off since god knows when; who knows when I'll get another? So tonight, I'm celebrating." Allman nodded, taking a more graceful sip from her drink; rosé champagne garnished with a mixture of summer fruits.

"And look at all these people who've come out to celebrate your day off." Jay mocked, panning his arm across the field of around sixty guests.

"I know. It's almost as if something else is going on." Allman smirked at her friend, finding comfort in their measly jokes.

"It's a great turnout. You and Mike will have done her proud. When will Julie be here?"

"Well, by my calculations, we wanted to allow a good two hours for welcome drinks and everyone to mingle first, so she'll be here within the next hour."

"Who's bringing her? I can't see your Dad or Mike."

"My Dad. He's treated her this morning with a boat cruise on River Weaver, followed by a picnic. God knows where Mike is, probably being a nuisance to some poor woman."

"God help them." Allman laughed before continuing.

"Only your dad could've put this much thought into everything. Your mother's a very lucky lady." Allman tried not to sound salty, but she couldn't help but feel jealous over everything Julie Anderson had; the big house, the doting husband, the perfect family. She tried her hardest to push any thoughts of her being a charity case to the family out of her mind. She knew The Andersons loved her as their own, but spectating across the wealthy sea of suits, she couldn't help but feel somebody was already thinking it.

"Hello, Louise." His voice soothed her away from her anxiety-fuelled search. Goodrick stood facing towards her and Jay with both his hands in his pockets, looking, if possible, more attractive than ever. Allman had always seen him in a full suit, something she was expecting tonight, but the casually unbuttoned shirt, no tie, and the way he had immaculately trimmed and styled his hair took her breath away. She froze, completely stunned at how he was able to have this effect on her.

"Jay, I presume?" Goodrick extended a hand outwards. Jay glanced across to Allman before uncertainty extending a hand also and clasping onto Goodrick's.

"Yes, and you must be The detective. What is it, Rudick?" Jay sarcastically asked.

"Goodrick, but please, call me Gregory if that's easier for you to remember." Goodrick stretched a smile that Allman knew all too well, he knew what game Jay was playing, and he'd already be two steps ahead. Their stare between one another intensified as Allman was speechless and eye-goggling at the specimen of the man Goodrick is. Allman watched the swaying of a blonde ponytail flick side by side past Goodrick's shoulder before shouting for the server to break the tension.

"Excuse me!" Allman waved her hand to beckon the server to retrace her steps so she was to the side of Goodrick, holding the same silver platter with freshly poured drinks. Goodrick took the opportunity to retrieve his hand back from Jay and look down at the offering. Allman pursed her lips when she saw the girl sheepishly smile when Goodrick locked eyes on her to retrieve a drink. It seemed he had that effect on all women.

"Thank you very much, eh…" Goodrick exaggerated to look for a name badge. From Allman's perspective, it looked like he was able to get more than an eyeful from the low-cut top.

"Lizzy, my friends call me mad Lizzy." The girl giggled childishly. It was easy to be caught up in a powerful man's gaze, especially someone as attractive as Goodrick.

"Well, to you, Mad Lizzy." Goodrick smoothly smirked, lifting his glass to her. Allman was expecting her to take a bow and kiss his feet, becoming slightly jealous watching how slick he was. *He could have any woman he wanted.*

"So, there's not really much point in me asking what you do, is there." Jay shrugged, trying to make small talk whilst Goodrick diverted his look back at them now his new fan made a brisk exit.

"And if you know what I do, there isn't much point in me asking you the same, is there," Goodrick smirked, swirling the fruit around in the flute glass. Allman smiled, knowing how alike they both really were; they just didn't know it yet.

"Right, well, I think it's only fair if I give Gregory the grand tour, don't you think?" Allman reassured her friend whilst linking her arm with Goodrick to whisk them both away now the pleasantries were exchanged. With a nod of Jay's acceptance, Allman turned Goodrick away from the path as they began their adventure down a dirt trail.

"Well, he seems nice," Goodrick said sarcastically.

"He is, believe me. He just has his guard up, that's all." Allman tried to reassure him as the path opened up to a freshly mowed square garden; sheltered by overhanging oak trees on every edge.

"And is that because of what you've told him about me?" Goodrick sounded sad enough for Allman to stop and turned to face him, lowering her hand to his wrist. She could tell his hand was clenched into a fist, no doubt holding the locket of his father he always kept in his pocket.

"I haven't told him anything you wouldn't say about yourself. Does that make you feel better?" Allman sweetly gazed into his concerned eyes. Staring back at her wasn't always the cocky, self-important detective he made out he was. She saw a vulnerable side to him, the side that kept pulling her in.

"So, he knows I'm an egotistical, bigoted, attractive, know-it-all detective?"

"I never said you were attractive." Allman broke Goodrick's pity-me frown as they both chuckled.

"Come, I have something I want to show you." Allman tiptoed in front of him, trying her best to keep the pressure on her toes to avoid her heels sinking into the soft ground.

She felt she pulled the catwalk off with grace, but from Goodrick's perspective, she probably resembled a wobbling goose. She stopped and looked into the great archway, that was cut away into the bushes, to showcase an earthly picturesque scene. Hanging lanterns dotted the tree's branches that entwined from above. Logs were sliced and placed around a raised palette with a dirtied teapot and plastic cups. Every tree had at least three wooden beams screwed into their trunks to act as a ladder to the branches above.

In the centre was Allman's pride and joy, a tyre swing. The den she and Jay built as children held a special place in her heart. To her, she didn't see the dirtied cups and plastic plates they left behind from their last tea party, instead, recounted the flower cakes they baked. They consisted of mud for flour, pond water for milk, and flowers for, of course, the taste, which was never tested. The fun was creating the mess, certainly not cleaning it up. She glanced behind herself as Goodrick made his way into one of her special places, gawking above him at all the string lights.

"It's more magical at night when it's all lit up, still a bit bright out at the moment," Allman said, trying to reserve any judgement coming her way.

"It's perfect, Louise." Goodrick humbly said, draping his jacket over the closest tree branch and joining her in the centre, with the swaying tyre swing between them. Allman was grateful for the break in Goodrick's intense eyes, with the frayed passing rope distracting her, although Goodrick seemed to look straight through it.

"It's a little after-school project that kept us busy." Allman began to explain, grabbing the knot at the base of the hung rope.

"Seems more than a little. Looks like any child's dream place. I wish I had something like this."

"Yeah, I don't envy my upbringing at all, I mean, yes, it wasn't great that my mum worked a lot, but she was a single parent after all, and I had this."

"I feel the same way about the café, the one I took you to. I'm worried it won't be around much longer." Allman frowned, seeing the look of despair drain Goodrick's face.

"What makes you say that? Is Eileen okay?" Allman inquisitively asked as Goodrick nodded his head, gulping as if the thought was too much to bear.

"Yes, she's fine, getting on a bit now. She mentioned it may be the time to sell up and retire, which at her age, I couldn't think of anything better. But is it greedy of me to want her to carry on, so I have an excuse to be there?"

"Surely you'll visit her, with or without the café. You can still spend time with her, even more so once she's retired."

"Of course. It's just, theres a lot of memories of my Dad at the café. Fun and laughter you can't capture, but when you're there, you feel it. That's what I'm worried about, not feeling his presence anymore. I only ever feel it there. I know that's where he is."

Allman gulped, knowing now he had meant the café itself was important. She could feel her heart become heavier, hearing how sensitive he'd become, knowing the pain. Imagining the tyre swinging in her hand suddenly burning, lighting every tree on fire, watching it crumble into ash. All her fond childhood memories of playing Robin Hood, swinging like Tarzan, and digging for gold, all ignited in an unforgiving fireball, the thought of the damage was unimaginable.

"I know how you feel, to be attached to a place, building, or even a room because it holds so many fond memories, but those memories won't go away, even if the place does. Believe me. Your Dad is always around you. I know it."

"And how'd you know that?"

"Well, I don't know for certain, but it's nicer to believe they are, right?"

"You never struck me as a religious person."

"What, me? No." Allman scoffed at the thought.

"I was brought up with the saying, let people believe what they want to believe. They will anyway, but always stay humble and kind."

"And whose saying was that?"

"My mum. She was full of wisdom one-liners. She used that one quite regularly because I was always obsessed with what others thought about me, and I still am to a degree."

"See, that's where we're a little different. I don't give a fuck about what people think of me."

"You must do, even a little. Everyone does."

"I only care about what you think of me, Louise." Allman lowered her shoulders, looking at the near-shattering stained glass eyes of Goodrick. He made her feel she was the only person he'd ever truly opened up to, a responsibility she didn't take lightly. She knew enough of him to know it was difficult for him to do so.

"And why would you care about what I thought?" Allman asked, tilting her head to the side, she knew full well, but she wanted to hear him say it. No, she needed to hear him say it.

"Why would you think I wouldn't?" Goodrick batted the caring game back into her court, neither of them wanting to admit it. With a sigh, Allman decided to let loose first.

"I care about you, Gregory, more than I should, and I don't know why but you have this overbearing, fixation spell over me where I question everything you say and do. It's like there's always another motive with you because I cannot begin to talk myself into believing someone as attractive and smart as you, is into someone like me."

"Someone like you being like what?" Goodrick's question came as Allman had begun spilling her conclusions.

"Oh, come on, Gregory, we both know I can be weak. I'm not always this well put together, detective; I make people believe I am."

"You could say the same about me."

"I never see you as weak, vulnerable maybe, sometimes. But then it's as if you cut the line just when I begin to walk across it and then have to pretend it never happened because you throw sarcastic remarks, knocking me off balance. I question if it was real or if I was looking into things too much, like I always do."

"My intention is never for you to question yourself. I know I'm sarcastic in any situation, but that's who I am, and I'm myself around you. I'm not good with words, but actions speak louder than words. I'm sure your mother taught you that one." Both Goodrick and Allman smiled at one another. He did certainly have a way of reassuring her over-imaginative mind from trailing off sometimes. She'd been so worked up over the case and fighting with herself. Was The Dragon taking her along for the ride like Goodrick thinks, or was she one step ahead of the know-it-all? A ruffling behind Goodrick concerned them both as Mike stumbled into their sight.

"Oh, hello, don't worry, I wasn't watching or anything." Mike chuckled as he walked up to them both.

Allman bit the inside of her mouth, knowing full well he was already attempting to get under her skin by referencing one of her favourite pastimes. She couldn't help but admit the sight of seeing both Mike, her first childhood crush, and now Goodrick, both equally pleasing on the eye, only a metre away from her shaking hands; her mind began to spiral with desirable thoughts.

A shudder tickled up her spine, making the connection to The Squirrel's story. Multiple Goodricks all there to please her. The Squirrel now appeared to be a narcissistic version of herself. Would that be what her week was like if she was a Creature?

"Lou, have we lost you?" Mike's persistent grin made Allman shake off all thoughts completely.

"Sorry, no, I was thinking." Allman nodded. Although Goodrick frowned his eyebrows, he could tell something was on her mind, distracting her.

"Well, don't try too hard, may hurt yourself." Mike sniggered whilst Goodrick nodded, giving him a reassuring, 'great joke kid' smile.

"We need you out front. She's only minutes away. Come on." Mike led the way and bounded through the bushes, disappearing from sight. Goodrick grabbed his jacket and linked arms with Allman, which she was thankful for. The extra support made walking across the soft grass easier.

"So, that's the older Anderson brother?"

"Mhm." Allman muttered.

"There's something you're not telling me. Is he an old fling? Is that it?" Allman smacked her lips apart at Goodrick's question. Acting appalled, although there was secret truths within it.

"Of course not! I see him as a brother, as I do Jay."

"Hm, some people are a bit prone to some incest, well, sort of a step-brother and step-sister sort of vibe."

"Believe me, that's not the case here," Allman stated, hoping that'd be the end of it.

"No? I'm grateful to hear that, though." Allman looked up at Goodrick feeling a sense of empowerment, knowing if something like that bothered him, he must like her more than he'd ever admit.

"Grateful for what exactly?" Allman asked.

"Well, I appreciate it when porn directors cast the brother and sister to at least resemble each other. You and he look nothing alike." The outburst of Allman's laughter was captured in a wave of numerous people screaming.

"Surprise!"

CHAPTER 30

July 26th, 2015

"Hi... Adriana, no, Superintendent Cross, it's me, Louise, I mean, Detective Allman, Detective Louise Allman, fuck!"

Allman sighed, frustrated at her incompetence in stringing a sentence together. She paced the length of her office back and forth, repeating the same speech over and over again.

"I've decided it's in the best interest of myself and mostly to the other victims that I – fuck!" Allman was caught off guard by an unknown knock at her office door. Being a Sunday and knowing Goodrick was at Eileen's, she wasn't expected to be disturbed so quickly by anyone.

"What?" Allman frustratingly shouted. A sheepish Jade shuffled her way inside.

"Jade? What are you doing here today?" Allman quizzed and took a seat, saving her legs from the relentless walking, thankful now she was in the best company to rest her mouth also. Goodrick had sure found a way to keep that area of hers occupied all night.

"You haven't seen our Paul, have you? Just don't go mad, but he kind of told me he was at yours the other night, and you cooked for him, I was wondering if he was with you last night?"

Allman could recognise the panic in her trembling voice, the white complexion of her dreary skin.

"No, I haven't, not since he dropped off some files for me Friday night, but then he told me he was going out drinking with some old friends?"

"Yeah, I know some of his college friends were over during the weekend, but he hasn't been home yet, and he hasn't returned any of my calls or texts. That isn't like him."

"He was very excited to rekindle with some of his friends. I'm sure he's passed out somewhere on somebodies sofa with bread and water, recovering." Allman didn't look like she'd convinced Jade enough, who slowly nodded her head whilst staring at the ground.

"Look, I'll send a memo out for his whereabouts. In the meantime, have you tried contacting any of these friends he was out with?"

"No, I don't know any of them. You think he's drunk somewhere still?" Jade asked with teary eyes. Allman sighed and placed her hand over Jade's shoulder, trying to comfort her.

"I think he's hungover somewhere. Nothing to worry ourselves with yet. It's only half past nine in the morning. Since when were you up and about before noon after a weekend of binging?"

"I've never binged. I've never binged anything. I can only watch two episodes of anything at a time. Apparently, that's not binging."

Jade sounded exhausted from a sleepless night worrying over her cousin. Allman sighed, chuckling softly at Jade's innocence, knowing she was overdramatic at times, but until Paul returned, she wouldn't be convinced.

"How about you go into Paul's office, look through everything you can find that may be able to help locate these friends of his, okay?" Allman dangled a set of keys in front of Jade's sunken face that lifted slightly. Allman knew anything she could do to keep her mind occupied would make her feel she was helping. Anything to keep her occupied whilst she sat down with The Dragon. Allman led a shaking Jade out of her office, feeling slightly guilty she couldn't engross herself more, even if she did have the tendency to overreact.

Allman knew she had to focus. She only had today left to advise Adriana that she'd decided to go forward and press charges against Superintendent Flatdick for the sexual abuse and rape she'd suffered. *Enough was enough.*

She'd spent too many years blaming herself for something that repeatedly happened. It wasn't because she was the weak, pathetic girl he tried to make her feel. He was a persistent predator that wouldn't stop at any cost, and Allman wanted to bring him down personally. The affection Goodrick had shown her in the past couple of days proved she was worthy of love, to know the difference between somebody idolising your body and using it for pleasure than using it for greed. Without any further interruptions, she gulped her newfound confidence and rang Adriana.

"Superintendent Cross, it's me, Detective Allman," she said as strongly as she could.

"Louise, I'm glad you called. Is this in regard to our last meeting?"

"Yes. I've decided I'll go forward, along with the other victims, and testify against Daniel Chadwick."

"And you have thought this through? Once we're off the phone, I'll call it in."

Allman took a couple of brief seconds, racking her brain to make sure she tallied all the pros and cons. It didn't matter if people knew; no reason to be ashamed. Plus, she'd be leaving that office in a couple of weeks and transferring to Tannoch. She had Goodrick, the incredible altogether detective, by her side. She felt invincible.

"Put the call in," Allman hung up the phone. For a moment, she was hoping it came across as cool and slick, like in the films, but realised she'd just hung up on her soon-to-be superintendent. Maybe it wasn't the best time to test that theory. Stabbing her fingers onto the phone pad, another knock at the door alerted her.

That can't be Jade again.

"Hello, Detective Allman." Goodrick chirped as he pushed the door open and slinked his way into her office. Allman couldn't help but blush at his big cheeky grin and reminisce about their most recent night together. Before she could remove the smile from her face, he'd already locked his lips over hers. It had felt the most natural thing in the world to her, to be embraced by him, finally to have no awkwardness, she was his, and he was hers, well, only in private.

Deep down, she knew they could never make anything official or public with how Adriana would react. Could you imagine the Internal Affairs meeting? She was most definitely sexually abused at work but it started as consensual knowing it was against the rules. But hey, now look at her, with her tongue so far down Goodrick's throat, she can taste the ginger biscuit he had with his morning tea.

"We do need to set some boundaries, Gregory," Allman said when he released her.

"I couldn't agree more." Allman was shocked at the realisation they were on the same page, something that happened very rarely.

"You do?" She asked for reassurance.

"Yeah, I mean, I know my way around a bondage knot, my safe word is banana, and I haven't forgotten it's a Sunday. I'm willing to take you up on your anal Sunday policy, remember?"

Both Allman and Goodrick smirked before chuckling. She knew now never to expect a realistic answer from him. It made anything he said humorous and not look at it as him being difficult or hiding from the truth. It was him being his usual, sarcastic self. Knowing now he truly cared about her, she was willing to take everything he said with a pinch of salt, and she'll need to think of some quick, witty remarks to bounce back to him if she wanted to keep up.

"Well, I didn't think you'd remember that, but that's something we can discuss further tonight."

"We will most definitely be discussing that subject tonight." Goodrick boasted, nodding his head vigorously. Allman stuttered to remember her words now he'd transfixed her on the highly anticipated evenings activity.

"Well, for now, I want to make sure we're on the same page, about us, about this."

Goodrick took a step back, taking a gulp. It looked as if he was ready to begin building his walls back up.

"What about us?" he fearlessly asked.

"You know we have to keep this a secret?" Allman began to explain. She wanted to continue with no interruptions so he didn't need to jump to any unsettling conclusions knowing his tendencies to do so.

"I need us to be kept quiet, but it isn't because I'm embarrassed or regretting anything. I love this, I like what we have, but there are too many obstacles at the moment. We need to both focus on this case, pinning our thoughts together if we're to move forward on The Dragon stories. I mean, he already has the images of us. Yes, we can deny it's you because, thankfully, you can't be seen, but now with the trial that's about to happen with Flatdick-"

"Flatdick? Trial? Have you decided to testify against him?" Goodrick's stare was intense, the tensest she'd seen him for a while.

"Yes, I told Adriana moments before you arrived. I'm going to nail that son of a bitch."

Goodrick leaped forward and took all of Allman's weight into his arms as he exhaled harshly.

"That's the best news I've heard all week. Well, besides finding out you are a squirter last night but I mean, very close."

Allman laughed loudly and hit him playfully on his arm to release her. Although she couldn't deny it, his strong hug reiterated to her that she'd made the right decision, a decision she made all by herself, well, subconsciously down to Goodrick helping her find her inner strength again, but she felt she deserved the credit this time.

"So, you're okay with us being a secret for now?"

"You can keep me as your dirty little secret for as long as you need. I'll be here for you, no matter what."

Looking at his watch, Goodrick announced it be best they go and wait for The Dragon's arrival as much as Allman wanted to remain in their bubble. Allman and Goodrick both walked side by side through the sparse Sunday staff, one being Jade, who was flipping Paul's office upside down with boxes stacked against the wall.

"What the hell's going on in there?" Goodrick asked as he shot a look inside.

"Nothing to be concerned about yet," Allman reassured him.

A policeman was stood watching over the doors, Allman nodded her head in his direction as she and Goodrick walked into the room and took their seats. The Dragon was escorted in by the same policeman, and the door abruptly closed behind him.

Unlike last time, The Dragon seemed a little occupied as he gawked around the room before taking the singular seat that was centred opposite both Goodrick and Allman. Each time he carried a new persona that was eerily presented across in the stories. Allman put it down to him maybe 'getting into character' to tell his tales, but she couldn't help but question if there was more to his personality traits she should be focusing on.

"No pleasantries this time, Dragon?" Allman asked as she watched The Dragon shuffle backwards awkwardly in his seat.

"Well, seeing as last time you couldn't wait to drag me out of the room, and you couldn't clear your diary for me yesterday, I think it best we get it over and done with."

The Dragon muttered, folding his arms together, a standoff body language trait he'd yet displayed to them, until now.

"Have you begun to realise you may slip up?" Goodrick asked.

"I'm sure if I'd given you any reason to do so, you would have already arrested me."

"You said you wouldn't talk if you were in handcuffs?" Goodrick asked.

"You're right. So, until that happens, I'm here to tell you another story, and I hope you listen carefully. I highly appreciate you are now following the rules."

He darted a deathly look towards Allman. She squirmed slightly in her seat, knowing the photos were his ammo, his blackmail and perhaps their punishment for them trying to record him that time.

"Well, let's get stuck in. What fucked up Creature metaphoric fuckery have you got planned for us today?"

LEECH

CHAPTER 31

By now you know what to expect, the magazine arrived like always, co-ordinates included along with our way of travel for that week and a clever article about Leeches. It wasn't quite fulfilling the budget The Network provided for transportation. It was a rundown minibus that came to collect each of us. I recognised the driver instantly; he'd been the same driver of the bus in Ducky's week. Do you remember the one in Portugal who drove me out and left me by the dirt road? The Network has a way of subtly reminding you they've always been there, one way or another, and I doubt they pretended to hide it.

The driver stared at me as I climbed on, taking a seat at the back, with a strong Scottish accent, told me.

"I'm Kenny. I'll be your designated driver, be ready by noon on the 3rd December."

At this point, I'd become relaxed about The Network and how they run things. Although seeing that Runt, knowing they had fooled me the first week with him, I was paranoid all over again. This time I couldn't wait to get off and see the other Creatures following The Squirrel's week, it brought the group closer together. I mean, what else brings people together other than being tortured for an entire week?

The venue for this week was by far the most accommodating. I was surprised to see The Lizard and the elderly woman, I'd yet to attend her week, were there along with Ducky and The Squirrel. When they hadn't participated in The Squirrel's final scene, I presumed they had broken the

2nd rule of participation and were ultimately dead, but no, there they were, full of life. The Lizard and The Squirrel had already began breaking the rules, talking amongst each other. It was evident they had a good relationship.

"I can't believe she's chosen the same venue again."

"She's a creature of habit; if something isn't broken, why fix it?"

That's what they said to one another, so I obviously felt out of the loop, they knew exactly what to expect, and The Lizard particularly looked eager to start. Ducky was itching to join in on their conversation, but the elderly woman shook her head and held her forearm in place, hindering any movement. She acted like the group's Nan, if you will, seeing as there was a vast age gap between us.

The Leech welcomed us into a magnificent spa retreat. She firstly showed us round like an open house tour. Clearly knowing her stuff from pointing out the hand-carved marble sculptures on the walls, the width of the hardwood floor apparently proves it's expensive. For a moment, I genuinely believed the week would be a game of trying to guess the value of the property, the way she hawked on at its grand gesture. It made sense to me now where most of The Network's budget had been spent.

The rooms, well suites, were a millionaire's dream, although it was a bit over the top for me. We were allowed to get 'comfortable' first in our suites. I couldn't fault her because she'd been the most welcoming host out of them all and would be bouncing around the resort, checking we were all okay. To put into perspective how grand this suite was, I was given a lower-end room she described because I'd been the newest. I mean, I wasn't going to argue.

A king-size bed levitated a floor up with a connecting set of stairs to the right of it. Watching The Leech demonstrate how to gain access to the bed and which button to press to operate the stairs, I was in awe. You could sit on the bed, and with a press of a button, the steps would stack into themselves against the wall, removing all access. It made for a comfortable night's sleep, knowing nobody could get to me. The shower was as unique and complicated as the stairs.

On the bottom floor, directly underneath the suspended level above, was a rectangle grid with stones and potted plants. I did find it odd there was an outline of what looked like a mini garden in the middle of the room, but I took it as some abstract art piece. On that first night, The Leech showed me how it was a pressure pad, so when you step over the stones and plants, fresh water would fall from the edge of the level above you, and it felt as if you were in a waterfall. It was by far the greatest shower I'd ever had, a lot different from the one I had during The Squirrels week.

The Leech also gave us some timetables. They were pushed through the door and described hour by hour what we were doing. The first few days were an absolute delight. Nine o'clock, breakfast was served to your room. Ten o'clock, we had to be showered and in the robes provided to us. Eleven o'clock, we were to meet at The Grand Hall, which was the centre of the resort, circular in shape with a dolphin fountain in the middle. We would then be taken to the treatment rooms on the other side of the complex. These included two-hour body massages, an hour in a mud bath, and facials – the beauty-focused kind, I feel I need to clarify – given the nature of the group.

This felt like a real holiday, a week to relax, and I suddenly felt silly for worrying, having the sleepless nights beforehand with the tight chest of anxiety crushing my heart. I felt it all slip away as if all my problems were gone. The Leech wanted us to relax. With her being the only one to do all the treatments, she was run ragged, making sure everyone had what they needed.

The Lizard and The Squirrel sat by the bar all day and laughed and joked, occasionally taking a dip in the hot tub or the mud baths, keeping themselves to themselves. I was automatically grouped with the girls and ended up taking part in all the girlie pampering, which I didn't mind. It was a complete change of emotion from the previous years of being hungry, tired, and beaten.

There was only one time I indulged in a full-body massage. I was excited to begin with, that maybe that was all her week was, you know, giving happy endings. After my first one, however, a rash began to show on the inside of my elbows. The Network knew everything I was allergic to, so I was surprised if they overlooked a detail.

The sixth night quickly came around, unfortunately, and we were given the schedule pushed through the door that morning. Same old same old, up until five. That would normally be the time we would all sit and have our evening meal together and make small talk about what subjects we were allowed to discuss. It was mainly centred around the food, knowing what everyone liked, what they didn't, and so on. It was a nice feeling that the group was finally bonding and beginning to include Ducky and myself as one of them.

It made me wonder that for the first few years, maybe it was only me who was stuck in their rooms whilst all the others were able to talk freely and join in conversations. It was eye-opening that these Creatures were actual people, just ordinary people like me and you, with some bizarre and sexual fetishes, too obscure for mainstream, so they have to hide in their ordinary life, and I was beginning to like them, strangely.

The Leech took us that final evening into an area of the resort we'd never been to before. She opened the double doors and began to slip out of the robe as she walked through onto the polished marble floor. The room was decorated like a roman bath house, with two sunken dried pools on either side of the long walkway. Carved columns pressed against each wall of the rectangular room with chipping painted frescoes between, also filling the entire ceiling above us. I was amazed, looking up, taking in the detail of the thousand faces. It had been the only thing that felt real and authentic in the over-the-top lavish resort.

We were ordered to remove our white robes and sit naked next to one another in a line, cross-legged, with our hands on our knees and spectate.

The Leech had a tremendous body, I'm not keen on any type, but I could appreciate the others liked what they saw. An olive complexion, toned flat stomach with perky breasts that were sheltered by long thick black hair. The little dance she did between the two pools was mesmerising. Every member of the group was hooked. There was no music, but there didn't need to be. The beauty of the ballerina moving majestically through the room was captivating. She was in front of us all as she did a tiptoe back and forth motion, I've no idea what it's called, but that's when the dancing stopped.

We all began clapping when she took her bow which was her signal for what was to follow. Blood began pouring from the ceiling. The heavy gloop hit my arched back like a bullet. The Leech still had her head down as it continued to rain red. I smeared my glasses and tried to frantically make sure I was with the others as we all sat in a flash flood of blood. The Lizard was sitting to my left. He was patting the ground between us to coat his entire hand with blood and began pleasuring himself. Part of his elbow had been sheltered when the blood poured over us, and I recognised the same rash I had, yet I knew he never received a massage.

Frantically, I looked across to the others who were all beginning to cover themselves in blood, and they too all had the unfamiliar rash. I stretched my skin as tight as I could, and that was the first time I realised it wasn't a rash, they were needle marks. It's no wonder she'd been so accommodating in making sure we were taken care of properly, feeding us, and keeping us constantly hydrated. The whole nursing week had been another smoke screen manoeuvre to her twisted pleasure, and all she wanted us for was blood.

I should've seen it coming. I mean, it's what Leeches are famously known for, but I believed that she was a Leech to us, like it was a metaphor for her clinginess to be around us all. I didn't have time to calculate how much blood there was. I concluded by the vast amount that was splattered against the horrifying drawings, she must've used Runts to create such a blood-soaked room.

The rest of the Creatures left me to my own devices as they began to 'play' in the blood. Ducky was matting her hair in it whilst creating 'blood' angels. The Lizard, which I'd already known wasn't squeamish about a blood scene, was splashing around like a child in a water park. The elderly woman, Nan, was dipping her toes in the partially filled baths and humming to herself as if she was dipping them in the ocean. The Squirrel had found himself a mirror to gaze into and all I did was watch. With my legs crossed and hands on my knees, I sat in the middle of a thick puddle of blood and watched.

CHAPTER 32

Goodrick repeatedly gulped as he told the final part of the story, imagining the stench of blood, the texture of its tackiness, completely absorbed by it. *No.* The constant slurp of the water, primarily for The Dragons use that he hadn't yet taken a sip from, was difficult for Goodrick to swallow.

"Are you okay, Detective Goodrick?" The Dragon asked, seemingly concerned.

"Fine, just not good with blood, that's all." Goodrick coughed.

"A detective who isn't good around blood? Now, that's a first." The Dragon said wearing a smug smile.

Goodrick knew better, so pressed on with questioning before Allman could force him out like last time. He did again make a reference to something Goodrick had seen for himself, the dolphin fountain that was outside the Fingask School, but, like the door described in the Villa on Ducky's week, it was out of place, out of context.

"You say there's a budget set by The Network? You hadn't previously mentioned that."

"I thought that'd be obvious, and you'd presume they would fund it. The only thing we pay is the sum of £5.00 a week for a 'magazine' subscription." The Dragon air quoted.

"And you don't pay anything else? All the food, all the transport, everything in these weeks, is always provided?"

"Yes." The Dragon confirmed confidently.

"But why? Why does The Network do all this, why do they do any of it?" Allman began to ask.

"That's what I'm hoping you can tell me." The Dragon responded.

"We need you to give us a little more. You depict what seems to be small details of each week and skip past information that could be useful to us?" Allman began to sound desperate, either that or tired of The Dragon's story-time.

"I told you, I'll tell you the stories in my own way, I'll tell you everything you need to know. Of course, there are details I miss out, not on purpose but because they're unnecessary to your crime scene, and I don't wish to waste any of your time."

"You have a real way of showing that, coming to us each time, sitting down with us both for an hour or so, and then disappearing. You won't allow us to take notes, record, or reflect on what has been said. You can't expect us to remember every single word in every single order once you are gone for us to piece this together ourselves. What you say happened doesn't make sense!" Goodrick shouted, slightly losing his patience.

He wanted definite answers, and he needed them now. Who are these people, if they really exist, their names and where to find them. Who controls The Network and where are they?

"It might not make sense to the ordinary person because what happens on these weeks is anything out of the ordinary. I've said all I wanted to say about that week. Now you know about The Leech. Hopefully, it may give you better insight into solving your case. Now, if you excuse me for today, I'll see you both tomorrow morning."

Both detectives stood up in defiance.

"All you've told us is you watched a ballerina prancing around some blood orgy?" Goodrick shouted over to him as The Dragon reluctantly already pressed the buzzer, requesting his immediate release.

"Hmm, a bloody ballerina you say?" The Dragon eerily asked with his back towards the standing detectives.

"Tell me Detective Goodrick, have you seen a bloody ballerina recently?" The Dragon cracked his neck to showcase a teasingly frightful smirk before walking out of the released door, putting his hands in his pockets.

Goodrick stood frozen, attempting to pick his brain with what The Dragon could be insinuating. Allman didn't seem phased as she walked over to the buzzer and gently pressed a piece of tape over it.

"What are you doing?" Goodrick asked.

"Prints. Only found a partial of one on the envelope with the pictures."

This was news to Goodrick. He'd never known she retrieved any, if only partial prints. Why wouldn't she have told him? Why would she keep this from him?

"And you didn't think to tell me?"

"It was when you ran of. You know when you went to Fingask alone?" Allman raised her eyebrows in his direction with Goodrick taking a step back.

Allman – 1, Goodrick – 0.

"Which, by the way, I can't find a report for. You have submitted a statement regarding Fingask, haven't you?"

He could hear the dissatisfaction tone in her voice. Suddenly, she was back to being the professional – do everything by the book – detective, not the carefree, up all night, tongues tied together girl he left this morning in bed.

"I thought it be best not to, I mean, I know it's in a way connected to our case, but through The Dragon's words, I thought we were both under the assumption these meetings are kept quiet between us."

"They are. But we need to think of a plan now. I mean, he only has two more Creatures to talk about, the weeks that happened during the year of 2014 and 2015."

Both Allman and Goodrick leaned against the table with their arms crossed, trying to unravel what they knew thus far.

"Well, we know the week Ducky attended was The Dragon's. We know that from the magazine and the coordinates, her murder happened during a week he hosted, and surely that's enough for us to warrant an arrest now?" Allman asked, biting her index finger.

She was eager to have this case locked down. Goodrick, on the other hand, knew there must be more to it. From what he'd seen, it didn't make sense; different aspects of what The Dragon told them were real, but it all centred around Fingask, the door, the fountain, and even the song.

"Have there been any more reports about Fingask? I know you enquired about the building, but all I've seen is the same old; it's demolished, it's gone bullshit."

"I've researched on it, off the record," Allman admitted. Goodrick was relatively relieved she wasn't doing *everything* by the book. Unknown to Goodrick, it had been Paul's hard work that uncovered what Allman knew. His hacking skills outsmarted most computers, if there was something electronically stored, he would find it one way or another.

"Well, don't leave me hanging." Goodrick said with a massive grin on his face, intrigued to know he wasn't the only Detective that didn't play by the rules.

"It was a research centre primarily. Archives relating to a doctor called Professor Albert Chiocchi, who used the facilities for independent research. This research included sleep deprivation, limb removal, starvation, and, get this…exsanguination."

"To drain somebody of blood?"

"Yes, he'd practise on mentally challenged children and adults who would be given to the school, cast away from their families. They would offer the families huge, vast amounts of money to take them away for 'scientific research'. Genuinely believed they would be cured and returned, but I couldn't find proof if they indeed discharged patients."

"And I'm presuming they found out what was happening there?"

"I'm guessing so. After 1932 when the professor died, some of the children he'd been researching continued to live there, and a sister building was erected on the same grounds to act as a boarding school. I could only find one archive newspaper clipping that supported this, an article essentially offering to house troublesome children away from their families and provide them with a career of a scientific nature. I mean, what parent wouldn't want their child to grow up either being a doctor or a scientist? Even today, parents would throw themselves at the prospect of it all, especially when it was aimed at the lower class."

"But there are no official reports from the council to confirm this building was actually built or not?" Goodrick questioned, delving into the mystery.

"No, but we'll have your testimony as well. I believe that's the building you saw and the other was in fact, demolished following a fire. Maybe a child who had been sent there to be tortured had caused the fire, or maybe it was a freak accident, and the council had no other choice but to demolish it. Who knows?"

"We need to know how The Dragon is connected to that school," Goodrick demanded.

"What, other than what he told us? That a man in a car took him from the train station, and he watched another man dismember him? I mean, what isn't believable about that?"

"Here's what we do, seeing as you know more about this professor and the schools history, I'll run the prints and try to piece together who The Dragon is. You continue to look into the school. We need to find records of every person that was used for research. All researchers write down their findings even if it's done off the books."

"I've already tried, and everything was burnt in the fire."

"Then find out how the fire started!" Goodrick shouted, clenching his fists. He didn't mean to come across as aggressive. He was chasing the thrill of finally having leads. He shook his head as Allman stared at him, gobsmacked.

"I'm sorry, I'm getting ahead of myself. I just really need this case closing Louise."

"Okay, you find out what you can on The Dragon, and I'll find what I can on Fingask. We recoup tonight?" Allman smiled sweetly whilst passing him the piece of tape that could hold a thousand secrets.

"Say eight o'clock at yours?" Goodrick asked.

"It's a date."

CHAPTER 33

Papers, photos, and multiple coloured sticky notes were scattered around her living area like a patterned medallion fabric. In the centre of it all was Allman, rotating herself in each direction and frantically labelling each idea and thought process as it entered her head. Back and forth she swung her body round to a new realisation of something and then whiplashing her neck back around to find connections. She was talking out loud, presenting each trial of thought to herself.

Manoeuvring on her behind, using the silk pyjama material from her shorts, made it easy to glide her across her wooden floor to any lead she wanted to follow. A final twirl stopped her abruptly as she yelped at the sight of Goodrick standing in front of her. Clutching onto her chest as she tried to restore herself, he leisurely chuckled at startling her as he placed a brown paper bag on the kitchen island.

"Didn't mean to frighten you, I know I'm a little early, but I brought us some food. I kinda guessed I'd walk into something like this." Goodrick explained as he pulled one of the bar stools out and took a seat facing her direction.

"Yeah, well, a knock would be appreciated next time." Allman brashly said, gaining herself in an upward motion. She delicately tip-toed through her spiralling circle of thought processes and observed each note, unable to control her brainstorming mind.

"I did knock. You were muttering away to yourself too loudly," Goodrick explained whilst retrieving a paper-wrapped parcel from the bag.

"What did you get me?" Allman was instantly redirected to the sweet smell of fresh food, painfully watching Goodrick ruffle the paper down to reveal a ciabatta sandwich.

"I asked Eileen to make us a goat's cheese and red onion marmalade sandwich, a bit like those tarts you took a fancy to at the party," Goodrick said whilst taking his first bite. Allman smiled to herself whilst retrieving her own. She found it thoughtful he'd noticed something so minimal but developed the observation into a grand gesture.

"Thank you, and thank Eileen from me. It's very kind of her."

A grateful Allman said as they both began to tuck into their evening meal. You could almost hear the echo of the bread hitting Allman's hollow stomach. She'd ignored the rumbling thunder of it for the past several hours as she dived deeper into what she could find about the case. Without wanting to lose her train of thought, she walked back over to the epicentre and took the stage whilst wielding a half-eaten sandwich.

"Right, so we start with Ducky." Allman pointed at the first row.

"What do we know about her?" She asked, taking another mouthful of the delicious creation.

"Well, she was a white female, aged twenty-three, cause of death asphyxiation-"

"We'll get to her body later. What do we know about *her*?" Allman exaggerated before catching Goodrick up.

"From what The Dragon has told us, she was a rule breaker, the first of her kind to drag these Creatures to another territory. A cheeky, young, free-spirited girl."

"Who liked rape?" Goodrick questioned.

"More reason why she had to be killed."

"What?" Goodrick stood up, taking his hands in his pockets, fully engrossing himself in Allman's speech.

"Bear with me." Allman held up a finger to pause him in his stride, rubbing her greased fingers against her thigh. She continued by picking up pieces of connected evidence from the floor.

"Right, she bended the rules, seemingly more than once, from what The Dragon has told us. The Network was forced to change tactics by restricting them from their phones after her week. I believe this was more of a safety net for them, so The Creatures were completely cut off from the outside world, which is, after all, what all The Creatures wanted. To solve this case, we need to get into the minds of each of these people. From what we've been told, Ducky was the one most likely to cause trouble for The Network with her persistent rule bending. Maybe she took it too far on the last week, and The Network removed her with the only way they contractually could, by death."

"Remind me of the rules of the contract he's mentioned," Goodrick asked. Allman scattered through some loose post-it notes until finding the one she needed.

"Right, from what I remember, every member needed to sign, thus making them a fully participating member. They must participate each week. Strict discretion is upheld at all times. Once you sign, the only get-out clause is death. There was also a sub-ruling for the use of extras, well Runts as they refer to them, like the drivers, they must also sign a contract but don't host a week."

"Okay, well, we know Ducky attended each week from what we've been told. Maybe she didn't attend the year 2014?" Goodrick pitched in his suggestion that Allman battered away.

"No, she must've attended as The Dragon said, she was one of them and if that was the case, she would have never made it to The Dragons week in 2015. Maybe there was a fight or an argument between her and another Creature that resulted in her death?"

"You think another Creature could have possibly killed her, not The Network?"

"Well, this is another theory I'm thinking of. This is what The Dragon's week of festivities was, he seems to comment on being the left one out, the watcher of the group. It's possible his week always intended for this to happen but all The Creatures must've participated in her killing."

"How so?"

"Lets take The Lizard first. What do we know about him?"

"He likes to throw a broadway dismemberment show?" Goodrick sarcastically said.

"And what's remarkable about that relating to Ducky's body?" Allman asked, seeing Goodrick's eyes lighten.

"Her left hand."

"Correct. Her left hand was severed," Allman confirmed before moving on.

"Next, take The Leech. What did she like to do?"

"Play in blood?"

"And Ducky's body was-"

"Drained from blood," they both said in unison.

"The slicing and removal of the skin from her face must be connected to The Squirrel. The skin suits with his printed face on them like The Dragon described. I hate to anticipate the next story clue," Allman paused, gulping hard as Goodrick looked as tired as she did.

"Did you find any more on Fingask?" Goodrick asked.

"No, I didn't. I'd already told you everything I could find." Allman said, scratching her head, taking a well-deserved rest on the sofa, and allowing Goodrick to take centre-stage.

"Would you like to hear my theory then?" Goodrick smacked his lips apart. Allman eagerly sat upright and leaned closer to him.

"There are no Creatures," he began. Allman scrunched her face, appalled at the thought.

"Before you object, listen to me. I examined the prints, and I got a hit."

Allman jumped up with excitement.

"You did? Who is he?" She could feel the pounding of her chest as her heart rocketed with the information but felt almost disappointed her partial prints didn't come through for her.

"Sit, sit." Goodrick beckoned her that she submissively obeyed.

"The Dragon, formally known as Kiefer Black." Goodrick took a case file that he'd rolled up inside the lining of his jacket and slid it across the floor to Allman, who eagerly trapped it under her foot and retrieved the contents. She opened the flimsy file to see a photo of The Dragon outside their office building, leaving one of their meetings, as he was wearing the same clothes, she recognised.

"Who took this photograph?" Allman asked, knowing Goodrick had been with her moments after each one of the stories. She understood nobody else had known about their meetings besides Adriana and her own team that Goodrick certainly didn't know about.

"I have a surveillance team, I asked them to take one, only that photograph exists of him, but they don't know anything about the case," Goodrick explained.

"A surveillance team?" Allman asked for more, looking up at him.

"I've had them watch over you as well as others, truth be told, for my own peace of mind," Goodrick confessed.

Allman frowned her eyebrows, not knowing what to do with this information. A churning feeling tumbled around in her stomach. The fear she'd recently been watched was true. She didn't quite understand why she was only being informed of this now. Although through good intentions, she felt unsettled.

"You've had people follow me?" Allman queried with a shaky voice.

"No, god no, only surveillance around this building, only in case anyone turned up again, you know, from after the photos were taken of us."

"Oh." Allman sheepishly said, tucking her legs against her chest. She couldn't quite understand why the troubling worry wasn't going away with his explanation. If anything, it intensified. It was, after all, the only reason she told her immediate team about The Dragon, so more eyes were on her for safety. Allman fought with herself why she didn't feel grateful for Goodrick's actions; it was certainly something she could have done herself if she was that worried. Was she still finding it difficult that somebody cared about her as much as to do something like that, or was it done for another motive?

"Anyway," Goodrick quickly tried to resume before Allman's overactive mind could churn.

"Kiefer Black. Prints came up from an enquiry made back in 2010 of a strange-looking male watching children on a merry-go-round. The file you're holding is insubstantial because although Kiefer provided his fingerprints willingly, a letter that's also photocopied in there was sent in." Allman flicked to the second page of the file and began reading.

"Unlawful confinement and obtaining a minor's DNA without the representative of a lawyer or guardian." Allman read whilst looking at an overexposed scan of an ID with the only recognisable information being Kiefer Black, date of birth 28th April 1996."

"That would've made him fourteen at the time and nineteen now, but how can that be if he's already attended four weeks from the age of eighteen? He's between twenty-two and twenty-three?" Allman's eyes battered left and right, trying to work out if she'd done the maths correctly.

"If you believe the week's existed," Goodrick stated. Allman stood up, throwing the empty file to the right of her in surprise at what he was suggesting.

"What on earth do you mean if they existed?"

"I'm going from facts here, actual evidence, not from what he wants us to believe. This is him; Kiefer Black. We know that now. He was detained by police; what else was uncovered, we don't know. His file was erased due to the proof of him being a minor, so we know he is indeed nineteen."

"This whole file could be faked? It was 2010 when the first week happened, he was already a Creature, and it would be pretty easy for The Network to cover a blimp like this up. In reality, this should never have been traceable. His prints should have been destroyed."

Allman was more sceptical about police tactics and how, even though she knew it could be fabricated, how a simple procedure wasn't executed lawfully. She should have felt relieved it hadn't because she might not have a name for the mysterious Dragon, but typically for her, it threw up more questions than answers.

"This might not even be linked to the same man who sits in front of us, the photocopy of the ID is badly smudged, it could literally be anyone." Allman resisted believing it.

"Well, this is what his fingerprints brought up, but you are right to a certain degree. There's no other information about any Kiefer Black, nobody that matches the age range from this ID to whom we see in front of us. No known addresses linked to that name. The only clue is when he mentioned Ducky was tracking them and that he was in the centre of the country at the time. But I do want to explain why I think he's leading us on a wild goose chase if I can."

Allman watched as Goodrick pleaded with both his hands open towards her. She reluctantly took a seat now. He admitted even with this illegal piece of evidence, that shouldn't exist, she seemed to be on the winning side of the argument so far.

"Enlighten me." Allman graciously allowed him to continue.

"Right, the school he mentioned, we know that also exists, well, from what you have found, did exist, I may not have been at the actual building that was demolished, but I'd seen what we believe was the sister building. I saw the grand door he'd described in Ducky's week. You know the old, out-of-place door he mentioned? I thought I heard a chainsaw but definitely remember the song that he described was playing in The Lizard's week, the fountain, the dolphin one that he just mentioned in The Leech's. That's there also. Little bits of details that he's given us seem to all be connected to that school from what he's seen there. He's probably researched it himself. Maybe he knew about The Professor and learnt about what he was doing."

"We know he's been there and seen it. He told us he had! If the council records are correct, it was indeed demolished in 1952, so that week he described The Lizard's must have happened in the same building you saw, and maybe he never knew it was a sister building erected in 1937. I mean, I had to dig very deep to even find the article. Someone tried very hard to bury any evidence both buildings once stood. Yet nothing to prove one still stands. Only you and The Dragon have that in common."

"Somebody in the council knows it's there as well. That's why there was an eviction letter for squatters dated the same year that The Lizards week apparently took place."

"How can you say these people aren't real then, Gregory? Is it so difficult to believe that The Network exists?"

"Yes! Because if they did, do you really think they'd be letting this freak talk to us? No, they'd kill him if we're led to believe they're as powerful as he says they are."

"Unless they have someone working on the inside, and this is part of their plan?"

Allman's stomach dropped as she spoke the words. She feared accusing dirty cops but wasn't obnoxious enough to believe rogue officers and detectives existed. Even superintendents don't always play by the rules, Superintendent Flatdick, for example. She saw the eyebrow raise of Goodrick, judging her for revealing another possible theory.

"If that was true, Allman, it must be one of us." Goodrick's stare unnerved her. Even after his eruption of hysterical laughing that followed, to try and break the tension, didn't ease her nervousness. She pushed a smile to humour him as he walked closer to her.

"Believe me, it's good we have different views and opinions on this. It just means we can come at it from both angles; one of us must be right after all."

Goodrick said as he brushed her bare shoulders. Allman bit the inside of her mouth because her gut was telling her she was right. *They do exist.* All the carvings on the doors at the murder scene depicted these people who she'd spent days learning about and connecting the dots.

"You really don't believe they exist?" Allman asked, looking up at Goodrick, feeling drained. She couldn't doubt herself now, not after all the brainpower she'd used to reach this conclusion. A troublemaker was ousted by the group, and all the Creatures attacked her, but what The Dragon's involvement was, she'd yet to work out. The night hadn't brought what she thought it would. She hoped Goodrick had changed his opinion in recent stories and started to believe in them as much as she did.

"I believe The Drag- no, Kiefer Black is a very sick and twisted individual who killed a young girl. Maybe lived out his own fantasies from what he knew about this school and that professor, did his own awful experiments. It's possible, Louise, we're just dealing with an illusionist whose using these stories, made-up people, because he can't come to terms with blaming himself for what he's done."

Allman rolled her eyes slightly. She knew Goodrick's theory had probable cause, as did hers. One way or another, she hoped they'd both end at the same conclusion for her own sanity. Goodrick's reputation alone will overshadow hers. No matter what evidence she brings to the table, he'll always trump her, and unfortunately for Allman, Goodrick knew that perfectly well.

CHAPTER 34

July 27ʰ, 2015

Goodrick sat patiently, tapping his foot to the beat of passing footsteps of officers walking back and forth in the corridor. Softly whistling to the clock ticking the seconds away from the remainder of the morning. He'd left Allman early that day with her hugging her pillow to make it in time for his morning breakfast with Eileen. Now he sat in the interrogation room alone, awaiting an arranged debriefing with Allman before expecting the highly anticipated visit of The Dragon - Kiefer Black.

A sudden rushed pace alerted him as he picked himself up from the table, now unable to keep up with the stampede. Sheepishly leaning his head into the corridor, anticipating to be guillotined, he darted concerning looks as people began running. Goodrick filtered his way into the march that took him to a familiar section of the building, the heart of what surrounds Allman's team. Detectives stood up from their desks, open-mouthed, as he tuned his ears to her voice.

"Okay everyone, listen up." Allman roared from the centre of the room. Hushed whispers became increasingly louder from the crowd gathering from each adjoining corridor.

"Quiet!" Goodrick shouted, unable to control his temper. A wave of shocked eyes darted in his direction, and they parted ways to make a beeline between him and Allman. He smiled softly in her direction as she reciprocated the gesture, unsure if she'd be thankful or not. He was sure he'd hear about it afterwards, regardless.

A teary Jade joined Allman. She took an arm around her and pulled her closer as her cries became unbearably louder.

"If you haven't already been told, I've officially declared our colleague, Paul Baxter, a missing person. We believe he was last seen leaving a local pub in the North District of the city centre, The Helmsley Lodge, at 2:15 Saturday morning but we've yet to confirm anything definite. Ben Deven will be the lead detective on this case so any enquiries or information, please liaise with him." Goodrick's eyes darted towards the large gut of Ben emerging from a desk, as Allman completely wrapped her arms around the inconsolable Jade.

"I know this information isn't what we wanted to hear on a Monday morning, but we all must be hands on deck and work together. We all know Paul. We can already say this is extremely out of character of him not to turn into work. I know emotions will be high at the moment, but lucky for us, we have the best goddamn set of detectives this country has to offer, and I promise I won't sleep or rest until I've found him, our colleague, our friend."

Ben was showered with a round of appraisal clapping from his speech. Goodrick clapped also as he made his way through the thinly dispersing crowd. He put his hand caressingly on Allman's back whilst Jade clung around her waist.

"Oh, Gregory!"

Jade cried as she felt his presence and instantly draped her body around him. Reaching as high as she could, she dragged Goodrick down to her painfully small height and wrapped her arms around his neck. Goodrick tapped her back as comforting as he could be; he wasn't one for hugs at the best of times, let alone now having bubbling snot and drenched mascara streaks rubbing against his suit jacket. Allman looked on from behind her and looked to be teary-eyed herself at the news.

"Don't worry, Jade. You know we'll do everything we can," Goodrick tried to reassure her whilst prising her arms from around him as she choked up.

"Thank you, Gregory. I know everyone will do their best. It's just difficult to remain positive. I had a bad feeling about him yesterday; I knew something was wrong. We have cousin's telepathy: I knew he was in trouble."

Both Allman and Goodrick shared concerned smiles, with Goodrick trying his hardest to refrain from smirking regarding their 'telepathy connection'. Jade shook her head and began being consoled by other members of the team, who all expressed their spiel of concerns and empty promises. The first rule you learn as a detective is to never promise something you can't deliver.

It reminded Goodrick of the first case he couldn't solve, a fifteen-year-old cold case that loomed over him of a missing seven-year-old boy. Snatched from what appeared to be an empty car park as his single mother loaded the car with groceries. The rest of the department believed the boy had run away. It was impossible for them to comprehend a mastermind was capable of keeping a young boy quiet just feet away from his mother and simply vanishing without a trace. Goodrick spent hours comforting the heartbroken mother. She pleaded with him to promise the safe return of her only child. He knew if he'd said those two words, it would have calmed her indefinitely, but he couldn't.

He felt worthless, watching as each of her tears corroded his rock-hard exterior, he ran before he crumbled himself. Now, all her hopes of knowing were now buried in a coating of dust in an archive storage unit that housed other gravestones of unknown truths. A graveyard that haunted each detective who simply admitted to not being able to crack the case before cracking themselves. A streak of solved cases, from then on in, egged him to keep going. Natural competitiveness; kept him running away from that one case. He hoped in time another young and brave-faced detective would dust it off and claim it as their win when he couldn't.

One thing he knew was that he wouldn't be losing this case. It had now been dubbed as '*The Fiddlers View Murder*' by the media. Goodrick would shake his head at every 'breaking news' report. Every article being the same as the last, alternating between photographs and different arrangement of the facts because since the first story emerged, there had been nothing new since. Only he and Allman knew the real depth of what could have transpired there.

Even Adriana kept her distance, knowing Goodrick had her whole, complete trust and compliance in him to deliver, but he knew time was running out, even for him. She wasn't amused their plan to record The Dragon didn't transpire and ultimately made her lose faith in his capabilities. They had dragged the days out to listen to The Dragon, and ultimately, both he and Allman ended on two completely different outcomes. Goodrick knew all too well when he was dealing with a psychopath. He only had to compare all their meetings, observing different characteristics and charisma from day to day. The Dragon was playing the leading role in each of his pantomimes, expecting Allman and Goodrick to play along.

"I'm not the killer."

Allman and Goodrick screamed back in their theatre seats.

"Oh, yes, you are!"

"Oh no, I'm not!"

"Oh yes, you are!"

Goodrick would turn in his sleep dreaming of that scene over and over in his head, watching The Dragon prance across the stage in clown make-up, making a joke of them. He skips from side to side, wielding a chainsaw as a prop, throwing a bucket of red confetti to symbolise blood over them until the final curtain is drawn. Goodrick had normally seen a chain of people taking the final bow, all holding hands and depicting the people The Dragon had described. Allman shrieked like a fangirl, throwing flowers along with her underwear on stage, jumping with joy.

For the first time last night, when that final curtain was lifted, Goodrick only saw the sad joker in handcuffs, alone with a single interrogating spotlight dangling above him, swinging side to side as he looked defeated across the empty theatre with only Goodrick as the audience. Goodrick was daydreaming with Allman in his arms, a little too long as people began to stare.

"Thank you, Gregory." Allman pulled herself away from his hug, now with drier eyes.

"There she is!"

A screeching voice roared behind Goodrick, making him turn quickly on the spot to an old colleague of his called Sandra, who was now bulldozing her way through the crowd.

"You have some nerve!" She screamed in Goodrick's direction. It took him longer than necessary to realise she was talking through him, aiming her finger at Allman, who stood sheltered behind him. The dynamics in the office changed with every set of eyes now focused between Sandra and Allman.

"Excuse me?" Allman asked sheepishly, moving forward as more people began gathering around them.

"You've accused my boyfriend of raping you! We both know you had a relationship that he ended because you were a boring shag!" Sandra spat.

The entire office gasped at the very public accusation. Allman spoke back in a hushed tone, attempting to avoid drawing anymore attention.

"Let's take this off the floor. We can talk privately in my office."

Her plea fell on death ears as Sandra moved towards her. Goodrick took a step forward, feeling the sense of danger increase, now she was nose to nose with Allman, who stood her ground.

"You'd best drop your charges or else," Sandra threatened.

"Sandra, you are talking to a lead detective here, remember your place."

Goodrick fired a warning shot, not trying to agitate her further, but didn't want things to escalate. Emotions were rife as it was with the worry and the unknowing whereabouts of Paul. Sandra darted her stare at Goodrick recognising he was out of place and probably until now, didn't realise he was there.

"Well, let's hope Internal Affairs do a better job at dissecting this bitch's lies before I have to get my hands dirty!"

Sandra stormed off in her extremely tight pencil skirt that caught the attention of every man's gaze, although Goodrick's eyes were stitched on Allman, who stood like a statue.

Even Jade began to stop looking sorry for herself as she tried to console Allman, who wafted her hands away and began stomping to her office. She appeared to everybody else to be unnerved by the words of Sandra whilst Goodrick knew all too well. She was breaking and needed to escape to a safe zone. Everyone began whispering and gossiping as they stood around. Goodrick gripped the locket of his father to try to calm his rising temper before following Allman.

"You lot not got work to do? One of your colleagues is missing, for fuck sake. Now, get to it!"

Goodrick barked his orders at Allman's team, who rightfully so, did as they were instructed, and their whispering transitioned into ruffling papers with the usual office lingo.

Goodrick erupted through Allman's office door to see her slumped over her desk, bawling uncontrollably. Without hesitation, Goodrick dropped to his knees and turned her chair towards him, feeling the weight of her head hit his shoulder with streams of tears running down his back. Her cries became louder as he tangled his hand through the long strands of her hair and hushed into her ear. With all his being, he wanted to make everything right but knew he was best keeping his mouth shut, knowing this wasn't the time for any sarcastic remarks.

How would he even begin to start to joke about her colleague going missing or being publicly accused as a cry rape victim, confirming most of the office's gossip? Allman began to recompose herself, sitting back in her chair with her tear-streaked face in her hands.

"It's all fucked, Gregory," she whispered.

"It's not Louise. You know it's not. That was uncalled for. I can have a word with Adriana regarding Sandra's behaviour in there if you want me to."

Goodrick offered, but Allman shook her head before taking her hands through her hair, tying it back to regain some posture.

"One battle at a time, Gregory. Right now, I need to focus."

"Yes, I know, but I have the power to get her suspended. Let me just take this off your shoulders, at least." Goodrick pleaded with her.

"The damage is already done, Gregory. Everybody in there will be saying I made the whole thing up. They'll have all sorts of people wanting a piece of the action, offering statements on his behalf to confirm I was compliant. He'll already know there are numerous people who'll say the office fling was well known. Even if they hadn't seen anything, they would say they did, anything for entertainment."

Allman huffed whilst Goodrick frowned, feeling defeated. He knew no matter what he offered or said wouldn't make her feel any better. He was grateful, surprisingly, for a knock on the door to stop the silence of Allman's self-loathing. He stood upright and dusted off his pants with an unfamiliar numbing sensation on his knees. Sam, the youngest of Allman's team, poked his head inside the room.

"Sorry to bother you both. The interrogation room is ready for your meeting."

Allman turned away to look outside at the bleak, burdened view of the car park.

"We'll be there shortly."

Goodrick responded, allowing Allman a few valuable seconds before tackling the next obstacle.

"We can take as long as we need, Louise. There's no rush." Goodrick said, placing his hand on her shoulder, which surprisingly rose quickly as she stood up.

"Let's get it over and done with. I don't have the time to be moping around in this office, feeling sorry for myself. There will be time to rest and cry when I'm dead."

Allman abruptly said before leaving Goodrick in her shadow and taking the lead, existing her office to a sudden, unnerving wall of silence.

CHAPTER 35

Using the corner of her polished nail, Allman scratched away hard lumps of mascara, that dotted her cheeks like freckles, as both she and Goodrick made their way into the all-familiar room. Her mind was fogged with an internal dialogue, repeatedly reminding her everyone was watching them. All likely thinking the same, it was apparent there could be more between Allman and Goodrick. *No one will believe me.* Why did she go ahead with the charges? Was she too wrapped up in whatever toxic romance Goodrick was somewhat providing her? She was easily influenced around him and would do almost anything he asked of her. Now she questioned herself, was she ever this strong independent woman she believed she was? Glancing behind herself to watch him follow in her steps, she couldn't make up her mind. How was she ever going to know what was good for her, if she was now too scared to trust her instincts?

The Dragon, Kiefer Black, welcomed her with his face-splitting toothy grin. This seemed to be the happiest he made himself appear to them, which unnerved Allman. *How can someone be this happy if everything he said was true?*

"Welcome, welcome all!" The Dragon cheered, greeting them into the room as both Allman and Goodrick took their seats in silence. This was a day she didn't care for his theatrics. All her thoughts were consumed by what could have been the last time she saw Paul's smile, how excited he looked before disappearing, but to what fate? Would Sandra follow through on the threats made about her? Why did Goodrick leave her in her bed this morning with nothing but doubt to wake up to? She knew he was a creature of habit with his morning ritual, but her gut was telling her something was wrong.

Her thoughts were consuming, she stared straight ahead unconsciously, not caring that her mood was infectious. It's difficult to channel out the only voice you'll ever hear inside your head. If you can't trust yourself or don't like what you hear, whose voice are you supposed to listen too?

"Well, you both seemed to wake up on the wrong side of the same bed," The Dragon joked, with a hissing laugh. *If only he knew.* Both Goodrick and Allman didn't bite knowing he was after a reaction. He was the only other soul who knew of their encounter, an encounter which most certainly be Allman's downfall. What if Sandra got wind she was now having a relationship with Goodrick? What if Flatdick would use this as evidence to discredit her statement? What would Adriana think? *Would anybody, anyone at all, believe me?*

"Anyway, this one isn't too bad..." The Dragon continued, sitting upright in his chair.

"Too bad?" Goodrick mocked.

"It did seem to get better each year, I can't lie about that. Unless I was just becoming custom to The Network and how their organisation worked." The Dragon shrugged.

"What have you lied about then?" Goodrick took charge, which Allman was grateful for. If there was ever a day she couldn't entertain The Dragon, todays the day. Her mind was elsewhere, questioning everything and anything that remotely worried her, things she hadn't questioned until now. That time Goodrick left, the first time, The Witch called him, a nickname she believed he called his step-mum following their conversation in the café, but what if it wasn't? A whole ten days for a short fall as he described it and no text or phone call? What if he couldn't physically use his phone?

There was an eerie silence, with darting looks between their acute triangle they formed around the table. The Dragon appeared to be uncomfortable with the blunt question. He began running his fingers through his floppy, dirty blonde hair.

"Please, Detective Goodrick, questions must be saved till last and only asked once I've finished the story. Haven't you understood that by now?"

"I've understood perfectly fine, well mostly, unless your willing to confirm some details beforehand?" Goodrick asked.

The Dragon shuffled in his chair, looking unimpressed with the request but nodded, folding his arms crossly.

"The Network, a governing set of somebodies, groups people together, odd-balls and weirdos like yourself…"

The Dragon looked on, unphased at the insult.

"…To give them a week where they can divulge into some freak party. Which so far you've mentioned rape, dismemberment, mental torture, I wouldn't know what to call someone stealing blood, but that vampire or leech whatever prancing ballerina…"

The Dragon bit the inside of his lip becoming irritated with Goodrick's disrespect.

"…No explanation as to why The Network does this because you don't know yourself and that's why you have come to us, but I need clarification on how this all started, how did you even become part of this?"

Goodrick paused briefly during his bombardment of questions. Allman attempted to listen intently at some of the things he was bringing up, she'd been questioning herself too much but now was intent involving herself in the presence. Why was Goodrick asking him so much about this if he believed these people didn't exist? Was he just trying to find holes within her theory and hope The Dragon confesses or slips up?

"The Network invite you, or, should I say give, you an ultimatum. You wouldn't not want to sign to their agreements if only you knew what power they hold over us."

"They blackmail you? Is that it? They have evidence on some freaks of nature and use it against them to…do as they please?" Even Goodrick frowned knowing it didn't make logical sense either at the suggestion.

"The Network doesn't see us as freaks of nature as you lovingly describe, we are Creatures, creatures of habit. If we cannot control our instincts, isn't it not best to contain us?"

Goodrick relaxed, folding his arms as he leaned backwards. Allman couldn't help but agree with The Dragon's logic, it may seem far-fetched to Goodrick but it made perfect sense to her why these groups of people were formed. If they intended to use disposable people, Runts, as The Dragon described Reggie, it would make sense to use nameless people of society, homeless and most likely addicts, to live out their sick fantasies. It's a classic case of using peer pressure and blackmail to control the masses. They were all infiltrated, driven by their own sick diverse pleasure to bear witness to the known illegal activities on one another, making them all accomplices. *Anybody could be a Creature.*

With an abrupt knock of Goodrick's knuckles on the desk, both Allman and The Dragon sat upright.

"Okay, I'll entertain it for a bit longer. What have you got to tell us about this time?" Goodrick unenthusiastically asked. The Dragon tore a grin looking eerily enthralled.

"I thought you'd never ask."

BEETLE

CHAPTER 36

I was almost at the end of attending all The Creatures weeks, this would be my last one before I could host my own so I was exceptionally keen to get it over and done with. It was a bright and cheery day on the 15th September 2014, the year of The Beetle. You probably guessed who she is now from the group, the plump older lady who everyone loved and doted on. She was the one that puzzled me the most, as with every year, came new surprises, this year being the most.

If The Network could nominate a star Creature, it'd be her. She followed the rules and did everything and beyond what was expected or asked of her. I knew this meant no matter what this week would entail, all of us would fully engulf ourselves to repay her. We all did anyway due The Network's contract, but she seemed so polite despite holding people down in Ducky's week, to splashing in our blood during Leeches. Nothing seemed to be too much for her.

I learnt she was an elder for The Network. This had been her third group of people, signed up from a young, experimental age and had a record of forty-six years. It seemed The Network had different rules back then for what age people joined. I mean, grooming isn't all that popular now, is it? Maybe it helped them sleep better at night, thinking because they're over a certain age to consent legally, they were somehow not the truly awful people they are.

The travel, again, was provided. It did grate on me not being able to jump in my car and go, but there were a few reasons for that. The Network had to be in control at all times. They couldn't risk someone up and leaving.

The other reason; we aren't suppose to grow deep, personal relations with one another. We're only there for a 'fun' week to live out the host's fantasies and then leave. I learnt from the previous year, whilst I was having blood sucked from my body, The Network used my car. They had been racking up parking and speeding tickets, providing alibis, it seemed, for if anything went pear-shaped. A picture, plain as day, caught speeding travelling the M6 with my face in my car, although I was hundreds of miles away. I was foolish to believe when we had to disappear for a week, we had control over it, but no, they always did.

So, there I was again, being chauffeured by the Scottish Runt called Kenny. We drove far out into the countryside with picturesque hillsides, and the fresh smell of livestock lingering in the breeze. A beautifully converted barn would be our home for the next seven days. French farmhouse window shutters, painted in tiffany blue, accompanied by a rainbow of potted pansies on every window sill. The Squirrel, wearing a velvet suit, tore one of them as we all walked through the gravel courtyard. He casually swirled the flower between his lips before spitting it on the floor as we came to an abrupt stop before The Beetle.

She stood poised with rosy cheeks, hands together, wearing a red picnic tablecloth apron. Unlike the eeriness from the previous years, this week felt homey. She greeted us all with open arms and looked genuinely pleased to welcome each of us into the cosy accommodation. Warm, open fireplaces throughout, stone pebbled walls, great oak four poster beds to rest on. It really was a holiday home, somewhere you could feel safe. How the other weeks transpired was always the same, we would spend the first day listening to the host's plans, some would hand out leaflets as The Leech did, and others would be a live presentation like The Lizard's. As for Ducky's week, well I was welcomed into hers like a wrecking ball.

The Beetle's welcoming day was subtle. We had a handful of time just pacing the bedroom, ready to be summoned. I know I miss a lot of information during these weeks, but I do tell you the most important parts, the only parts that should matter to you, that is. I could talk in great depth about how this was the week we all really came together as a group and shared heart-warming stories of our personal lives over an open fire. We all knew we shouldn't, but even I, who didn't have much to tell, was absorbed into the warmth and the unfamiliar feeling of being surrounded by strangers who, at times, felt like the only family I ever really knew.

We all had our unusual perks, and I don't understand it, even to this day, but it worked. We were all individually crazed and perverse, chastised out of society, but we slotted together like a beautiful jigsaw. Sure, we were all warped and rough around the edges, but when everybody is, you choose to ignore the imperfections.

The Beetle's week was difficult to interpret. I learnt from previous years to take the week as it comes and try not to anticipate too far ahead. We sat down on the second night to a grand, solid oak table dressed in linen with brass candelabras. Beer and wine were poured, and smiles and laughter were shared. The best I could describe it would be a very dysfunctional Christmas dinner with an estranged family.

Ducky would be the wild child, the single one who brought a new date every year. The Lizard would be the dad, eat himself into a coma and be asleep in his armchair before we would all finish. The Squirrel, well, he's obviously the uncle knob head, the show off who you wouldn't leave around your children. The Leech would be the cool, sophisticated aunty who was more likely onto her third divorce but busy opening a fourth company. The Beetle, head of the family, the Nan, kept us all together as a unit. As for me, I didn't see where I belonged in the family of Creatures, maybe I was the troubled one they sent away to some convent. That would explain why I wouldn't be involved much with nothing to say.

Plate by plate, The Beetle set out an extravagant five-course meal where we were able to dish it out ourselves, and it was very much a 'pass the salt' situation. Ducky placed herself by me with The Beetle next to her at the head of the table. The Squirrel was to my right, and much to my dismay, he was still the only Creature I couldn't tolerate, even as a person. Every time I'd pass a plate for him to then pass it across to The Leech, he made a point of tediously stroking my finger and smirking out the side of his mouth. The Lizard piled his plate high, it was difficult to see him behind it. All three types of meat with multiple selections of vegetables, and he claimed his mountain of food with a Yorkshire pudding balanced on top.

Nothing was too untoward until I saw The Beetle place a cup of tea in front of the Leech. The Squirrel and Ducky flirted across me, and I was desperate for a distraction, so I watched intently as The Leech swirled her tea, and for a while, I was transfixed by the vortex of steam clouding above her. The Leech picked up the teabag by the string that was hooked around the mug handle, delicately dunking it a couple of times before removing it.

A giant thud hit the table as she dumped it on a nearby napkin. The tea bag wasn't anything I'd seen before. It was almost the same width as the mug when she dragged it out and looked fluffy in texture. My eyes burned into the tissue, which was now becoming transparent from soaking up the moisture of the red dye from the tea leaves. It was The Leeches unnerving glaring eyes as I watched her slurp her first sip, which made me realise it wasn't tea at all. The Beetle had brewed a bloody tampon.

I felt a little sick bubble trap itself within my windpipe. I felt the need to compose myself and tried to turn on my chair to escape for a bathroom break. A sudden jerk from my right shoulder glued me straight back down as The Squirrel poured the gravy boat over my dinner. Heaps of gloopy brown liquid splashed across my plate, saturating every inch of it until a puddle formed around the edges. The gravy had a distinct odour to it. I couldn't quite tell if it had been made with something else like mint. Onion gravy was what I concluded in my head as that was most common and would explain the lumps that now scattered across my much-anticipated dinner.

The Squirrel passed the gravy boat to Ducky once he'd finished drenching mine and stretched his arm across the back of my chair, leaning into me. That all-familiar stench of his cologne lingered across my nostrils. Feeling his heavy breath brush across my neck, he whispered softly to me.

"Please, let me introduce you to Scat Nan."

CHAPTER 37

"What?" Goodrick blurted. Allman darted concerning looks towards him, trying to soak up the story herself.

"Scat Nan? And this was the best week for you, supposedly?"

Goodrick scoffed with his arms outstretched on the table with his palms open. The Dragon looked unnerved and wiggled back in his seat, most likely annoyed that Goodrick knocked him off his stride.

"Is that what you did? Take part in a mad hatters shit party?" Allman couldn't help herself but smile, trying to mask her laughter. She found it humorous how defensive Goodrick was becoming.

"Is this really the most surprised you've found yourself, Detective Goodrick?" Allman smirked humouring his outburst.

"I just don't get it. Why, who, what would make somebody want to sip on a tampon tea and order a side of lumpy shit gravy?"

Allman couldn't help but erupt in a fit of giggles towards Goodrick's complete baffled expression, fighting to understand the week's festivities, which to her didn't come across as the most startling. She could understand why to The Dragon, the weeks seemed to become less intense.

It began with him detailing a brutal rape scene, witness to dismemberment, tortured, swan lake blood bath to now the mad hatters shit tea party, which made her chuckle the more she thought of it. Goodrick seemed to gleam with happiness watching her, unable to control her laughter intensifying. The troubles that had been weighing her down were slowly lifting with every giggle.

"I'm not wrong, though, am I? Imagine, oh please, pass the apple sauce and anyone for a menstrual pad?" Goodrick charmed as Allman hugged her stomach. She might not have found it as funny if she didn't need an excuse to be happy, but she needed this. She needed a reason to smile, even if it was short-lived and to somebody else's dismay. She and Goodrick passed smirks to one another that she forgot to look at The Dragon, who had remained perfectly silent. Allman gathered herself with a couple of final wipes of tears from her face and coughed as she sat upright in his direction.

"I apologise for our interruption. Please continue, Dragon."

The Dragon stared deadly between Allman and Goodrick unnervingly for a few seconds with his arms crossed. Allman gulped, not quite sure if her laughing took him over the edge.

"Dragon?" Allman tried enticing him, but nothing. She glanced at Goodrick, subtly asking for help.

"Kiefer Black!" Goodrick said abruptly. Both he and Allman watched for his reaction, any indication that Goodrick was on the right path in obtaining his name, but nothing. This seemed to infuriate Goodrick further.

"We know your name is Kiefer Black. We obtained your prints that brought up a file that you were cautioned and interviewed by police for watching kids on a merry-go-round back in 2010. We know you are nineteen, born on the 28th April 1996. There are a lot of inconsistencies in your stories except for one place you told us about, Fingask. Ever heard or read about a doctor from there, Albert Chiocchi? He messed with young children and experimented on them for the sake of science. His research was into sleep deprivation, starvation, cutting off their limbs, and even draining their bodies of blood. Hell, I wouldn't pass on the chances he even raped them knowing the sick fuck he was. And you know all about him, don't you, Kiefer? Is that why you were staring at those children on that merry-go-round? Were you looking for your first victim?"

Allman shifted in her chair as Goodrick began to rattle his theory. It did sound convincing, and he had good circumstantial evidence to support his claims, but that's all they were, circumstantial. Allman couldn't help but feel in her gut there was more to it. They wouldn't be able to use his prints as evidence as that file was supposed to be discarded. Any judge would dismiss it as evidence. There was nothing linking him to the scene or to Fingask, only other than what he'd told them. Unless he changed his story, Goodrick was telling him everything they knew on a whim.

Allman began looking down at her fingers, becoming unsettled that Goodrick may have intentionally ruined her chances of getting more of the story. The more he talked, the more she could work on. The unsettling sobbing from The Dragon made her look up as she watched his face crumble and crease. His mouth was gaping, and his eyes were tightly shut as he raised his arms up to the air, signalling he was giving up. His cries began heavier as he pounded his hands against the table.

"I... I didn't want to hurt anyone," The Dragon choked out. Allman's eyes widened as she watched intently at the tears streaming down his face.

His lips were trembling with every intake of air he took. He was in pain, physically and mentally. Allman stared on, open-mouthed herself, unknown how to take his sudden reaction. *Was this it? Would this be his confession?*

"Just tell us the truth, Kiefer." Goodrick enticed further with a softer tone, knowing he'd gotten through to him. The Dragon began shaking his head erratically, becoming more distressed, to the point Allman frowned her brow. It was difficult to watch without offering any support.

"Tell us what happened. What did you do to the girl?" Goodrick was referring to Ducky, but he seemed to be removing any connection to what The Dragon had tried to make them believe.

"Nothing, I..."

The Dragon was choking on his tongue with how upset he was becoming. Allman began pouring a glass of water for him and pushed it closer to his side of the table. Within the same second of her reaching across to him, his whole demeanour changed. His face suddenly relaxed and all distress he had been portraying disappeared in a blink of an eye.

A blank expression with steady breathing. Allman held her breath as she stared into his teary eyes, which were seconds before becoming red and raw with sadness, were now dark with evil. Her heart began thumping through her chest with her hand clamped around the glass, terrified to move. She screamed as The Dragon grabbed her arm and pulled her closer to him.

"Ask him, ask him how his wife and child are. He's not who you think he is!"

The Dragon whispered hastily as she struggled to get her arm away from him. *What wife and child?* Goodrick raced and began to drag The Dragon away from her, with his arms wrapped around his chest. Allman was able to release her arm from his grip as Goodrick planted him on the floor, smacking the panic button on the side of the wall. He had The Dragon pinned down, digging his knee into his back. Allman was transfixed with The Dragon's eyes, he never took his glare from her whilst being detained by Goodrick, nor did he look away when two other police officers erupted into the room to help him.

"I told you! I told you when I'm in handcuffs, I won't talk!"

The Dragon threatened as Goodrick, along with the help of others, wrestled his arms behind his back. Goodrick began rattling his rights as he was arresting The Dragon. All the while, Allman and The Dragon shared an unusually long connection, he was attempting to tell her something from his eyes.

"I warned you! That lanky detective got himself in trouble by snooping. I told you of the dangers of The Network!"

Allman gasped, knowing he was referring to Paul. For such a small man, three officers were struggling to get handcuffs on him. Allman fell to the floor by his face, giving herself carpet burns on her knees, as she desperately came close to The Dragon.

"What have they done to him?"

She desperately needed to know how to help Paul. She knew she was the reason he took it upon himself to do his independent, off the record research. She'd inadvertently put her team of closest detectives all in immediate danger.

"You don't get it, Detective Allman! You're not fucking listening to me!"

She darted concerning looks back and forth as The Dragon's mouth frothed, becoming tired from resisting.

"Get what? Where is he? Tell me!" She desperately cried as she watched The Dragons face tear with a chilling grin.

"Welcome, your in a Creatures week."

Clink.

You are invited.

Join us for one week, yours, theirs, ours.

Participate each week once a year, and enjoy, for, in return, we will give you one week to be your true self.

You set the boundaries. You disclose the information.

All we ask is that everyone involved is a signed, participating attendee.

This automatically renounces any involvement of anybody under the age of 18 and any animal to attend.

You will only be referred to the name The Network provides you once you join the appropriate group.

Your membership will only be revoked upon death.

If you wish to complete your application, sign below and await instructions.

Signed _____   Dated _____

_____

Print full name in CAPITALS

Printed in Great Britain
by Amazon

24674222R00178